Pathway to Home

A Becker Family Novel

Pat Wahler

Evergreen Tree Press

Cottleville, MO

Book Layout © 2017 BookDesignTemplates.com
Book Formatting by Jeanne Felfe
Editing by Joy Editing
Cover design by Jenny Quinlan, Historical Editorial

Publisher's Cataloging-in-Publication Data
provided by Five Rainbows Cataloging Services

Publisher's Cataloging-in-Publication Data
provided by Five Rainbows Cataloging Services

Names: Wahler, Pat, author.
Title: Pathway to home : a Becker family novel / Pat Wahler.
Description: Cottleville, MO : Evergreen Tree Press, 2020. | Series: Becker family, bk. 3.
Identifiers: LCCN 2020920698 (print) | ISBN 978-1-7323876-6-9 (paperback) | ISBN 978-1-7323876-7-6 (ebook)
Subjects: LCSH: Life change events--Fiction. | Man-woman relationships--Fiction. | Fire fighters--Fiction. | Kansas City (Mo.)--Fiction. | Women--Fiction. | Romance fiction. | BISAC: FICTION / Romance / Contemporary. | FICTION / Romance / Romantic Comedy. | FICTION / Romance / Firefighters. | GSAFD: Love stories.
Classification: LCC PS3623.A35646 P38 2020 (print) | LCC PS3623.A35646 (ebook) | DDC 813/.6--dc23.

First edition: December 2020
Printed in the United States of America

"Features excellent dialogue, great writing, and a good plot. Pat Wahler combines suspense with humor to create scenes that capture the reader's attention."

—Romuald Dzemo for *Readers' Favorite*

"Readers who enjoy wholesome romances with a splash of drama will love this novel."

—Peggy Jo Wipf for *Readers' Favorite*

Praise for *On a City Street* (A Becker Family Novel, Book 1)

"Wahler provides a heart-warming roller coaster of emotions and sparks…and who doesn't love puppies?"

—Jeanne Felfe, author of *Bridge to Us*

"I found it really hard to put the book down and loved the twist ending." —Trudi LoPreto for *Readers' Favorite*

"A delightful read for fans of contemporary romance with a touch of real-life angst."

—Louanne Piccolo for *Readers' Favorite*

Praise for *I am Mrs. Jesse James*

"A vivid, moving tale of the woman behind the man of myth and legend. This is a book not to be missed!"

—Nicole Evelina, *USA Today* bestselling author

"*I am Mrs. Jesse James* tackles the Jesse James story from a new and heartbreaking perspective." —*Missouri Life*

"This is a fantastically researched historical piece that many readers will enjoy, even if the historical genre is not their first choice." —*InD'tale Magazine*

Praise for *Let Your Heart Be Light: A Celebration of Christmas*

"The stories are short and engaging...A fun and enjoyable read, especially around Christmas time." —Gisela Dixon for *Readers' Favorite*

"*Let Your Heart Be Light* is rich and sweet and will warm your heart." —Donna Duly Volkenannt, winner of the 2012 Erma Bombeck Global Humor Award

Dedicated to the readers who survived 2020 with a hopeful heart and a sense of humor. I salute you all.

Chapter One

A small blue box bobbed with the surge of each wave. Mira Gordon glanced toward her mother's best friend, Dinah, and nodded. As though they had rehearsed it, the two women leaned over the boat's railing to toss a handful of hot pink hibiscus petals into the sun-dappled water. Even though Mira's vision blurred with unshed tears, the flowers brought a smile. They were her mother's favorite, plucked straight from the tree Pauline had planted in the front yard of the canary-colored rental home they'd lived in for as long as Mira could remember.

The box quickly disintegrated, just as the funeral director had promised it would, releasing her mother's ashes into the salty waters off Key West. Dinah raised her cell phone and snapped several photos. "What a beautiful sendoff we've given her. I'm sure Pauline's smiling down on us."

Mira watched as the petals drifted away. It had been more than two weeks since her mother had passed, preceded by months in hospice care. Pauline had made her last wishes known in a matter-of-fact fashion—at peace with her decision—long before the end came. She'd only been fifty-seven. Far too young to be taken. The utter finality of the moment knotted Mira's stomach and her chest tightened. She closed her eyes long enough to take a deep breath, as her mother had taught her to do whenever an anxiety attack threatened.

"You okay, lovie?" Dinah put an arm around Mira's shoulders.

"I'm fine." A gust of air loosened Mira's thick braid, and she pushed strands of hair away from her face. "What a breezy end to the day. It's a good thing we chose the water urn instead of trying to scatter ashes. We might have waited forever for the wind to be still." She managed a weak smile. "Air currents aren't favorable for a dignified exit." Macabre as it might seem, the resurrection of whimsy brought a welcome sense of comfort. Everything else in her world had gone topsy-turvy, but at least her sense of humor hadn't abandoned her.

She had a feeling she would need it in the coming days.

"Wind's picking up. We should head back." Ernesto, owner and captain of the catamaran they sailed on, boomed out his comment at full volume.

"I'm ready to go," Mira said. "Thanks for your help. I really appreciate it."

"No problem, *chica*," he replied. "Anything for Pauline. We're all gonna miss that little lady."

"Yes, we will." She swallowed hard and turned her face away from the water. Shadows had lengthened as the sun melted into the sea, setting the sky ablaze with shades of gold, pink, and crimson. "What a glorious sunset. I don't think I've ever seen a prettier one."

"I'll bet Pauline had it painted especially for you." Dinah massaged her lower back and stretched her spine. "She always brought a good day, didn't she?"

A good day. Mira considered her life with Pauline, in the lazy congenial atmosphere of the Keys. Small as the island was, Mira had only ever left Key West twice to visit the mainland, and while the experience had been fun and an eye-opener, she'd still been in the familiarity of Florida—a state teeming with tourists, snowbirds, and an occasional 'gator. But her haven with Pauline in Key West, the place they called home, kept her centered. She filled her lungs with sea air and turned her palms up to Dinah in an agreeable shrug. A single hibiscus petal clung to one of her fingers. She brushed the petal off into the water.

"I suppose you're right, but now I need to figure out how to *keep* the good in each day."

What to save? What to give away? Mira gently folded a long sundress into the box at her feet and opened another dresser drawer. A tangerine-colored scarf Pauline had often draped around her neck sat on top. She lifted the silky scarf to her nose and sniffed. The scent of bergamot, her mother's favorite essential oil, clung to the fabric and quieted her spirit. *This one stays.* Mira placed it on the creamy quilted bedspread. If only all decisions were so simple. She caught her lower lip between her teeth and allowed herself a moment to think about how much she missed her mother.

In spite of everything, they'd had a happy life, filled with an interesting mix of people. Pauline had the knack of making anyone feel at home, a fact that drew many to her door. Yet even with a generally cheerful nature, there were evenings when her mother had turned toward the west and sighed. In those moments, Mira could have sworn Pauline's expression took on a mournful look— one that disappeared almost as quickly as it came. Mira had learned not to ask any questions.

The front door banged open, and Mira jumped. "Yoh!" Dinah called out, a bit of Jamaican spicing Dinah's speech as it often did. Moments later, she appeared at the bedroom door, her ample figure draped in a loose sundress, and her graying hair coiled into its usual messy bun.

"I told you I'd help pack Pauline's things. Why didn't you wait for me?"

"I needed something to do." Mira decided not to mention how fiercely the quiet had agitated her mind. It replayed too many images of why she no longer needed to tiptoe into her mother's room to see whether another dose of morphine was required. Or the difficult final day when she and Dinah had held hands and prayed for the end to come quickly. Mira remembered how she'd wracked her head until it ached for any topic that might help ease her mother into eternity with a smile.

Her fingers clenched into a fist. It wasn't fair. Nothing about this silent invasion of illness made any sense, especially for her mother. Pauline had based her entire life around the tranquil philosophy of clean living. Yet cancer had still found a way to launch an attack.

Then again, who said life held any promise of fairness?

"You look mighty solemn," Dinah said. "Packing can stir up a lot of emotions. Why don't you let me handle this?"

Mira willed the burning sensation to leave her eyes. "I'm glad you're here, but I want to be the one to do what needs to be done. Besides, I may want your help later with my own things." Her gaze strayed away from Dinah's. "Isabel told me the real estate market in Key West is so hot right now that she plans to put the house on the market as soon as possible."

"What?" Dinah's eyes opened wide. "This place has been in Isabel's family forever. Why would she want to sell?"

"She'd like to do something different. Like traveling." Mira smoothed the frayed hem of Pauline's nightgown and laid it carefully into a second box. "Whoever said, 'When it rains it pours,' wasn't kidding."

"What terrible timing. Do you have any idea where you'll go?"

"There are so many things to think about. I suppose it would make sense to stay close to work. Walking or riding my bike beats the heck out of driving."

Dinah marched to the closet and pulled out an armful of hanging clothes. "A place to stay isn't a problem. You can bunk with me for as long as you'd like."

"I'm sure Joe and the grandkids would be thrilled to share the bathroom with a house guest," Mira said with snark, working to suppress a chuckle over the thought of adding one more person to the snug fit inside Dinah's lime green bungalow. "Actually, I've been tossing around several ideas this morning. Some of them are kind of radical—for me."

"What? Radical isn't at all like you." Dinah dropped clothes on the bed and stared at her. "Wait a minute; your face is flushed. Are you sick?"

"I feel fine, but you touched on what I've been thinking. My entire existence has been this island, and if you're counting, that's twenty-four years. Don't get me wrong. I loved growing up here, and I'm proud of being a conch. Pauline and I had a wonderful life, just the two of us together," she smiled at Dinah, "along with a circle of good friends. You know she was more than a mother to me. She was my best friend. Now that she's gone, I can't help wondering what I've missed. Could there be something else out there for me?"

"I can see how you might think that way, but it's too soon to make such a big decision. Do you really want to leave your hometown? Leave your job?"

"Le Croissant Français is a wonderful place, but do you realize I've been there for three years? I can't tread water as an apprentice forever." She held onto her mother's satin blouse and rubbed her thumb across the silky fabric. "I'd love to open my own place. One where I could use Pauline's ideas to make food that not only tastes good but is good for you too."

"Hmm. In theory, this sounds great, but taking on something like that means a lot of responsibility and tons of cash. You'd probably have to go to a bank." Dinah shuddered.

"Believe me; I'm not crazy about the idea of going into debt. Pauline left me a little money, but certainly not enough to do what I have in mind. To tell you the truth, I don't know how in the universe she managed to squirrel away anything."

Dinah's eyes twinkled. "She told me that she'd scraped together a small nest egg over the years. That woman cut a lot of corners so that she'd have something to give you besides her old van."

Pauline's 1970's-era VW van had been around almost as long as Mira. She had bought it used and then had one of her friends paint the body bright pink, adding a rainbow-colored fresco of flowers, peace signs, swirls, and hearts. On the rare occasions when she would re-move the car cover to drive her van around the island, she'd wave at the tourists who snapped pictures. The memory tugged the corners of Mira's mouth up.

"She was one of a kind. But you're right. It might be too soon to leave my comfort zone. Maybe I'll find an apartment and then decide what to do. Who knows? Maybe Pauline will give me a sign." Mira sighed and placed her mother's satin blouse into the box.

An interesting thought. What *would* her mother want her to do? Pauline had never been afraid to share her opinion, although Mira had to admit she hadn't been pushy about it. Even her circle of unabashedly bohemian friends—from artists and writers and musicians to her co-workers at The Water's Edge Healing Spa—appeared to appreciate the advice she dispensed. Or more accurately, they appreciated not being hit over the head with it. Pauline had a way with people, a talent Mira envied.

For Mira and her mother were as different as sand and sea. A high-spirited woman with a quiet mouse of a daughter—a girl prone to periodic anxiety attacks—who always trailed behind in Pauline's impressive wake. As an adolescent, Mira had once blurted an openly insecure question to Dinah. "How can she and I possibly be related?"

Dinah had only laughed and pointed to a mirror.

The blaze of red hair, forest green eyes, and spatter of freckles across the nose clearly branded Mira as her mother's daughter.

"You're even both left-handed," Dinah had retorted.

True, they did look alike—except, of course, for Mira's snub nose and dimpled smile, which had clearly been cut from a different cloth. But not even Dinah could claim Mira had inherited Pauline's wide-open personality.

Or was it more accurate to say wide-open in all ways except one?

"Seems like you're light-years away. What are you thinking about, lovie?"

For the past few weeks, Mira had spent hours and hours turning over the news Pauline had shared with her, like she was kneading a batch of bread dough. *Can I talk about this?* The concern etched into Dinah's forehead made the decision.

Mira rose from the floor where she'd been sitting and walked to the window. She pulled the lace curtain aside and scrunched her eyes against the bright sunlight. "There is something I'd like to tell you." A breeze set the bamboo wind chimes on the patio to softly tapping. "Pauline gave me a letter the day before she died. It was one she wrote last year—after she got her diagnosis. She told me not to read it until she had passed."

Dinah's mouth dropped open. "No lie? What does it say?"

"The one thing I thought she'd never tell me." Mira let the curtain fall back into place. "You know how long I've wondered about my father. Any time I asked her, she always said the same thing. 'One of these days we'll talk.' And then she'd change the subject. If I pushed, she'd flinch like I stuck a pin in her arm."

"Are you telling me she wrote you a letter about your dad?"

"Listen for yourself." Mira took an envelope from the dresser top, removed a piece of paper, and slowly unfolded it. Pauline's familiar curlicued handwriting in vibrant purple ink made it feel like her mother was standing right beside her. The thought formed a lump in Mira's throat. She cleared away the lump and began to read out loud.

My dearest darling daughter,

If you're reading this letter, it means I've left you—although certainly not voluntarily. We've had such a sweet life together, for which I am deeply grateful, but I'm greedy. It hurts me to miss the years yet to come. I wish I could cheer you on as you bloom into the amazing woman I know you will be and realize the dreams you've shared with me.

I wish I could see you find your soulmate and give me grandchildren—along with the chance to dream over their future. I wish I could be there for you whenever a problem that seems like a mountain arises.

But the doctor tells me it's not to be. There is no clear answer to this muddle of feelings I have, but it occurs to me there is one important gift I can give you. One I've resisted. Until now. I can tell you about your father.

Mira's throat tightened. She paused long enough to lift her gaze to Dinah's and inhaled a full deep breath. When she knew her voice would be steady enough, she read on.

His job was to travel around the Midwest and sell medical supplies for a company in Kansas City, where he also lived. Years ago, his employer sent him to a tradeshow in Key West. One where I presented a workshop on holistic practices in medicine. After my speech, he sought me out to say how much sense it made to him. We went out for coffee and found we couldn't stop talking or laughing. He was such a kind man. Gentle and smart. An Old Soul harbored in a young man's body.

Within a finger snap, it felt like we'd known each other since the beginning of time. No one had ever touched my heart as he did, and we both understood the truth right away. Something new and important and magical had blossomed between us. By that same evening, he packed his suitcase and moved out of the hotel to stay with me.

We spent the entire week together. The experience was heaven—and so spiritual I could barely breathe from the weight of all that had happened. When it came time for him to leave, he said he loved me, and promised to come back as soon as he settled things with his boss and his family. I asked no questions. The fact that we'd be together again was all I cared to know.

Days turned into weeks. I tried again and again to contact him but he never answered his phone or returned any of the messages I left. I began to wonder if I'd only dreamed of us and what we felt for each other. Once I realized he wasn't coming back, I truly thought I'd rather die than be without him—until the impossible happened.

I learned I was pregnant. The news floored me. When I wasn't much older than you are now, I'd had surgery, and the doctor told me I'd never be able to bear a child. You are the proof doctors aren't always as smart as they believe themselves to be.

After you were born, I held you, and your tiny hand wrapped around my finger. From that day forward, you were all I needed in this world. The truth resonated clear as a cloudless day. Life must continue, and it was my job to live it in the richest way I could manage. For your sake, for mine, and yes, even for your father's.

As I write this, I'm smiling, knowing what you must be asking yourself now. Here is my answer. His name was James Todd. I apologize for waiting so long to tell you these things. I thought it would hurt you less to keep the truth to myself. Please try not to judge him or me too harshly. I couldn't bear it, for I have no regrets and am at peace with what happened. How could I ever be unhappy about an experience that gave me an amazing daughter like you?

There is one promise I can make. A fundamental principle, really. Forgiveness heals. May this be as true for you as it has been for me.

With my love now and forever,
Pauline

Mira folded the note into careful thirds and placed it back inside the envelope. Even though she'd now read her mother's words a dozen times, she wished there were more. The letter wasn't enough for a last good-bye—let alone an explanation.

Dinah pulled a tissue from the pocket of her dress and wiped her cheeks. "Do you know how many men had their eyes on her over the years? I always wondered why she never looked at them as anything but friends. Now I know."

"If you've figured all this out, then please explain it to me. She seemed so resigned over everything. Wasn't she mad about him deserting her? And if he was the love of her life, why didn't she try harder to find him?"

"Your mother was a level-headed woman. How did she handle any problem? She meditated until she received an answer. It would be like her to decide that if he'd changed his mind, she wouldn't try to force him to return. Not to mention, she had more important priorities than an absentee lover."

"I suppose you mean me."

"Of course, I mean you. And her friends, too. Her job and her life here in the Keys. It was all part of her. And let me tell you, miss, no one would ever have labeled Pauline miserable or bitter."

"I know. But it's just so sad that she spent her life missing a man she's only known for such a short time. I have more questions now than I did before. I wish she'd told me this when I could still ask her." Mira chuckled ruefully. "Maybe if I meditate, I can get some answers."

"Meditation isn't a bad way to clear your head, lovie."

"Do you know how many times I've heard Pauline say those exact words?"

"Because they're true." Dinah patted Mira's back. "Why don't we finish up here? Tomorrow we can donate what you don't want to keep."

"What about Joe and the kids? Won't they starve if you don't fix them dinner?"

"I told Joe he's in charge. Today is all about you and me and Pauline."

Chapter Two

The next day, a gull squawked as it glided over the café patio, heading toward the water. Late morning had arrived, and the sun already blazed with heat. Mira and Dinah spotted a small puddle of shade and scooted their table and chairs into it as the spicy scent of freshly prepared fish tacos curled around them. Mira reached for one, nearly upsetting the salt-studded goblet next to her plate. Sweet golden-colored liquid sloshed onto the table.

"Nothing like a margarita to brighten the day," Dinah said, sipping her drink.

Mira nodded, too hungry to focus on anything but food. She took a bite, and in no time, there wasn't a scrap left on her plate. It had been a while since she'd had an appetite. Her loose-fitting waistband proved it. She took a sip of her drink and caught sight of their young server as she approached the table with a dessert plate. On the plate rested an enormous slice of key lime pie, topped with sky-high meringue. One of the restaurant's feathered inhabitants, a red hen, darted across the server's path with a frenzy of clucking.

Dinah took custody of the plate. She picked up her fork and quickly lifted a bite of pie to her mouth. Closing her eyes, she said, "This little slice of heaven melts on my tongue." She pushed the plate toward Mira. "Try some."

"No, thanks," Mira replied. "I'm stuffed as it is. I haven't been hungry lately. My taste buds must have gone numb. But they are back in business big-time today."

"I know why you feel better. Clearing out Pauline's clothes is a good first step toward moving forward." She pointed her fork at Mira. "Do you realize how much it would please her to know we took her stuff to a homeless shelter?"

Mira had decided to donate everything except for the tangerine scarf. There wasn't any need to become lost in sentiment. Especially since she knew an apartment would give her even less space than the small rental house she'd soon be vacating. The prior night, she'd spent hours on her laptop but hadn't had a shred of luck finding a place to live. Possibly because another subject holding much more interest had kept her occupied.

As if reading her thoughts, Dinah asked, "Have you found an apartment yet?"

"Nothing that grabbed me. Luckily, Isabel has been gracious. She said she'd wait to put the house up for sale until after I move, but I don't want to take advantage of her good nature."

"I'm glad she's being reasonable. Isabel knows you need time to get your bearings before you make a decision." Dinah scooped another bite of pie into her mouth.

Mira set her goblet on the table. "As a matter of fact, I've been considering the possibility of going in a new direction."

"What do you mean? I thought you said you didn't find another place."

"My lack of success was probably due to me being on safari for something else."

Dinah's eyes narrowed. "The look on your face makes the hair on my arms stand at attention. What are you up to?"

"I can't stop thinking about Pauline's letter. It's like giving a teaspoon of water to somebody who's dying of thirst. A little isn't enough. There's so much more I want to know." Mira lifted the glass to her lips again and took a deep swallow to make what she had to say easier. "I spent the evening hunting for information on James Todd. There were all kinds of hits, but nothing seemed to fit with Pauline's letter. I tried linking his name to medical supply sales with no luck. Then I searched for his name and Kansas City. Still nothing. I expanded the search to include Missouri and scrolled forever until I ran across an old article in the society section of a Saint Louis newspaper. It associated him with a woman, apparently his sister, who married some up-and-coming lawyer."

Dinah leaned forward. "That sounds promising. What did you find out?"

"Not much. Apparently, he was best man at his sister's wedding. I practically went cross-eyed staring at the screen, but no matter how long I looked, it was the only scrap of information that fit."

"Uh-huh. Well, too bad you couldn't learn more about him, but it's probably just as well. The way he up and ditched Pauline, who knows what kind of person he is? Maybe he's a con man. Or maybe he turned state's evidence and got put in a witness protection program." Pauline's scowl left no doubt as to her opinion of the man's moral fiber.

"Wham! See what I mean? Now you make me wonder whether I ought to worry about the genetics of inheriting criminal tendencies. There could be big clunky convict shoes in my future instead of flip-flops."

"I was only kidding." Dinah patted her hand. "Anything shoddy you inherited from him would be doubly crossed out by what you got from Pauline."

"Still, it begs the question. No one could have had a better mother than I did, but there's a part of my heritage that's missing. I don't know anything about my father. And," she added emphatically, "it's time I find out."

"Where would you even start, Mira? The trail sounds awfully cold to me."

"Not when I got smart and changed my focus." Mira took another sip of liquid courage. "I hunted for his sister."

Dinah's eyebrows disappeared under her bangs. "And?"

"Bingo. I found her. Elise Becker. A big fish in a big pond. She and her husband, Tom, live in Kansas City.

There were a ton of articles on them. He owns a major law firm. She apparently organizes lots of charity events."

"I don't want to be a killjoy, but high society people aren't likely to give you the time of day. She probably won't even take your call."

"Most likely, you're right. That's why I plan to talk to her in person." A hot itch at the crest of her back made Mira hope she wasn't getting ready to break out in stress hives.

"Mira Gordon, don't you dare mess with me. I know you as well as anybody, and here you are talking about heading off on a," she took a moment as if searching for the proper words, "wild goose chase. You're not the type to do something as foolish as that."

"Exactly what type am I? I've stewed over that question before, but my life was lazier and a lot more comfortable when I didn't think about it at all. Now there's one thing I can tell you for sure. My world has been shaken up, and it'll never be the same again."

"Keep in mind your life hasn't been as lazy as you seem to think. You earned a degree in…What was it, again?" She snapped her fingers. "Culinary Management. You have a job. And you have goals."

"A degree won't disappear if I leave for a while. Neither will a goal. Right now, all I need to do is get answers."

"So…This is temporary? You're coming back?"

Good question.

Too much had happened in a short span of time. Until she knew more, how could she make any commitment? The hopeful look on Dinah's face reminded Mira she wasn't the only one who missed Pauline. Mira finally lifted and dropped her shoulders. "Why wouldn't I?"

"Then I guess you better go, lovie. Soak it all up and learn what you can. Sometimes, you gotta take risks. Even though you'll always be a conch, it doesn't mean you can't venture out to discover your roots."

The VW van sat parked in front of the house, newly washed and all but shimmering in the sun. Pauline had adored lively colors, as her van clearly proved. With the assistance of Dinah and her husband, Joe, what remained of Mira's belongings had been crammed into Pauline's teal-colored suitcase, a couple of large boxes, and an oversized canvas duffle bag.

"You sure you don't want to keep any of your furniture or other things?" Joe frowned at her. "We can hang on to them until you come back."

Mira turned away from the cheerful yellow house she and Pauline had shared all her life. It wouldn't do to get emotional now. Already her chest felt tight, and her hands tingled. "I think it's best to sell everything else. Isabel is putting up a 'For Sale' sign tomorrow, so nothing can stay. You don't have room to store any of this at your place. What doesn't sell can be donated to a shelter."

"All right, lovie," Dinah said. "We'll do it your way. Just say where to send the money. Or we could put it under the mattress for you." She grinned.

"I'll tell you as soon as I know." Mira laughed and turned to hug Joe. "Thanks for your help. Do me a favor and watch out for my friend. Don't let her work herself into a dither worrying about me."

"Of course, I'm gonna worry." Dinah yanked Mira away from Joe and into a big hug. "I want you to hurry up and get answers so you can come back home to us. While you're away, I'll keep my eyes open for a nice apartment. And I'm sure you could get your job back in a minute." Dinah's eyes were watery as she said goodbye.

"Don't cry, or I will too." Mira sniffled. "This feels strange, like it couldn't be happening. Key West is so small everybody knows everybody else's business. Now I'm heading for a new world that I'm completely clueless about."

"Yeah, well, you better keep your eyes peeled. I listen to the nightly news and see the awful stuff that happens. Here, you know exactly who to stay away from; but you won't have a clue about other places. There are bad people out there. Don't get mixed up with them."

"No worries. I'll be too busy driving to get into trouble. According to the map, KC is over sixteen-hundred miles away."

"Lordy, I get the shivers thinking about it. From here to Kansas City? That's a long pull to tackle all alone. What if the van breaks down? Or you get lost? What if you run out of money?"

"The trip is all mapped out, and the van is fine. You know how Pauline babied it. I've got enough cash, and the VW makes a great mobile hotel room. Plus, there are a thousand rest stops and gas stations and anything else I'll need between here and there. I don't speed, so before you even say it, I won't drive too fast. All the new scenery will keep me occupied. I intend to check everything out as I go."

"Seems weird for you to be off on your own." Dinah exhaled heavily. "But you probably need to do this. Otherwise, you'll spend your whole life wishing you had. See you soon, lovie. Bless up."

Mira smiled and stepped away from Dinah. "Bless up," she replied and gave Joe a wave.

She climbed into the driver's seat and started the engine. A tremor of apprehension mixed with excitement made her shiver despite the day's heat. Mira took one final glance at the place she'd called her home and then aimed her vehicle toward the Overseas Highway.

The road spooled out before her like a long ribbon surrounded by the sea. It would be over one hundred miles before she passed through each of the Keys and reached the mainland. She took a deep breath to blunt the sharp edge of her nerves. The van chugged along like a champ, inspiring her with a sense of freedom. She settled herself into the present moment and the pure beauty of the drive.

By the time Key Largo—the final island before the mainland—loomed ahead, Mira's palms were no longer damp. Depending on the number of stops she would make, she'd be in Kansas City within a few days. The thought lifted her spirit higher than it had been in months.

Chapter Three

Aiden Stewart turned his truck's wipers to the fastest speed but still had to hunch forward and squint his eyes to see the road. As usual, the weather in Kansas City had changed quickly. The current downpour started with a middle-of-the-night sprinkle. By morning, it turned into a Costa Rican rainforest kind of day. On a straight stretch of road, he glanced toward the sky. From the looks of a thick wall of dark clouds, it would be a while before the storm let up. Aiden rounded a corner, and his pickup splashed through water that looked like a pond on the road. The tires of his sturdy Dodge Ram held tight to the pavement as he kept a firm grip on the wheel. This beauty of a truck was worth every penny he'd paid for it, despite the expression on his father's face when Aiden had driven over to show off his new purchase. His dad was too deep in the Ford camp to be impressed by any other brand.

His mind moved on to today and what lay ahead at work. With all the rain, it was bound to be challenging. Aiden stretched his head toward his right shoulder and then to the left, his neck crackling. He'd once thought firefighters spent all their time battling flames. Now he knew better. Duties included a multitude of diverse incidents—traffic accidents, medical emergencies, and sometimes a task as mundane as installing a child's safety seat for a nervous new parent. Crazy as it sounded, his station had once even gotten a frantic call about a kitten who'd climbed a tree. Really, people?

Nevertheless, he loved his job. The excitement and the challenge outweighed any negatives. "Ready for anything" was his captain's motto. And so they were. With equipment cleaned, polished, and checked at every shift change. Despite the endless bantering—usually at the expense of a fellow crew member—when the phone rang, they got serious fast. Everybody knew a call could bring—quite literally—anything.

The rainfall lightened from torrential to moderate, and Aiden turned the wipers down a notch from the breakneck speed setting. Maybe the storm would ease up sooner than he thought, which would be a relief, especially since he'd gotten out of the door later than he wanted. His eight-year-old daughter, Lily, hadn't felt well when she woke up, complaining about a stomachache. He'd brought her a glass of apple juice and glanced at the clock, trying to be patient. It was his goal to arrive at work thirty minutes before his shift started—the least he could do for the guys waiting to get off.

After forty-five long minutes, Lily finally announced she felt better. Aiden had handed her a banana to eat while he drove to his parents' house and then dropped her off—with the ever-present shadow of guilt hanging heavier than ever over him.

His thoughts were swept away when he spied a curve in the street ahead of him that marked the half-way point to the station. With no other delays, he'd arrive only a hair later than the dot of seven-thirty. He let up on the gas pedal and twisted the wheel to make the turn. But no sooner than he rounded the corner, he drew in a sharp breath. A van was parked on the side of the road, not quite out of the traffic lane. A girl stood next to it, directly in his path. Aiden slammed on the brakes and blared his horn. She jumped out of the way and flattened herself against the van. His truck skidded to a stop within a mere foot of where she'd been standing. He must have splashed a rooster tail of water on her. She looked soaked to the skin. Realization sunk in, and Aiden's heart pounded in his ears. *I almost hit her!*

He took a minute to catch his breath. Why would anyone be foolish enough to stand in the street? What was wrong with her? Shock and fear mutated into righteous anger. He positioned his truck to protect the girl from oncoming traffic and turned on his emergency flashers before opening the door. Fueled by the aftereffects of his alarm, Aiden charged straight toward her. "Are you out of your mind? What the hell do you mean by standing in the road? This is a blind curve, and it's pouring rain. What's wrong with you?" Words fired from his mouth like gunpowder.

Her eyes met his, and she blinked. "One of my tires blew out, and I was getting ready to change it. I guess I didn't think about the traffic."

Aiden could barely hear her voice over the drum of rain. The girl—young woman, he amended to himself after closer inspection—had huge eyes and an expression that registered panic. She glanced around her as if looking for a place to flee, and he felt a pinch of regret. No wonder she seemed so scared. He must look—and sound—like a maniac. Aiden brushed a sleeve across his rain-soaked forehead. "Look, I apologize for coming on so strong, but the fact is you could be laying underneath my truck right now instead of on your feet and alive. You scared the crap out of me."

His change in demeanor didn't erase the suspicion from her wide green eyes. She said nothing and watched him warily as the rain continued to patter down. A sedan honked and swerved around his truck while Aiden took a moment to assess her. A couple of inches over five feet tall. Slender. Paler than she ought to be. Red hair twisted into a thick braid that hung, dripping, over her shoulder. Arms crossed tight over a drenched denim shirt. He tried to figure out what he could say that might bring color into her cheeks and noticed her shiver. His gaze left her to settle on her vehicle; it was a van painted like photos he'd once seen on a 1970's record album cover. A psychedelic VW? He looked lower and saw the proof of what she'd told him.

The tire on the front driver's side formed an airless rubber splotch under the rim.

Aiden heaved a sigh. He'd be late to work anyway. Might as well make himself useful. "Okay, this is a dangerous corner with poor visibility. How about I give you a hand? We need to clear your van off the road before something bad happens." In a semblance of politeness, he forced himself to smile as benignly as he could. "My name's Aiden Stewart. What's yours?"

Ignoring his question, she replied, "I don't need any help. I can change my own tire."

She obviously didn't want to offer a name. The idea of her trying to use a jack in the rain struck him as a lousy one. What if the vehicle slipped off and crushed her? Come to think of it, the last thing he ought to do was allow *anyone* to crawl under a van in not-so-great weather conditions. "This is no time or place to be messing around with a car problem. I'm fast at switching out tires. Unless you're part of a Daytona race crew, why don't you let me take care of this?"

The redhead waited for a minute like she was weighing his words before she pointed. "The jack and the tire are in the back of the van." She shivered again.

"You're soaked. Would you like to wait inside my truck?" She shook her head emphatically at his offer, so he shrugged and went to retrieve what he needed. The first thing he noticed was the Florida plates. When he opened the door, a folded sleeping bag and suitcase caught his eye. *I bet she's been traveling for a while.*

Aiden grabbed the jack and slung it over his shoulder. He rolled the spare to the front of the VW with his free hand. Near the deflated tire, he clunked the equipment on the pavement. Grabbing a couple of jack stands from the back of his pickup, Aiden got to work. Thankfully, the rain had enough decency to drop off to a light drizzle. She stayed close beside him while he jacked up the vehicle. When he started to remove the bolts, she cupped her hands to take them.

One lug nut stuck tight, and he had to twist it so hard that he worried about stripping the threads. He jerked it a few more times before the nut moved. After that, the job went fast. Once he had the spare bolted securely, he lowered the van back to the ground, and then checked his handiwork. "You might want to put more air in that tire. It looks low. Most gas stations have an air pump you can use."

He thought he detected a hint of humor form in her eyes. "I know. I'll take care of it. Thanks for helping me." Now that her van was mobile, she looked much more at ease. "I'd like to pay you for your trouble."

"No, ma'am. I'm glad I could be of assistance." He heard himself slipping into firefighter persona. What was wrong with taking a moment to be polite and respectful? Oh yeah. Captain Zampella. Aiden ought to be burning rubber for the station, where Zamp would most certainly be waiting to chew him out. As little as one minute past shift start time was considered beyond unacceptable.

"Then I suppose all I can do is thank you again." For the first time, a broad and beautiful smile lit her damp face before she turned toward the ridiculous-looking vehicle.

He watched her climb in. Obviously, his initial impression had been wrong. Her pale skin didn't mean she was a candidate for a fainting spell. It marked her as a true redhead. The VW's engine exploded into life, which reminded Aiden of his job and his boss. He dashed toward the truck, vaulted to the driver's seat, and revved the pickup's engine before he realized he still hadn't gotten her name.

A strange sense of disappointment followed.

After thirty minutes of catching hell in Captain Zampella's office, Aiden was finally dismissed to slink away to the locker room, shaking his head. He peeled off his wet clothes, toweled himself dry, and donned a clean uniform. Zamp had been much hotter under the collar than usual, acting as if Aiden didn't already know the rules or the fact that being five minutes late to his shift wouldn't win any popularity contests among the crew. Keith Puno, his best buddy and co-worker, had warned Aiden via text message about Zamp's mood only minutes before Aiden's arrival. The chewing out he took proved Puno hadn't been exaggerating.

Puno joined Aiden in the locker room and nudged his shoulder. "What happened, man? It's not like you to be late."

"I nearly hit a woman who was dealing with a flat tire. I helped her because I thought that would be better than someone running over her and creating another call for us."

"Nice. What'd Zamp say?"

"He just gave me a warning, since it hasn't happened before." Aiden leaned over to tie his shoe. "This whole mess wasn't much more than lousy timing, but I didn't have any choice. Even knowing the consequences, I couldn't just drive off and leave her stranded."

"Always the hero, aren't you, Stewart?" Puno eyeballed him. "A woman, you say? Was she young? Pretty?"

Aiden considered the question as he tied his other shoe. Truthfully, even soaking wet, the redhead was stunning. She was probably in her early twenties. But he wasn't about to give Puno any ammunition. Instead, he grumbled. "Oh, knock it off. So far, this day's been hellacious, and the shift has barely started. I hate to think what we're in for over the next twenty-four hours."

"Well, let me fill you in. First, you missed out on the equipment check, with Zamp reading us the riot act because when he inspected the pumper he found a smudge of mud on the floor. We all got our asses handed to us. Then he pointed out there better not be any sluffing off during the staff meeting at 0900 hours. But you? Maybe you ought to grab a nap instead of attending something as boring as a meeting. I'm sure Zamp wouldn't mind if you got a little shut-eye after rescuing a damsel in distress."

"Go stuff it, Puno," Aiden growled. Today he wasn't much in the mood for the typical ribbing that made up a fair amount of his daily work life. There were two sure-fire stress relievers at the station. One: teasing each other unmercifully. And two: working out. Preferably both, in equal measure. Either choice was effective in minimizing tension and cementing solidarity between crew members. Even though he knew how much the men needed an outlet, he wasn't in the mood for hearing it now. He took a deep breath. "The meeting's still on?"

"Yep. And as far as I know, it's a general Come-to-Jesus event."

"We'll have to make the best of it, but I have a feeling eyes will be rolling like marbles. As soon as Zamp finishes sharing whatever pearls of wisdom he has, I'll be ready. When he asks if there are any questions, I'm going to bombard him. You know how much the captain loves questions."

Puno broke into a guffaw. "Zamp's always been under the impression guys who ask questions are the ones paying attention. That'll be a great strategy to get back in his good graces—and set yourself up as a target for big-time retribution. Because of you, the meeting will run longer. There's nothing we all love more than long meetings."

"Yep. That's the way I see it," Aiden said. "And I don't have any problem with handling the guys. What I need to do is cut my losses and make the boss happy with me again."

"Man, you are such a brown-noser. If the meeting runs longer than normal, I hate to consider what's in store for you tonight. Better sleep with one eye open, pal."

"Don't I always? You showed me that the first day we worked together by dusting my pillow with flour. Just enough so I woke up the next morning looking like Bozo the Clown in full makeup."

Puno slapped his knee and bellowed with laughter. "That was a good one. Do you remember what Zamp said?"

"How can I forget? He took one look at me and yelled, 'Is this what they're teaching now in the fire academy? Things have changed since I was there.' He knew exactly what had happened, but he stayed totally deadpan."

"The first of many bonding moments between us. Glad you didn't hold it against me. Hell, you and I have pulled some of the dirtiest tricks this station has ever seen."

"Better keep that quiet. Remember, I'm trying to get back on Zamp's good side."

"You don't have anything to worry about. I've got your back."

Aiden snorted and then broke into a grin. It was the honest to God truth. He didn't have the slightest doubt Puno would always have his back.

Chapter Four

Mira sat in her vehicle and waited for the man in the silver truck to zoom away before she cautiously eased back into traffic. Wet and chilled to the bone, she cranked up the heater. Until her tire blew out in Kansas City, the trip had been almost like a vacation. Her mind replayed the string of memories.

She'd admired plants with lovely purple flowers growing along the roadside as she crossed the state line of Georgia, charmed by the view until she hit a traffic snarl in Atlanta. After breathing her way through a mild anxiety attack, the snapshot views of Tennessee and Kentucky had made up for it. Then there were the impressively hilly and rocky vistas of southern Illinois, leading straight into St. Louis, where she'd ogled the silver arch, a gigantic curve of steel against the sky, reflecting the sun like a polished mirror. Pushing on through the last leg of her journey, she had cut through a route clear across the middle of Missouri, past an eclectic mix of towns and farmland until she'd reached the final leg of her destination.

That's when the storm had hit, with rain pummeling the roof of her vehicle. She'd tried hard to see the road, but the windshield wipers could barely keep up with the deluge. Between the tempest and the knowledge that she'd almost reached her destination, Mira had forced herself to relax by breathing in and out ten times. She'd just turned the wheel to round a curve, when an enormous boom shook through her steering column. With a death-grip on the wheel, Mira had braked to a gradual stop. The flopping noise and distinct lean of the vehicle had clearly shown that her van suffered a blowout. In the rain, no less.

"Oh, cha." Mira had automatically blurted the word she'd heard from Pauline on the rare occasions when someone ruffled her mother's normally patient nature.

Changing the tire would be a challenge under perfect conditions, but during a storm and on an unfamiliar road? *Stop the drama, and count your blessings. This could have been much worse.* Come to think of it, somebody—Pauline?—must have been looking out for her. If the blowout had occurred on the highway instead of on a low speed limit road with less traffic, who knows how things would have turned out? The gentle reminder had returned her serenity. Rain or not, there wasn't anything she could have done but get out of the van and take care of the problem.

Then it happened. As she'd stood in the rain staring at what used to be her tire, a huge pickup truck had careened around the corner at warp speed, sliding on the wet pavement right in her direction. She had leapt toward the van for safety. When the truck came to a stop, the driver had burst out the door of his pickup and charged toward her like she was a red flag and he a bull. As though his carelessness had been all her fault.

Recalling Dinah's warning about dangerous people, she'd gone straight into defensive mode, keeping her eyes on the dark-haired man who wore a black t-shirt imprinted with some sort of emblem. He had tucked the shirt neatly into khaki pants making the outfit appear to be a uniform, but that didn't lessen his unnerving behavior. He had marched right up to her with his eyes blazing while rain pelted them both. The man must have been at least six feet tall. The rain-dampened fabric of his shirt had clung to muscular arms. That, along with the menacing look on his face, had been enough to make her consider dialing 911.

Just when she had been on the verge of bolting to her vehicle and locking the door, he'd stopped shouting, and then…apologized. At first, she'd wondered if he was one of those Jekyll and Hyde types until she recognized hints of sincere regret in the aqua-colored eyes that reminded her of the sea.

When he'd offered to change the tire, she'd hesitated only a short moment before taking the chance to trust him. He'd grabbed Pauline's spare tire and ancient jack without any fuss, completing the work quickly and efficiently. It would have taken her twice as long, and she knew it. *What was his name again? Aiden Stewart?* Maybe she'd misjudged…Aiden. He'd been nothing but a gentleman once he calmed down. His initial reaction must have come from their too-close-for-comfort encounter.

But she had no more time to dwell on what had happened.

Checking her phone's GPS, Mira forgot about the attractive Good Samaritan. She had a much more important—and, she had to admit, unsettling—situation ahead of her. The Becker home was a short distance away. Throughout her road trip, she'd rehearsed various approaches out loud while she drove, but none of them felt quite right. In the ideal scenario, her father would just so happen to be at the Becker house when she arrived. He'd answer her questions with a perfectly plausible reason for his absence—maybe amnesia?—but a photo of Pauline that Mira carried in her purse would bring memories flooding back. The knowledge of her identity would shock but then delight him. They'd hug as tears glistened in their eyes.

For the first time, she'd have a father. They could spend time getting to know one another. They'd make plans to keep in touch with phone calls and even schedule a visit from time to time. On Father's Day. She'd always felt left out on Father's Day.

Wouldn't it be nice if everything worked out so neatly? Yeah, right.

The onslaught of rain slowed to a stop, and Mira put aside her overly optimistic notions to take in the scenery. Small lots with moderately-sized homes were crammed close together but soon transformed into an area with larger pieces of ground, kept as meticulously as the luxury landscaped hotels in the Keys. This wasn't a surprise, given the palatial homes she saw. Homes that could easily be mistaken for a country club. She checked her GPS again and guided the VW into a gated community—thank goodness the gate was open—with an immense stone sign at the entrance.

The development was built next to a golf course. She'd never seen so much wide-open space, unless you counted the expanse of the sea. Slowly, she navigated the pristine avenues, craning her neck until she finally found the correct house number. Mira stopped her van and stared at the residence. An itch started on her right shoulder. She nurtured a vague hope the itch would go away while she continued to take in the colossal Becker home.

A large driveway curved up to an ornate Italian-looking fountain that sat in front of a palatial two-story structure built from warm-hued stone. Reflections from impressive arched windows welcomed her, with golf course greens visible in the background. Two tall columns framed a set of doors at the entrance, with an attached four-car garage on the house's left side. What looked like a small cottage was tacked on to the other side of the garage. Mira inched forward, half-expecting a security guard to stop her vehicle, but no one appeared.

She braked again and shut off the engine. Her gaze glued on the entrance, she got out of the VW, still thoroughly wet and shivering. Fighting an urge to bite her thumbnail, she squared her shoulders and plodded toward doors embellished with fancy stained-glass windows. Mira touched the doorbell and realized a camera mounted on the wall was aimed straight at her. The itch on her shoulder moved to the back of her neck.

A woman opened the door. She had brown hair frosted liberally with gray and looked friendly enough, although her eyebrows arched up when she glanced from Mira's soggy hair to the van in the background, its bright colors clashing with the artfully neutral surroundings. What a delightful picture they must make.

The woman finally spoke. "May I help you, Miss?"

"My name is Mira Gordon." She took a breath. "Are you Elise Becker?"

"No." The woman smiled. "I'm Mrs. Caldwell, the household manager. Do you have an appointment?"

"Do I need an appointment?" It hadn't occurred to Mira such a formal introduction would be necessary.

"If you let me know what you need, I can check to see whether she's available."

"Well…" Mira struggled for the proper words. "I'm trying to locate someone, and I hoped Mrs. Becker might be of help. I drove a really long time—all the way from Key West—just to speak to her."

Mrs. Caldwell's eyebrows lifted again. "That is a long way. Why do you think Mrs. Becker can be of help you?"

"I'm looking for a man by the name of James Todd. I think he's her brother."

The woman's mouth opened in surprise, but then her facial expression returned to unruffled politeness. She opened the door. "Please come in and have a seat. I'll find out if Mrs. Becker can see you."

Mira stepped across the threshold, and her footsteps echoed across the marble floor. Mrs. Caldwell pointed to a leather chair near the door.

In the regal surroundings, Mira realized again how out of place she must appear. She smoothed her damp hair. "I'm sorry for how I look. I got caught in the rain. I don't want to ruin the floor…or the chair."

"Don't worry about that. Do sit down."

Mira settled on the edge of the seat as Mrs. Caldwell began to ascend the lovely staircase that wound in an upward curl. This place looked more like a hotel lobby than someone's home. Her eyes strayed around the room. The floor under her feet gleamed. Each wall was painted a pale gray, accented by white baseboards, columns, and recessed ceilings. A sitting room just off the foyer caught her attention. It offered plush gray chairs along with a white coffee table, all arranged under a massive chandelier. The entire space made her feel like a soggy blot on the landscape—as out of place as her vehicle in the driveway. She rubbed her hands together nervously to warm them.

Movement from the corner caught her eye, and she swiveled her head back to the staircase. A slim blonde woman dressed in a cream-colored turtleneck and well-tailored black slacks came down the steps. Her meticulous appearance had Mira squirming uncomfortably, feeling like something she'd once seen a cat carry in after a night on the prowl. Mira stood and waited as the woman stepped closer, her perfectly ruby-red lips pressed together in a grim line.

"I understand you'd like to talk to me. What does this concern?"

Mrs. Becker's tone was curt, but Mira didn't want to miss out on what might be her only chance to get badly needed information. She kept her voice low and steady. "My name is Mira Gordon. If I'm not mistaken, James Todd is your brother. I was wondering if you would tell me where I could find him."

The woman narrowed her eyes. "Exactly why are you looking for my brother?"

Cha. Maybe the two of them didn't have a warm relationship. "It's sort of a long story."

The woman held up her hand. "Before you even start, let me warn you. I do not tolerate hearing nonsense or lies. If it's money you're after, you should know my husband is an attorney, and you won't get far." Her words were dipped in skepticism.

Mira shook her head. "I promise you I'm not after money. Please let me tell you the short version of what I came here to say." *Can I really make this into a short version?* Since the woman didn't order her out, Mira felt encouraged enough to plunge in.

"As long as I can remember, it was always just my mother and me. I never had a father in my life. She would never even speak about him. A few weeks ago, just before she passed away, she gave me a letter she'd written. It said my father was a man from Kansas City named James Todd. I searched online and found what information I could. As you might guess, I had a lot of questions, so I decided to drive here. There are so many things I've always wanted to know. I'm hoping you'll help me."

Elise Becker's face went white as the baseboards. Her hand held on to the staircase railing as if to steady herself.

"How dare you come to me with such a fabrication. Get out."

"I'm telling the truth." Mira lifted her chin. "Exactly as my mother explained to me in her letter. If you'd only give me a number or an address for him, I'll leave and not bother you again."

Mrs. Becker narrowed her eyes. "Did your mother's letter say anything other than what you've told me?"

"Well," Mira figured she might as well expand on the details. "She said she'd met him when he came to Key West for a sales conference years ago. They must have fallen for each other right away because they spent the entire week together. Before he left, he said he had to go back home to settle things with his family and asked her to wait for him. They apparently were planning a future together, but she never heard from him again. She called and left messages. He didn't answer." Mira swallowed past an enormous boulder lodged in her throat. "And I came along nine months later."

If Elise's face looked pale before, now it was colorless. She opened and closed her mouth, staring with such intensity that Mira wanted to back away and run out the door. Yet she couldn't leave now—not if she wanted answers.

"I'm sorry," Mira continued. "I know this must be a shock. It came as a shock to me, too. Please understand why I needed to come. All my life, I've wanted to know about my father. Even if he doesn't want to go beyond seeing me one time, I need to try." Her voice broke, and in the silence that followed, the sound of nails clicked across the floor.

A small white dog loped into the foyer. He saw Mira and barked himself into a frenzy. Elise said, "Louie, stop," but the pup ignored his mistress and charged right at Mira, who jumped at the chance to do something besides stand there and feel foolish. She knelt and held out her hand. Louie left off barking to sniff her fingers. He must have deemed her a non-threat because his tail moved back and forth, and he slurped her thumb with his little pink tongue. By the time she was sure they were friends, Mira felt more composed. She straightened to face Elise again. "Are you willing to help me?"

"This is…not what I expected to hear. Give me a moment. My head's reeling." Elise put her hand on her forehead.

Hope inflated Mira's spirit. She held her breath and waited.

"It's been so long. But I remember now. My brother did go to a conference in Key West. So many things happened later that I'd forgotten. He called me before he left the Keys and said he had something important to share with me."

Mira could sense a change in Elise Becker's demeanor. Her stomach fluttered with excitement, and her mouth stretched into a grin.

The woman tilted her head and examined Mira again as if looking for clues. "You have dimples when you smile. Just like Jimmy's. And…yes. You have the Todd nose. Like mine."

The comments pleased Mira more than anything she'd heard Elise say so far. It was finally happening. She'd get to meet her father. Get to talk to him face-to-face. "Do you think I could see him sooner rather than later? If he won't mind, that is."

A shadow crossed Elise's features. "My dear," she reached out and touched Mira's cheek as though checking to be sure it wasn't a phantom standing before her, "I'm afraid that won't be possible."

Mira's heart dropped to her toes. "Why not?"

"All those years ago, Jimmy was on his way home from Key West. He had a few customer visits he needed to make along the way." Her eyes moved away from Mira's. "A day after he and I spoke, a call came from the police in Tennessee. My brother had been in a terrible accident." Elise's hand dropped. "He didn't make it."

The bones disappeared from Mira's knees, and she plopped back into the leather chair. "He's dead?"

Elise winced at the blunt question. "Yes."

Mira's temples ached, and she massaged them. She couldn't think of a single thing to say. Why had she pinned all her hopes on finding her father? Now she felt as thoroughly deflated as her tire had been earlier.

"You brought back a time I try my level best to block from my mind. Jimmy was several years younger than me. In many ways, I felt like more of a mother to him than a sister."

"I didn't mean to stir up painful memories. It was a mistake for me to come. I wasn't thinking clearly. I'm sorry, Mrs. Becker."

"No. I shouldn't have been so harsh. I'm sure this is upsetting news for you."

Mira pushed her damp braid off her shoulder. "You forget; I never met him. I only just learned his name. My feelings aren't wrapped up in the past like yours." She extended her hand. "I'd better be on my way. It's a long drive back home."

Elise took Mira's hand but didn't let go. "Wait. What you said and what Jimmy told me fit together. I believe it's true. You are my brother's daughter, and that makes you my niece. Please stay. At least for a little while. I'll answer as many of your questions as I can." The corner of the woman's mouth curved into a half-smile. "I have pictures I can show you, and if you like, I'll make copies for you."

Mira considered the long journey home. The letdown of coming so far with little more information than she had when she left the Keys was unbearable. True, her friends were waiting in Florida, but Pauline was gone. If she stayed, there might be—as Dinah had said—the possibility of finding her roots and maybe even a family she had never known existed.

"I appreciate the invitation," Mira said. "And I'll gladly take you up on it."

Chapter Five

Aiden stepped through the front door and into the kitchen, where his parents sat at a round table nestled in a bay window nook. Each had a cup of morning coffee before them, part of their usual routine. His mom faced the window, where an assortment of multi-hued birds pecked at seeds in the feeder outside, while his dad stayed hidden behind an open newspaper, no doubt reading the sports section. Aiden caught a whiff of freshly baked cinnamon rolls. The luscious aroma hung in the air, and his stomach growled. This morning, rather than eating breakfast with the guys before shift change, he'd cleaned the pumper floor until it sparkled. When Zamp saw him working, the captain's eyes signaled approval, although he kept his mouth in a straight line.

"Any rolls left, Mom?" Aiden sweetened the request by leaning over to plant a kiss on her cheek.

"Of course," she said with a delighted twinkle in her eyes. "I'm surprised you asked. You know I always double the recipe. Help yourself. They're on the counter."

Aiden grabbed a decadent-looking roll, took a bite, and closed his eyes in a moment of sensory bliss. "These things are so sinful they ought to be illegal. Worth every extra hour it takes to burn off the calories."

Flattery won him a modest smile, as he knew it would. "Oh, what a line you have. Baking is how I de-stress. Sometimes I think I should find a healthier way of relaxing."

"Don't you dare stop making these rolls. Even if there is evidence of weakness in my waistline." Aiden's dad folded the newspaper he'd been reading to jump in on the conversation. "How'd your shift go, son? Was it busy? I figured all that rain would keep you guys hopping."

"Luckily, it wasn't as bad as it could have been. No more than three calls for minor stuff. The worst thing that happened was getting chewed out by the captain."

"Captain Zampella gave you a hard time?" His mom shot an indignant look at Aiden. "You're one of the most dedicated employees he has, always taking extra shifts or working longer hours whenever they ask. What possessed him to do such a thing?"

"He had good reason. I got to work late."

"Why were you late?" His dad's reading glasses slid down his nose. "When you dropped Lily off yesterday morning, you left in plenty of time. Was there a traffic snag?"

"No, a woman with a flat tire." An image of the red-haired beauty, thoroughly bedraggled, but still quite pleasing to the eye, came to his mind. "I rounded a corner, and she was standing right in my lane. I almost hit her. So, I changed the tire before somebody *did* hit her."

"Surely, the captain wouldn't hold that against you." His mom shook her head and got up to refill her mug. She normally limited herself to only one cup, so Aiden knew she must be seething. "I've never heard of such a thing. You're a public servant, and you were performing your civic duty for a person in trouble."

"Settle down now, Betty." Aiden's dad, always sensible, took off his wayward glasses and placed them on the table. "Rules are rules, you know."

"And there are exceptions to every rule. Helping someone certainly sounds like an exception to me, Robert."

Hmm. Robert instead of Bob. She was definitely peeved. Aiden shrugged. "It is what it is, Mom. I got a warning. It could have been worse."

"I certainly hope he remembers how lucky he is to have you." She huffed out a breath.

"Thanks, Mom. I'll have him give you a call if he has the nerve to forget."

"If the captain ever wants another one of my cinnamon rolls, he'd better keep it in mind."

"Okay, okay. That's enough, Betty." His dad cast a swift intervention. "Now that you've got your mom ready to boycott the station's cinnamon roll supply, shall we change the subject? Your daughter's upstairs brushing her teeth. She'll be down in a minute."

"How is Lily? Did she complain anymore about feeling sick? She seemed fine when I called to tell her good-night."

"That child is fit as a fiddle." Distracted from resentment at the captain, Aiden's mom's face softened.

"After you dropped her off, she said her tummy hurt, but she seemed perfectly fine only a short time later. I took her to school and didn't receive any calls from the nurse."

"This isn't our first go-round for these stomachaches. When I took her to the doctor, he couldn't find any reason for them. Still, I'm worried." Aiden put the rest of the roll in his mouth and wiped his sticky fingers on a napkin.

"My poor little Lily." His mom made a tsk-tsk sound of sympathy. "I know what ails her. She misses her mama. A traumatic experience can cause a lot of emotional pain for a child."

Aiden felt a sudden sharp throb of loss and rolled his shoulder, still a little stiff from last night's workout session. "I miss Rose too, Mom, but there's nothing I can do except get by as best I can and try to move on." For the millionth time, he considered his weary reality. *Always easier said than done.*

A swift patter of footsteps announced Lily's arrival and snapped Aiden back to attention. She appeared at the doorway, her light brown hair in pigtails, and her hazel eyes bright, pausing for a breathless second. She spotted him and shouted, "Daddy!"

Racing toward his waiting arms, the child's joyful tone booted out any lingering melancholic thoughts. He swooped her up into a big hug and nuzzled his cheek against hers. "How's my girl?"

She answered by locking her small arms around his neck. When she let go, he kissed the top of her head. "Were you good for Memaw and Papa?"

"Uh-huh. Are you taking me to school today, Daddy?"

"Yes, honey. Do you have your stuff?"

She waved her arm toward the door with the confident gesture of an eight-year-old who knew Memaw could be counted on to gather up the necessities.

"We're off, then." He redirected his gaze toward his parents. "I appreciate you guys watching her. Don't know what I'd do without you." With sole responsibility for double-duty parenting, his own parents' love and support made Aiden's twenty-four hours on, forty-eight hours off schedule possible.

"We love having her. It's a great excuse to spoil our only grandchild." His mother smoothed a tendril of Lily's hair from her forehead. "See you in a couple of days, sweetie."

She blew a kiss toward her grandparents. "Bye, Memaw. Bye, Papa."

His dad winked at Lily and then picked up the newspaper.

Aiden walked his daughter outside and got her strapped into the back-seat booster when she stiffened. "Daddy, I forgot Siggy!"

"Be right back." Aiden sprinted for the house to grab the precious stuffed animal. Siggy, a plush, three-toed sloth, and Lily were inseparable. He and Rose had bought the souvenir a couple of years ago during a visit to the zoo after Lily couldn't take her eyes off the real live version of the animal. The child's delight had made the purchase well worth it. She slept with Siggy every night and carried him wherever she went—except school, of course. Aiden feared the day when Siggy fell apart from all those enthusiastic hugs and kisses Lily bestowed on him. Or worse yet, if the creature ever got lost.

His mom met Aiden at the door with Siggy in hand. He snatched it and mumbled a quick thanks before dashing back to the truck. If they didn't hurry, they'd be late. He remembered Zamp's lecture from yesterday grimly, determined not to let the clock beat him two days in a row.

"Here you are, Lily-Lou." Aiden handed the toy to his child and then drove toward her school with the speedometer pushed to the posted speed limit. He pulled the truck into the parking lot exactly on time. Aiden ushered his daughter to the office, signed her in, and kissed her cheek before leaving.

Returning to his vehicle, Aiden turned on the ignition and sat a moment, staring at the brick building. An ache squeezed his heart. The past year had been every bit as difficult for Lily as it had been on him. How long did it take to recover from loss? More to the point, when did it become easier? As soon as he thought he'd extinguished the worst of the pain, embers would stir and flare up again. Those were the moments that left him wondering. Was a person only allowed a certain amount of happiness within their lifetime, measured out with a precise mathematical formula? Had he already used up his share?

For the truth was, he and Rose were great together. They had been deeply in love, content, and satisfied. After Lily was born, the addition of a daughter added a new dimension to their relationship. By the time Lily turned four, they had been trying hard to give their daughter a brother or sister. Rose had been an only child, and she desperately wanted a sibling for Lily. After months of doing what online experts recommended, Rose had become so discouraged that she and Aiden had scheduled an appointment at a fertility clinic. They'd both been poked, prodded, and analyzed in ways that tossed any semblance of modesty or privacy out the door. When the doctor had finally called Rose with results, the news was not what they had expected to hear.

Aiden pulled into the driveway of his tidy cedar and stone ranch-style house. He eyed the front yard and mentally added another item to his to-do list. Leaves from the sugar maple tree had completely covered the ground. Tomorrow he'd rake and bag them. Aiden grabbed his duffel, Lily's suitcase, and Siggy as he headed for the garage door entrance to the house.

When he stepped inside, the foyer echoed with each footfall. That's when it hit him. Walking into the empty house shot down all his defenses. He missed being greeted with a kiss. Having someone ask about his day and tell him about hers. He all but ached to have a conversation with somebody other than Puno, his parents, or the guys at work. Aiden put down the bags and paced toward the kitchen.

A miniature rose plant sitting half in and half out of a speck of sunshine on the floor caught his eye. *I forgot to water you again.* He filled a cup and hastily dumped liquid onto dry dirt. Instead of green and healthy, the plant looked more like twigs with brown leaves. This was the last of Rose's jungle of plants that he'd managed to keep alive. He hoped his negligence hadn't obliterated it.

Aiden sighed and turned toward the window. A clear sky and sunshine promised a much better day than yesterday's wet dreariness. How would it feel to get in his truck and go for a long drive, abandoning all his cares and worries for a while? He almost succumbed to the pleasant notion until a long list of duties changed his mind.

He decided to unpack the bags and start a load of laundry. Rubbing the itchy stubble on his chin, Aiden opened Lily's suitcase and pulled out her soiled clothes. The mindless task had him teetering on the edge of a foul mood. He tossed the dirty items into the washer and then reminded himself of his daughter—a small-scale version of her mother—and the pleasure that came from watching their child grow up.

Whenever Lily looked at him, he saw Rose's hazel eyes. It was a permanent reminder and one that made it practically impossible to do what he'd so flippantly said to his mom about moving on. True, he did need to think about a direction for his future rather than drifting along with the current of everyday life. But moving on? How the devil did one befuddled and more than slightly broken father make such a monumental thing happen?

He waited for a clever resolution to pop into his mind. A dumb thing to do since, as usual, no answers showed up. Aiden counseled himself to shuck off the attitude and get busy with more productive pursuits.

Gathering an armload of dirty towels, he carried them back to the laundry room.

Chapter Six

With a duffel bag in one hand and pulling her suitcase along with the other, Mira followed Mrs. Caldwell upstairs to the bedroom Elise had assigned to her. One step inside, and she had to stop and look around. Elegant, serene, and massive. It all but took her breath away.

The cream and gray color scheme echoed the rest of the house. Chic furniture was tastefully arranged around the room, like the deep gray fainting couch tucked between two corner windows next to a floor lamp. Mira could envision late-night reading urges satisfied on that couch, especially after she spied the wall of built-in bookcases. Dozens of volumes, accented by canine figurines and assorted other collectibles, sat on the shelves surrounding a large-screen television. Mira wasn't much for TV viewing, but she ached to check out the titles displayed before her. As if that weren't enough enticement, she spotted a gorgeous fireplace on another wall near an antique white queen-size bed covered with a thick charcoal comforter that looked incredibly tempting after nights of sleeping in a van.

"Let me show you the bathroom," Mrs. Caldwell said.

An attached white-tiled bathroom offered a separate shower and tub. A glance showed her that even the toilet was something special. It had a bidet. She held in a smile. Wait until she told Dinah about this.

"And here's your linen closet." Mrs. Caldwell opened a door where fluffy pure-white towels were displayed in neat stacks. "Over there is your clothes closet."

Closet? It looked more like a small country. Not even the most luxurious hotels in Key West were so spectacular. "All this seems too grand. I really only need a bed."

"Mrs. Becker is delighted you are here, and she didn't want anything less for you than the best suite in the house. I can see you're shivering. Why don't you change out of those wet clothes and relax? A warm shower or bath would do you a world of good."

"Thanks." Mira glanced at her soggy self. "I don't want to mess up this beautiful place."

"There's no need to worry. You should find everything you require in the bathroom. I'll check on you later and then give you a tour of the house." With a gentle smile, she turned and walked away.

Mira took a second look at the deluxe bathroom. She counted five whirlpool jets in the tub and could hear each one of them calling her name. A long soak sounded divine until she remembered she needed to wash her hair, too. With a regretful glance, she walked past the tub and turned on the shower. Once steam filled the room, she stepped in. Hot water pummeled her skin, forcing her tight muscles to loosen and her body to feel as soft as putty.

After toweling off, Mira put on jeans and the warmest shirt she owned. Fall in Kansas City was a lot colder than fall in Key West, although the hairdryer helped warm her. She ran her fingers through wet strands as the dryer hummed. Glancing toward the arched window that framed a pretty lake on the golf course, she wondered if any golf balls had ever hit the house. She decided against the possibility. Surely, no golfer would dare intrude on the sanctity of the Becker home.

Yawning, she put away the dryer and eyed the bed. It pulled her closer. Was it as soft and comfortable as it looked? She climbed on top without turning back the comforter and settled herself in. *Question answered. Feels like lying on a cloud.* Mira closed her eyes and allowed herself to drift.

A firm rap at the door bolted her upright, and she rubbed her eyes. How long had she been asleep?

"Miss Gordon, I wanted to let you know dinner will be served at six-thirty," Mrs. Caldwell's serene voice announced.

What must she think of me? Mira jumped from the bed and frantically smoothed the comforter. "Please come in. I fell asleep."

The house manager cracked open the door. "I knocked over an hour ago, but you didn't answer. I guessed you might be asleep. I hate to wake you, but you must be terribly hungry by now."

"Yes," Mira fumbled around to straighten wrinkles from her shirt. "I'll be ready."

When the sound of Mrs. Caldwell's footsteps faded away, Mira raced to a mirror. She ran a brush through her hair until the strands crackled and then plaited a long braid. Regarding her reflection, she hoped the yellow blouse and jeans she wore would do. Would her outfit be considered appropriate enough for a dinner served in such high-class real estate?

Stepping outside the bedroom, she hesitated. Which direction? Reasoning that the kitchen most likely would be on the first floor, she headed for the curved staircase. After a few steps down the hallway, the sound of voices behind a closed door stopped her.

"A stranger shows up on our doorstep, parks an ostentatious old van in the driveway, and gives you a ridiculous story. And what do you do? You believe every word she says and invite her to stay. This isn't like you, Elise."

Mira sucked in her lower lip. The man spoke in a voice tight with frustration. Could he be Elise's attorney husband?

"Everything she said fit with what happened. How could she know anything about Jimmy? Tom, she even *looks* like him."

Mira knew she ought to keep walking. Eavesdropping on a private conversation was rude and unethical, but she couldn't make herself move an inch.

"There are plenty of people who resemble other people. I could claim I'm the King of Sweden, but that doesn't make it true."

"Shh! Don't speak so loud," Elise admonished him. "She seems like a sweet young girl. And she just lost her mother. I think she's telling the truth."

"Look, dear," the man's voice became softer and more patient, "I understand how much you want to believe she's a link to your brother. I know what losing him did to you. But keep this in mind. She could have stumbled across information about Jimmy, connected him to us, and then manufactured a counterfeit story so we'd give her money. I can't in good conscience simply accept her claim without proof."

"What proof can she give you? All she has is a letter from her mother."

Now nothing could have convinced Mira to budge from the spot where she stood.

"Here's what proof she can give me. A DNA test."

Mira didn't wait to hear Elise's answer. She scurried for the stairs, her heart pounding so hard it thundered in her ears. Clearly, Mr. Becker considered her a liar, with nefarious ulterior motives. Her eyes stung, and she considered gathering her bags to leave for home. At least she was among friends there. People who cared about her. Trusted her.

Mrs. Caldwell appeared as Mira stepped to the foyer's marble floor, tilting her head slightly to one side. "Is something wrong?"

"I've been thinking. The offer for me to stay here is too generous. I really ought to leave."

"I can see something has upset you." Mrs. Caldwell's tranquil demeanor was so like Pauline's that Mira wanted to pull her into the comfort of a hug. The woman continued, "I'm sure you understand how painful a completely unexpected situation can be. Working through it may prove to be even harder. But that doesn't mean the process shouldn't happen."

Even Mrs. Caldwell's enigmatic comment sounded like something Pauline would have said.

"I guess you're right. There are bound to be raw feelings over anything related to Mrs. Becker's brother, no matter how long ago the accident happened. I don't have a clue how I feel about it myself."

"Try to be patient with us, dear." She patted Mira's shoulder. "Now, let me take you through the house, and then I'll show you to the dining room. Mrs. Becker ordered a feast to celebrate your arrival."

Awkward. That's the best way Mira could describe the atmosphere when she sat at the long dining table with Tom and Elise Becker. Even though the décor was designed for celebration, the atmosphere spoke otherwise.

A double set of candles glowed from within a floral centerpiece of yellow roses. Mr. Becker wore a suit with no tie, and his wife had on a form-fitting sheath dress. They looked like they were going to a cocktail party. Mira's jeans and slightly-wrinkled shirt were more suitable for the beach. She had hoped Mrs. Caldwell would join them for dinner, but when the house manager didn't appear, Mira figured the family took their meals without staff at the table.

Elise chatted in a euphoric way. "The weather's due to get much cooler this week. You mentioned you don't have any clothes for fall, and it can be bone-chilling here. I'd love to take you shopping tomorrow."

Mr. Becker assumed a disapproving expression but said nothing.

"Oh, that's really not necessary. I have a windbreaker. That'll be enough for now." Mira glanced at the handsome man forking a bite of steak into his mouth. "I won't be in Kansas City long enough to need warm clothes."

"My dear, we must have time to get to know you before you even speak of leaving. And please use our first names. I suppose you're too old to tack on the word 'aunt' or 'uncle,' but remember, we are family."

Before the start of dinner, Elise had made the effort to be been kind to Mira in a relentlessly determined way. She'd dragged out an album with pages loose enough to prove it had been viewed often, filled with pictures of James Todd. His childhood photos were cute, as with most little ones, but it was the grown-up images Mira wanted most to see. The man her mother had met. He had been tall and attractive, with blonde hair, and she understood what must have made Pauline swoon. In the photos where he smiled, Mira caught her breath. They *did* have the exact same dimples.

She nibbled at a bite of salad. The food smelled scrumptious, but, hungry as she was, she found it hard to eat. Every look Mr. Becker—Tom—gave her felt like a mini-version of judgment day. Mira took a sip of wine, a little drier blend than she preferred, before she spoke. "You mentioned making copies of photos. It would mean a lot to me. I'll pay any cost."

"Just say which ones you want, and I'll have Mrs. Caldwell take care of it tomorrow," Elise said firmly. "You don't need owe me anything."

Tom sliced into his steak. "Driving here from Key West is a rather big decision. Why did you come all this way alone? Did your employer give you a leave of absence?"

"There wasn't any reason to bring a friend. And as far as a job goes, I quit the bakery where I was apprenticing as a pastry chef." She saw the dubious look on his face and added defensively, "I majored in culinary arts. Someday, I'd like to open my own place."

"Ah." He leaned back and tented his fingers. "I see. It would take a fair amount of money to open a bakery, wouldn't it? Payments on the property, equipment, supplies, insurance. Not to mention employee pay unless you plan to never get sick or take time off."

"I haven't really checked into any of those things yet," Mira's cheeks grew hot.

"Trust me. You'd need money, and business loans aren't always easy to come by. How do you plan to go about doing this?"

"Tom, for heaven's sake, stop grilling her." Elise's swift interruption startled Mira. "Have you forgotten this is our dinner table and not the courtroom?"

"My apologies if I've offended anyone. I'm only trying to understand a few things."

Mira laid her fork on the table. "I think I get what you're driving at. If it makes you feel any better, as soon as I get the pictures copied, I'll be leaving."

"Oh, no, no, no," Elise interrupted, each word a swift and staccato sound. "You're my brother's child. I can't let you go before we get to know each other. I haven't even told you yet about your cousins—our two daughters. If there's no job waiting for you, there isn't any reason to rush away. I'd be delighted if you could stay a few weeks, or even longer. We have more than enough room, and we'd love to have you stay. Wouldn't we, Tom?" Elise swiveled her head toward her husband and speared him with a look.

Tom was the first to glance away. "Certainly. You are most welcome."

His tone was overly hearty, as if trying to convince himself—or his wife. Mira wasn't sure she'd ever heard a less sincere statement. What a relief it would be to go back home. She could stay with Dinah, despite the crowded conditions, until she found an apartment. It was a place where she'd be wanted. And, in many ways, much, much easier to deal with than this.

Embrace your fear, then let it go, Mira. Breathe.

Her mother had never run from a difficult situation. She faced it head-on. It occurred to Mira with sudden clarity that if Pauline hadn't wanted her to seek out James Todd, she'd never have written the letter disclosing his name in the first place.

Her chin lifted. "All right. I'd like to get to know both of you, too. And the idea of cousins? It overwhelms me. Here's the thing. I appreciate your hospitality, but I can't just sit around in your house all day. I've always worked. Maybe I can pick up a part-time job."

Elise lifted her forefinger. "I have an idea. Tom, you can hire Mira at your firm. Maybe she could work with your new attorney, Neal." Turning toward Mira, she added, "He's single and ambitious and quite attractive."

Mira jumped in before Tom could answer. "There's no need for that. I'd really rather find a job on my own. When I came into town, I noticed a lot of nice little retail areas and restaurants. I'm sure something there would work out for me."

"Fair enough. But if you change your mind, let us know." Tom's tone sounded a touch less harsh. "I do have one request, though. Your vehicle is rather…quaint, but would you mind parking it in the garage instead of in our driveway?"

Chapter Seven

Less than an hour until shift change. Aiden shot a look toward Puno, who was shoving items into his duffel. "You were in rare form last night. As far as I know, you haven't pranked anybody in months. What revved you up into overdrive?"

Before they had turned in, Puno had delicately covered the toilet seat with plastic wrap. An old but highly effective gag. Their bunkmate, Brody, got up in the middle of the night and staggered toward the bathroom. Shortly after, his shouts and curses had raised the roof. Aiden bet they could hear him clear to Canada.

"Yeah, well, what are you gonna do? Slow shift. Gotta have some excitement." He zipped the duffel shut. "Have you got any plans?"

"Just my usual. Catch up at home. Spend time with Lily. Catch some z's. What about you?"

"I'm taking Chrissy out to dinner tonight. The kids have been driving her nuts. She always needs a little extra attention when my shift is over."

"Rose felt the same way. She worried the entire time I was gone. I guess being married to a firefighter is hard on spouses. Maybe even harder on them than it is on us."

"Listen, Stewart, let me give you fair warning. Chrissy's all wrapped up again in her favorite pastime—finding you a girl. She has a friend who she says is sweet and real pretty to boot. She thinks the two of you should meet and have a few laughs. We can all go out to dinner together or to a movie if that makes you feel better."

Aiden felt his shoulders bunch. It wasn't the first time Puno and Chrissy had tried to play matchmaker. He'd given an excuse for each one of their offers. Too soon. Too distracted. Too busy. Was he ready to quit stalling and step out into the dating world again? The idea sent an icy chill down his spine. He was thirty-one years old. Men his age shouldn't be going on dates. They should be spending time at home with family. Barbecuing hamburgers. Working on a home project. Watching a movie. For somebody like him, dating was much more complicated. It meant hiring a sitter or asking his parents to watch Lily. Dressing to impress. A ton of painful small talk. It wore him out thinking how much effort dating took. On top of that, it wasn't only Puno and Chrissy jumping in. Even his own mother had tried to set him up with a friend's daughter. He'd put his mom off with excuses, too. And yet…Aiden raked his fingers through his hair.

"Tell Chrissy thanks," he finally said. "I'll think about it."

"Hey, you didn't say no right away. That's progress." Puno punched Aiden's shoulder lightly and grinned. "I'll tell her we're almost there."

The blare of a siren brought their conversation to an abrupt halt. An unruffled voice announced over the speaker, "Equipment fire."

"Oh, man." Puno shook his head. "I must have jinxed us. We'll be working overtime for sure."

"Yep," Aiden agreed as he grabbed his gear. He and Puno raced for the pumper where Brody, none the worse for his aggravating night, sat behind the wheel. "Come on. Come on, let's roll."

Aiden and Puno jumped on the truck. As it always did when responding to a call, Aiden's heart rate clipped up to a frenetic pace. "What have we got?"

"An oven fire," Brody replied. "It was called in by the owner. They used an extinguisher, but there's a lot of smoke, and she wanted us to do a check and make sure they're good."

"Cool. If our luck holds, we may only work an hour over," Puno observed as the pumper pulled from the garage.

"Yep." Brody activated the lights and siren. "I definitely need some good solid time at home to figure out how I'm gonna repay the smartass who jacked with the john."

"Schneider. I'll bet it was Schneider. Sounds like something he'd do." Puno offered the suggestion, oozing with helpful innocence.

"Uh-huh," said Brody, unconvinced.

His heart settling back into a normal rhythm, Aiden rolled his eyes.

A few minutes later, the pumper ground to a stop in front of a coffee house. Brody shut off the siren but kept the lights flashing. Aiden and Puno hopped off the truck and headed toward a front door flung wide open, where light wisps of smoke escaped. Out of the corners of his eyes, Aiden spied a psychedelic VW van parked in the side lot and paused a moment in surprise. The mystery redhead. It had to be her. Who else drove a vehicle as flamboyantly …odd…as that one?

Mira squirted the oven with a final blast from the fire extinguisher just to be sure. She coughed and peered inside, noticing a charred collection of ashes on the bottom. Tally Gillis, the owner of Steamin' Mugs Coffee Shop, must have overfilled the muffin tins. Blueberry? It was hard to tell when the baked goods were blackened rather than browned.

She moved toward the door connecting the kitchen to the customer area where Tally, a short woman wearing glasses who had hair the color of cotton, stood at the entrance, flapping a towel to shoo smoke from the room. "They're here," she yelled at Mira.

The screech of a siren announced the fire department's arrival loud and clear. Tally had been so distraught when flames appeared in the oven window during their interview that she had immediately run to the phone to call for help, even though Mira didn't think it was necessary. While Tally spoke to a 911 operator, Mira had grabbed an extinguisher mounted on the wall near the counter and doused the flames. She never dreamed that going in to inquire about a "Help Wanted" sign posted in the window would result in this. Timing was everything, she supposed.

Mira waited at the entrance to the kitchen as two men in helmets and waterproof jackets adorned with reflective tape raced across the threshold.

Tally pointed in Mira's direction. "She used the extinguisher on it. I think the fire's out, but I don't want to take any chances."

One of the firemen continued to speak with Tally, while the other followed Mira toward the oven. The door still hung open, and the firefighter, who appeared enormous in his gear, took a look. "What happened?"

"I'm pretty sure there was a batter spillover. See?" Mira pointed at the charred mess. "Looks like it caught fire."

"I think you're right." He turned an amused gaze from the oven to Mira. "You did a good job putting it out."

The voice sounded eerily familiar. She took careful stock of the man who stood before her, and his aqua-colored eyes confirmed her suspicion. "Aiden? So you're not only a tire-changer but a firefighter, too. You must be a man of many talents."

"That I am, but you've got me at a disadvantage. I told you my name, but you never told me yours."

He gave her an unforgettable grin that made her feel twitchy. She tried to think of a clever comeback, but none came to mind. "I'm Mira Gordon."

"And I'm surprised to see you here. With Florida plates on your vehicle, I figured you were only passing through."

Mira sorted through possible responses to the probing comment and ultimately chose a vague version of the truth. "There are things I need to do in Kansas City, so I'm staying for a short while."

Tally trotted toward them. "I hope my oven isn't ruined. It's too expensive to replace. You can see I need someone around with a calm head. I swear sometimes it seems like I'm all thumbs. I'm glad you'll be working with me, Mira."

Cha. I wish she hadn't given such a thorough report of my business in front of Aiden. He seems nice, but I barely know him. "I'm looking forward to it," she murmured.

"Do you think you could start tomorrow? The order I was working on has—as you can see—gone up in smoke."

Mira noticed Aiden observe their conversation as though he was absorbed in watching a scene from a car chase action movie. She didn't want to discuss her situation in front of a stranger, no matter how cute he looked wearing fireman gear and with a hint of dark stubble on his face as though he'd forgotten to shave. There really wasn't any reason for him to hang around. The fire was out.

"Why don't we discuss it later, Tally." Mira sneaked another glance at Aiden. "Is there a report to sign? We don't want to hold you up. I'm sure you're busy."

Aiden snapped out of whatever preoccupied him to give her his full attention. "I imagine my partner got everything we need. The oven could use a good cleaning, but I suggest you also have a repairman check it to be on the safe side."

He continued to stand there until the other fireman called to him from the door. "Brody's waiting. Let's head out."

"Thank you so much," Tally said to him. "I wouldn't sleep at all if you hadn't come. My apartment is upstairs, and I'd be worrying all night long over whether the oven would flame up again."

"You're welcome, ma'am. It's what we're here for." Aiden arched an eyebrow at Mira. "Maybe I'll see you again sometime soon. Hopefully not because of another predicament."

Heat rose from her neck to her face. "There's no need for you to worry. I can handle any problems that come up without your help."

She'd meant to sound confident and equal to any task, but by the slight smirk on his face before he turned away, she doubted he got the message. Not surprising, since he'd yet to see her without some sort of misfortune lurking nearby.

"What did he mean by another predicament?" Tally fanned her face with the towel.

"Oh, the day I came to town, I had a flat tire, and he changed it for me."

"What a gentleman. And to ice the cake, drop-dead gorgeous. He's a regular knight in shining armor." Tally's eyes glistened with rapture over the heroic image she'd created. "Sweetie-pie, I hope you noticed the expression on his face when he looked at you, because I sure did."

Mira couldn't help laughing at Tally's romantic assumptions. "I hardly think a fireman in the middle of doing his job wastes time flirting with someone he's there to help."

"I know what I saw, and I also heard him mention seeing you again. I'm not so old that I don't remember what a man's face looks like when he's smitten."

Tally's suggestion ignited an odd little pull of longing that coursed through Mira's body. She could feel it pulse all the way to her fingertips. Was this reaction what Pauline had once called chemistry? *No, it couldn't be. More likely a reaction from dealing with the fire.* "Tally, this is only the second time I've seen this man in my entire life. The only thought he'll ever have related to me is what trouble is lurking next."

Tally's knowing glance said otherwise, so Mira steered the conversation to a more important topic. "You mentioned tomorrow as a start date. That'll be fine. What time do you need me?"

"Could you be here by six? Mornings are usually busy, and I'm already behind on having enough baked goods to serve."

"Will do. I'll see you then."

Mira gathered her bag and waved goodbye to Tally before leaving the café. The thought of immersing herself in the utilitarian rhythm of a kitchen routine smoothed over Tally's speculation about the attractive fireman. More importantly, it reminded Mira how much she wanted to get back to work. Since Mrs. Caldwell planned and supervised all the meals in the Becker home, and Elise was forever watching her figure, Mira had been gently discouraged from the idea of baking her special chocolate croissants— or anything else for that matter—in the spotless kitchen. Only one issue worried her…what Elise would say about Mira working at a café.

Elise had twice more pushed the subject of accepting a job at her husband's law firm. Mira had a strong suspicion that news of her employment in a coffee house would not be celebrated with vintage wine and roses on the table. Things had been much easier with her mother. Pauline generally encouraged her daughter to think through a situation and then make her own choice. Waters were far choppier with Elise, who tried her best—Mira sensed—to help, but wound up coming across as presumptuous. Tom, on the other hand, continued to maintain his courteous but distant, and vaguely suspicious demeanor.

After nearly a week in KC, it crossed Mira's mind that if the Beckers treated their daughters the same way they treated her, it explained why Carolyn, a veterinarian and the oldest child, had moved to St. Louis following a broken engagement. The youngest daughter, Kathryn, a singer and songwriter, had left home to find a career in Nashville and never came back. According to Elise's report, a few months ago, Carolyn had married a man with a career in law enforcement while Kathryn was in a serious relation- ship with a doctor who worked in Nashville. The news didn't make it sound like either girl planned a return to

Kansas City. Apparently neither of them visited much, which infused Mira with a sense of dismal longing. *How I wish I could spend time with Pauline.*

The last thing she wanted to do was add to the sorrow she sensed in Elise whenever she talked about her daughters. It wasn't any secret how much she missed them. Mira pulled out of the parking lot and decided she'd find a way to soften the blow of her new part-time job announcement. There wasn't any reason to upset Elise further. But how to sweeten the notion of choosing a café position over one at a prestigious law firm? She pondered the question for a while and then groaned. There was only one thing Elise wanted to arrange for Mira even more than a job with Tom's law firm. Something she'd mentioned nearly half a dozen times in bursts of enthusiasm. Mira had gently resisted the request—up until now.

Her newly found aunt wanted to arrange a date for Mira with the law firm's young attorney, Neal Evans.

Chapter Eight

One look at Lily told Aiden his daughter had started out wrong when fastening her buttons. The left side of her jacket hung lower than the other. "Let me help you with that." He motioned toward her jacket, treading as lightly as he could. Lately, his daughter had been showing the dawning signs of an independent spirit, eager to do more things for herself, and growing sulky if they didn't turn out the way she intended. While he conceded this was better than dealing with another stomachache, he missed the days when she asked for his help.

Lily dipped her head down to look. "I can do it." She put Siggy on the floor and slowly undid each of the buttons. Aiden told himself not to give in to the urge to take over and do the job himself. He watched as she painstakingly rebuttoned her coat. The undertaking wasted better than five minutes, which felt more like thirty.

"There," she said with satisfaction as she scooped up Siggy. "What are we going to do now, Daddy?"

"Since you don't have school today, you'll need to come with me while I take care of some errands." At the disappointed look on her face, he added, "If you're good, we'll go to the bookstore. You can buy two books, and then we'll figure out something to do afterward."

This news perked her up, and she happily followed Aiden to his pickup. "Are we going to see Memaw and Papa?"

"Why don't we give them a day off? You and I will make our own fun." He buckled his daughter into her seat.

First stop was the dry cleaner to pick up his dress uniform, and then to a discount store for laundry soap and paper towels. He drove past the animal shelter, which triggered Lily to ask about going inside—only to look.

"Sorry, Lily-Lou. We don't have time today." He didn't have the patience today, either. Last time they'd gone to the shelter, they stayed for an hour, and she had a meltdown when he told her she couldn't bring home the puppy that licked her fingers with utter devotion.

He'd decided Lily was too young to take on the responsibility of having a dog, not to mention the imposition of handing another duty to his parents on the days when he was at work. He hated being the bad guy. It would be a pleasure to indulge his daughter, but he reminded himself of something his mother had told him after Lily was born. "It's easy to spoil them, especially when they're little, but you have to remember parenting isn't a popularity contest."

Aiden swiftly moved Lily away from pouting over his decision by directing silly questions about sloths to Siggy until the child giggled. On that much more upbeat note, he finished the rest of the things he needed to do and then drove to a small bookstore not far from their home. Lily loved spending time there. The place was a perfect retreat for children, with a large cozy nook upstairs filled with comfortable chairs, games, and books designed to delight. Lily browsed around the stacks until she found a picture book about sloths and an early reader featuring puppies. Aiden gave the saleslady his card to seal the purchase and Lily proudly carried her plunder to the truck. Sunshine beating through the windshield of the cab made the day feel much warmer than it really was.

"I'm hungry, Daddy."

"Me too," he replied. Where had the time gone? It was way past noon, their usual lunch hour. He thought a moment. "How about we go out to eat? Does that sound good?"

Lily squealed, "Yes! Where will we go?"

He considered the possibilities and ruled out their usual drive-through burger joints. Today he felt like sitting in a place where he could sip a hot cup of coffee and warm his fingers. An idea brought a grin. "It's a surprise," he told her. Aiden checked for traffic, then made a quick U-turn.

A few miles down the road, he caught sight of Steamin' Mugs Coffee Shop and pulled into the lot. There were only two cars aside from Mira's easily recognizable van sitting at the far end. The sight kindled a pulsation in his head as if he'd gulped a shot of Jim Beam on an empty stomach.

Aiden shook the feeling off and parked his truck before unbuckling Lily from her booster seat. "I'll bet you can get some hot chocolate here."

"Mmm. I love hot chocolate with marshmallows and whipped cream," she pronounced. Aiden hoped he wasn't wrong in planting the idea. He couldn't imagine a café without hot chocolate.

"Let's check it out." He took her hand.

A brisk breeze kicked them into a trot as they headed toward the entrance. He opened the door, and they stepped inside. Yesterday morning, when he'd walked through the entrance for the fire call, he'd been focused on the oven. Today, he took a moment to look around.

A faux brick floor and white walls made the place look clean but rustic. Two cases filled with baked goods caught his eye, and he sniffed. There wasn't a trace of smoke smell from yesterday's mishap. Instead, the scent of baked bread, along with hints of coffee, cinnamon, and chocolate, laced the air with a tantalizing aroma. There were a couple of chairs and tables near the counter with a small adjoining room that held more places to sit. The tables were empty except for one occupied by some guy who wore headphones and took occasional sips of coffee while typing on his laptop. At that moment, Mira emerged from the kitchen, her face rosy with—Aiden presumed—heat from the oven. Her head tilted when she saw him as if trying to remember his name.

"Hello, Mira," he said. "Looks like you've got everything under control today."

She broke into a smile and wiped her hands on a rag from the pocket of her apron. "Yes, we're fine. Thanks again for your help in checking everything yesterday. It made Tally feel a lot better."

"Is she well?"

"She's upstairs taking a nap. Probably dealing with the aftereffects of stress. I'm surprised you're here. I didn't know firefighters did a day-after check."

"We don't. I'm here to grab some lunch for my daughter and me."

"Your daughter?" Mira came a few steps closer and peered over the counter. When she spied Lily, a beaming smile set her face aglow. "How do you do, young lady? My name's Mira. What's yours?"

Lily could be shy with strangers, so Aiden prepared to prompt her, but he didn't need to say a word.

"I'm Lily Stewart. Can I have some hot chocolate with whipped cream and marshmallows, please?"

"You sure can," Mira replied. "That's my favorite, too." Her eyes moved from Lily back to Aiden. "Is there anything I can get for you?"

"Coffee, please." He examined the posted menu. "And we'll each have a slice of the cheese quiche."

Mira nodded.

Lily pointed to something in the display case and looked at Aiden with puppy-dog eyes. He couldn't say no and added, "Give us one of whatever that is, too."

"*Pain au chocolat*…chocolate croissants. They're my specialty." She melted him with a modest but pleased expression.

"Well, then, give us two."

Aiden settled his bill, and then Mira disappeared into the kitchen while he led Lily to a table near the counter. She placed Siggy on it and leaned him against the wall. Then she began to chatter about a friend at school. He nodded at the right places and asked a few questions. Then Lily had a question for him.

"Will you make a braid in my hair like Mira's?"

"I guess I can try," he said.

"Now?"

"Lily, we're in a café. People don't braid hair in cafés."

"Please, Daddy."

Sighing, Aiden got up. He gathered her hair and tried twisting it together. "I'm not sure I know how to do this."

He heard Mira's voice. "What don't you know how to do?" She placed their drinks on the table.

"I want a braid like yours," Lily said.

A smile played at Mira's lips. She glanced at Aiden. "Do you mind?"

"I wish you would," he replied.

Mira took over and quickly wove Lily's hair into a tail. "It will loosen up fast because I don't have any rubber bands, but at least you can see what it looks like."

Lily ran her fingers up and down the braided tail and giggled. The sight tightened Aiden's throat, and he swallowed hard before speaking. "You be careful with your chocolate, Lily. It looks hot."

The mug was piled high with whipped cream and shaved chocolate sprinkles. Lily's eyes became the size of a plate.

"I hope you like it." Mira dimpled at the child's obvious delight. "Your food will be ready in a few minutes."

Aiden fanned Lily's drink, keeping Mira in his side vision as she walked away.

His daughter took a sip of her cooled-off drink and promptly got herself a whipped cream moustache. His amusement turned Lily into a clown, and she leaned into the cream again. He handed her a napkin. *This is nice. No pressure to gobble and run. A good choice to come here.*

Mira returned with plates of quiche and croissants and set them on the table. Aiden and Lily dug in right away, with Lily keeping a sharp eye on the croissant. She could only finish half of her quiche, so Aiden polished off the rest. The quiche had been tasty, but the pastries looked delectable. He gave one to Lily, and even though he wasn't hungry anymore, he took a bite of the croissant anyway. A buttery flakey crust with melted semi-sweet chocolate in the center. Pure heaven. These pastries would give his mom's cinnamon rolls a run for their money, although he'd never dare admit such a thing to her. Lily took one bite, followed by another and another. He wasn't sure how she could handle so much food, but he wasn't about to stop her.

Mira made her way back to the table to gather the empty dishes. "How was it?"

Aiden wiped his mouth with a napkin. "Best meal I've had in a while. The quiche was delicious, but those croissants are a work of art."

"They'll be better next time when I can let the dough sit overnight. This is the shortened prep version."

"I don't know how they could get any better, but you can bet I'll try them again. You must be a fast learner. For a new employee, you seem pretty good at this job."

Mira laughed. "This isn't my first time in a bakery. I went to culinary school in Key West. After that, I apprenticed in a pastry shop."

Aiden put down his croissant. "You're from Key West? I hear that's an amazing place. What would bring you from paradise to Kansas City?"

"My mother was sick for a long time. She died a few weeks ago. I came here because," Mira paused, "because she had some business I needed to take care of."

Lily had wound down from her speed-eating phase. No wonder. Her belly had to be stuffed full enough to burst. She looked up at Mira, and her bottom lip quivered. "My mommy died, too."

With brows slightly furrowed, Mira knelt beside Lily and put an arm around the child's thin shoulders. "I'm sorry, honey. I know how hard it is to lose your mom. They say as time goes on, it gets easier."

"That's what Memaw says. But it still makes me sad."

"Of course, it does. That's normal. Anybody would feel sad when they can't be with someone they love. But remember this. Whenever you think about your mom, she's still here," Mira tapped her head, "and here." She touched her chest near her heart.

Aiden took a drink from his mug to ward off the burning sensation he felt behind his eyes. Lily seldom talked about her mother, and when she did, he tried to steer the conversation to another topic, fearing he'd only upset her—and himself. But Mira didn't seem to have any trouble holding a serious conversation with his daughter. The knowledge gave him a familiar and uncomfortable sensation. He wasn't very good at parenting. He ought to be able to speak of such things. On the other hand, maybe it was different with Mira and her mother. Maybe they hadn't been as close as he and Lily had been with Rose.

The hint of a smile that showed up on his daughter's face meant the world to him, but a glance at the clock told him they'd lingered at the café long enough. "I'm afraid we need to head for home." He lifted his gaze to Mira's and mouthed a silent "thank you." She nodded, and he read an abundance of understanding plus a dash of sympathy in the depths of her green eyes.

"It's nice to have met you, Lily," Mira said as she rose. "I hope you come back sometime soon to see me."

"Daddy, you'll bring me and Siggy here again, won't you?" Lily picked up the sloth.

"I imagine so." Aiden rubbed a finger across his chin. "Mira, you said you were in town for a while. Do you know how long you'll be here?"

"I'm not really sure. Maybe a month or so. It all depends." She didn't mention what it depended on, and he figured it might come across as meddling to ask.

"I…I mean, we—Lily and I, that is—would like to see you again. And have some more of those delicious croissants." *Good Lord. I'm stuttering like a teenager.*

"That would be nice." Color stained her cheeks a pretty shade of pink. "Hey, could you hold on a second before you go?"

Mira went straight to the counter and packed two chocolate croissants into a cardboard box. She handed the box to Aiden. "This is for you to take home. A belated thank you for changing my tire." Turning to Lily, she said, "It was fun to meet you." She pointed to the plush animal. "You too, Siggy."

Aiden took his daughter's hand and led her outside. When the cold air bit into him, he barely felt it. Something had stirred a flame in his core that heated him from the inside out. He hadn't felt this way since…he stopped to think about it.

Since the day he first met Rose.

Chapter Nine

Date night. Mira stood in front of the mirror and fussed with her hair. When nothing else looked right, she finally gave up and plaited it. As she worked the strands into a braid, she let her mind drift on other topics so she wouldn't think about this evening's dinner with Neal.

It had been more than two weeks since she'd started work at the café, and Elise still wasn't pleased about the part-time job. Not even after Mira had patiently explained how much she enjoyed it. Tally had turned out to be great, although at times a touch scatterbrained as if she had other matters on her mind. With each day, Tally passed on a few more responsibilities to Mira, and she seemed eager to hand over even more.

"I guess I'm wearing out," she'd said. "I can't remember the last time I had a vacation. My daughter and her family are out in Colorado. I'd love to head there for a visit one of these days. It's been an age since I've seen them."

Mira identified with the forlorn look on her employer's face, and her heart went out in sympathy. What could be worse than having a family you couldn't spend time with? She stoutly proclaimed she'd be happy to keep the café open anytime Tally wanted to go, and her boss's face brightened with gratitude. This gave Mira another reason to like her. Some people were set in their ways, but not Tally. She'd even agreed to a few of Mira's suggestions to change up the menu, adding more locally sourced organic ingredients to the food and drinks they served.

A soft tap at the bedroom door chased away her musing. "Come in," she called, and Elise glided into the room with Louie on her heels.

"You look lovely, darling. The color of that scarf suits you."

Mira's fingers went to the silky scarf. "It was Pauline's. Tangerine was one of her favorite colors." Louie pawed Mira's leg, so she picked him up, ruffled his ear, and planted a kiss on his curly head. She'd never had a dog before, and it touched her whenever the poodle jumped into her bed for a nighttime cuddle.

"If you don't mind my asking, why do you call your mother Pauline? In the conversations we've had, I've often wondered about that."

"I don't know. I guess it's because everyone around us called her Pauline, and she never told me not to."

Elise's eyes shimmered with dampness when she put her arm around Mira. "I'm glad you're here. How I wish Jimmy could see you. He'd be so proud."

"I'm glad to be here, too." Mira smiled. Elise had whole-heartedly embraced her as family, unlike Tom. Mira could understand his position, at least to a degree. She'd learned his quirks. Tom lived and breathed the analysis of data and facts. Since he didn't have any proof to draw a concrete conclusion—and Tom preferred concrete conclusions—he remained doubtful. Yet he'd never brought up a DNA test to her. She wondered if Elise had talked him out of it. Maybe Tom would eventually learn to do what Elise had done—take what Mira said on faith. Although as time went on, the chances appeared less likely.

"I think you and Neal will have a wonderful evening." Elise adjusted Mira's scarf. "I feel like a matchmaker."

"I'm sure he's a nice man." Mira had never been on a blind date before, and the thought made her palms sticky. It didn't help that an image of Aiden kept intruding on her thoughts. He'd stopped by to grab a coffee twice since he and Lily had come in for lunch. Tally got a kick out of teasing her about it. Mira gave another absent-minded scratch to Louie's ear. "When you talked to Neal, what did you tell him about me?"

Elise's mouth puckered. "We've been discreet. Tom and I discussed how to handle questions. He suggested we not say anything at this point so as not to put undue expectations on Neal or you. All we've told anyone is that you're the daughter of a dear friend and would be staying with us for a while. When the time is right, we can say more."

"I see." Mira considered the facts. Given the tenuous state of the situation, she hadn't disclosed the purpose for her visit either. Of course, Tom had other reasons not to speak the truth about why Mira had come to them. She had to admit it hurt a little. Her gaze roamed to a photo on the nightstand. Elise had framed a picture of the man Mira had been told was her father. Jim Todd's friendly grin subdued Mira's doubts.

"Darling," Elise interrupted her thoughts. "You really should have let Neal come to the house and pick you up. I don't like the idea of you meeting him at a restaurant."

"Since we don't know each other, meeting like this seems a better way to ease into things." *Plus, it gives me the option of leaving when I want. What if we sit there like two sticks with nothing to talk about?*

"Why don't you take my Mercedes? It's much easier to maneuver than your van."

"I don't mind driving the van. It's like a piece of home to me. Besides, he might as well know the person I am right away."

"All right. Just remember to park in the garage when you get back. Tom is worried the neighbors might complain."

"I only forgot once." She envisioned the van's mind-bending colors shaking up the decorum of the neighborhood. "I promise not to do it again."

Elise squeezed Mira's hand. "I'll wait up for you. I'm anxious to hear what you think about Neal. According to Tom, he's a rising star in the firm. He'd be a great catch."

Except I'm not fishing…

Elise looped her arm through Mira's and walked her to the top of the staircase. "Have a wonderful time."

It was a small gesture of affection, but one that filled an empty place in Mira's heart. As she maneuvered her VW from the garage to the street, she considered the fact that Tom and Elise had two daughters. They spoke to the girls on the phone occasionally, but their relationship didn't go much further. How could they have become so detached? It seemed such a dismal situation. Here she was, receiving the attention and affection that rightfully belonged to Carolyn and Kat—she'd picked up on the nickname Tom used for his youngest. The situation made her feel self-conscious and intrusive, like she'd poached Elise's attention.

A worry for another day.

Mira spied the bar and grill where she was to meet Neal up ahead and parked the van. She got out and strode toward the entrance. Tally had taken her to lunch there one afternoon, and Mira thought the casual ambiance would be more comfortable than the restaurant Neal had first chosen. She preferred a place that wasn't overly crowded, where the food was good, and the prices reasonable. Friendlier…that's how this little bistro struck her.

She swiveled her head to look around the room when a man rose from a booth. He gave her a long look, and then a friendly wave. *Could that be him?* Mira moved toward the table. "Neal?" She extended her hand, and he took it with a grin.

"You must be Mira. Elise told me to watch for a beautiful redhead. She was right."

The remark should have embarrassed her, but his tone was so amiable she didn't feel any heat in her face at all. She noted he had auburn hair, gray eyes, and skin as fair as hers. The handshake was solid. Not a limp noodle. Not a knuckle-crusher. "You're too kind. I hope I didn't keep you waiting."

"Nope. I only got here a few minutes before you did. I'm glad you decided to come. Tom said you were a little skittish."

"Oh?" The remark surprised her. If anything, she'd have thought Tom would have described her as a pushy stranger with a hidden agenda. "He's a busy man. We don't see each other nearly as much as Elise and I do."

"Yes, Tom mentioned you were visiting for a while. Elise, of course, was much more expansive."

"She usually does have a lot to say," Mira agreed as she opened the menu. "Are you ready to order? I've been here before, so I know what I'm getting—their house salad."

"We'll make it two." He motioned to a server who jotted down their order.

Elise had been right. Neal *was* nice with an open manner and friendly grin. Not the least bit pretentious either. Mira leaned back and relaxed as he chatted to her about his work with Tom, when the restaurant's front door clanged open. She glanced toward the sound. What she saw straightened her spine away from the bench. *Of all people!* Aiden and Lily walked into the lobby. Lily had Siggy in one hand, and her other hand clutched Aiden's. Aiden saw Mira, and their eyes linked. A surge of…something…sped up the rhythm of her heart.

"What's wrong?"

She turned back to Neal's puzzled expression. "A man I know just came in."

As soon as the words left her mouth, she heard Lily call out, "There's Mira!" The little girl released Aiden's hand and galloped to the table.

"Hi, Lily," Mira said. "How's Siggy?" She dipped her chin toward the sloth clutched under Lily's arm.

"He's hungry, so we came here for dinner."

Aiden joined them at the table, and his expression surprised Mira. His eyes were pinched tight, and a muscle twitched in his jaw. "Hello," he said and glanced pointedly over at Neal. "Sorry to intrude on your evening."

"Oh, you're not intruding," Mira rushed to fill the silence. "This is Neal. We're having dinner." *What a ridiculous thing to say. What else would they be doing at a restaurant?* "Neal, this is Aiden and his daughter Lily."

Neal rose to shake Aiden's hand, and it occurred to Mira they looked like two dogs sizing each other up. A little flattering, but a lot uncomfortable.

Lily obviously sensed no tension and began to jabber. "I told Daddy I wanted to see you again. I need another hot chocolate and some more of those chocolate things."

"You mean the croissants?" A cute child made the perfect diversion for an awkward situation. "If I know when you're coming, I'll be sure to have a fresh batch ready for you."

The child turned her eyes to Aiden. "Daddy, can we go see her tomorrow?"

"I'm not sure, Lily. We have a lot of things to do."

"I hope you can stop in for a few minutes, Aiden." *Cha. He wasn't normally so stand-offish. What in the universe was troubling him?* "If you're in a hurry, I can box everything for you to go."

"Pleeeeease, Daddy? You promised Siggy and me we could see Mira."

"I'll think about it," he replied in a tone that convinced Mira they wouldn't show up. "Come along, Lily. Let's go find a seat and stop pestering these two."

"I hope to see you tomorrow," Mira said to the little girl. Aiden didn't speak another word. He aimed a curt nod toward Neal, and then he and Lily settled at a booth directly in Mira's line of vision.

A moment of silence followed. "Well," Neal finally said, "I get the feeling your friend is ticked off about something."

"He isn't usually so abrupt. Maybe he had a bad day. He's a firefighter. I'm sure he sees some awful things."

"You could be right. That's a tough job and one I certainly wouldn't want."

His comment lightened the mood, and then, thankfully, their salads arrived. In between bites, Neal did most of the talking. Mira tried to answer him like a normal human being but found her attention drifting. She was too painfully aware of Aiden's presence to hear what Neal had to say, and when she did respond, she stumbled over her words.

"Seems like you've got something on your mind," Neal said with a sigh. He jerked his chin toward Aiden. "Ever since he came in. Is there something going on between the two of you?"

A direct question deserved a direct answer, except she wasn't sure how to categorize Aiden. An arbitrarily helpful stranger? A potential friend? A widower with a cute little daughter? She had no idea how to respond, other than the fact that Aiden frequently popped into her thoughts, which she wasn't about to admit. "Something between us? I don't suppose there is. We've only seen each other a few times."

"I'm going to conclude that maybe you wish you did have something going on with him."

Mira felt her skin begin to prickle. She breathed in and out. "I don't know. He's busy with his job and his family, and I'm still trying to figure out my life." That was certainly the truth. Relief made the prickly feeling disappear and also lifted Neal's mouth into a grin.

"That's good news because I'd like it if you gave me a chance. Can we go out again? I promise you a nice evening."

A movement from the other side of the room showed Aiden getting up abruptly from his booth. He took Lily's hand, and the two of them headed for the door. He didn't so much as wave goodbye or nod in her direction. The flat-out dismissal pained her.

She forced her expression into pleasant lines. "It's sweet of you to ask. I'd like to go out with you again."

After a pointedly casual goodbye in the parking lot, Mira aimed her van back to the Beckers' home and considered the evening. The blind date had been enjoyable, despite the appearance and odd behavior of Aiden. She still couldn't figure out what she'd done to perturb him.

Eventually she let go of the unanswerable question and followed an impulse to stop at a discount store and pick up a few things she thought Elise might enjoy. Tucking the items into her van, she continued home, careful to park the

VW in the garage—snickering at the assurance no neighbors would be upset by a glimpse of her colorful vehicle—and went inside the house.

She half-expected to see Elise standing at the door impatiently waiting for answers, but the kitchen was empty. Even though the clock read only a few minutes past nine, the house was quiet as midnight. Mira padded upstairs. A light showed from under the master bedroom door, and the low murmur of voices carried to her. She sprinted past it as quickly and quietly as she could.

No way did she want to overhear another conversation between Elise and Tom. Maybe they were discussing the DNA test again. If Tom insisted on the procedure, Mira couldn't decide whether she wanted to comply or not. If he felt her to be so untrustworthy, why would test results change his mind? Especially since he'd obviously persuaded himself she'd come to them under false pretenses.

A DNA test reminded her of a lie detector. Only necessary when one person refused to accept the word of another.

Chapter Ten

Not even the cinnamon roll his mother gave him when he arrived at his parents' house first thing in the morning after shift change to pick up Lily, sweetened Aiden's disposition. He'd been a bear for the past twenty-four hours, snapping at his best friend when Puno made another bold as brass remark badgering Aiden about the expression on his face as he—ogled?—the gorgeous redhead working at the coffee shop on the day of the oven fire.

The scenario had become a favorite target since Puno knew it would get a rise out of him. This time Aiden had to burn off steam in the workout room with extra minutes running on the treadmill, so he'd forget an urge to pummel the smirk off his pal's face. Worse, the image of Mira at dinner with some guy who wore a Brooks Brothers sweater and reeked of success had been burned into his brain, changing him from a rational man into an insecure kid. This was it. The reason why he'd refused whenever Puno or any other well-meaning person—like his mother—had tried to not-so-subtly push a woman in his direction. He obviously was not the dating type.

"You seem upset," his mom said, concern lining her face. "What's wrong?"

"Nothing." His reply sounded flimsy even to him, so he changed the subject. "Where's Dad?"

"He's downstairs with Lily. They're organizing his fishing lures. I swear your father must have a thousand of them."

"Yeah, well, it keeps him busy. Nothing wrong with that." Aiden hollered toward the stairway. "Time to go to school, Lily."

His call brought his daughter scampering up the steps and to his side, all smiles as she launched herself at him. Her enthusiasm softened his disposition. After she planted a damp kiss on his cheek, she said, "Today, Daddy? When you pick me up after school, can we go see Mira?"

She'd repeated the same refrain multiple times. At first, he'd been pleased over her enthusiasm, but not so much anymore.

"Lily keeps mentioning Mira. Who is she?" A deep groove appeared between his mom's eyebrows.

Swell. "Just someone we met one day at a coffee house."

"She must have made quite an impression if Lily wants to see her again."

"I like her, Memaw. She's nice and pretty, and she makes the best hot chocolate in the whole world." Lily beamed an innocent look at Aiden. "Daddy likes her, too; don't you, Daddy?"

"Um, sure." He cleared his throat. "Hey, I don't see your bookbag or Siggy. You'd better get them. We don't want to be late."

"Okay," she said as she dashed away in a burst of eight-year-old energy.

His mother eyeballed him in a way that made him shift from one foot to the other. "What's going on? I can tell there's more to this than what you're saying. Who is Mira?"

His mom could be like a dog gnawing a bone. Aiden exhaled in surrender. "Remember when I told you about being late for work after changing a woman's tire? It was Mira's. A few days later, the station got a call from a coffee shop for an oven fire. I found out she works there." He paused a moment. "The next day I took Lily to the coffee shop for lunch. The two of them seemed to hit it off."

"I see." Mom all but glowed with interest. "I have an idea it isn't only the two of them who hit it off. Are you attracted to her?"

"Geez, Mom, don't beat around the bush or anything."

"Why should I tiptoe? You know I loved Rose like a daughter, but that doesn't mean I want you to spend the rest of your life alone."

He couldn't begin to explain the long-dormant emotions Mira had stirred when he had no idea how to sort them out himself. "All right. I admit to feeling… something. It doesn't matter, though. She's involved with somebody else. I saw them together on a date a few nights ago."

"I haven't heard you express the slightest interest in any woman since Rose—God rest her soul—passed. You needed time to grieve. Time to heal. But, Aiden, I see signs that you're ready. Let me ask you something. Does Mira wear a wedding ring? Unless she and this man are married, you have as much chance with her as anyone else."

"I never thought to look at her hand, but she's never mentioned a husband. Or a fiancé. She told me her mother died, and she's only staying in KC for a month or so. Maybe the business she has here is related to the man she was with." He pushed the chair he'd been sitting in toward the table. "I'm out of my depth in the dating scene. Ever since high school, it was always Rose. I don't have any experience pursuing someone else."

"Well, I guess it's time you learn. Your life isn't over. You deserve more. And so does Lily."

Before he could answer, Lily burst back into the kitchen with her bookbag and Siggy, thankfully preventing any further discussion. "I'm ready to go, Daddy."

"Good job, Lily-Lou. We're going to have to hustle to get you to school on time."

He kissed his mother goodbye, and she whispered, "Think about what I said."

At the end of the school day, Aiden waited in the chaotic pick-up lane at school, watching for Lily in the group of children darting this way and that from the entrance. Her bright yellow jacket tipped him off. He relaxed when she saw him and waved a red-mittened hand. A truck came in handy when sitting in a line of traffic. His vehicle towered over most of the others. Lily skipped to the truck, and he jumped out long enough to settle her into her seat. She grabbed Siggy from his resting place and pulled the sloth into a hug.

His shoulders relaxed as soon as he drove away from the semi-organized mayhem in the school parking lot. He ought to have Lily ride the bus, but the idea rattled him. What if some bully wouldn't let his daughter sit down? Called her names that made her cry? Or—he gulped—threatened her? If anyone hurt his little girl, he couldn't handle it. He caught a glimpse of Lily in the rear-view mirror, smoothing Siggy's hair. She said something to the sloth he couldn't hear, and he decided to do something, anything, that would please her.

"Hey, Lily, guess what?"

Her attention shifted away from Siggy. "What?"

"We're going to get you some hot chocolate from Mira's coffee shop before we go home. How does that sound?"

Lily's squeal answered his question. Such a small thing to make her happy. Show her how much he cared. Besides, after stewing over his mother's early-morning advice, he'd finally given himself a mental shake while he folded the laundry. His resigned conclusion? *Why not? What have I got to lose?*

On the drive to the café, he and Lily played a round of "I Spy," with Lily winning because she gave him the color puce—she'd learned it during art class that day—and he hadn't a clue what it meant until she informed him it was brownish-purple. And he had guessed green. Who knew?

Rush hour traffic clogged the road, but it didn't delay their drive to the coffee shop. There were a few cars in the lot, but he didn't see Mira's van. His heart dropped like a stone. He'd have liked to see her, but it was too late to back out now.

"Where's Mira's rainbow bus?" Lily picked up on the vehicle's absence the moment her feet touched the asphalt. He marveled at his daughter's accurate description of the VW.

"I don't know. Maybe she isn't working today." He took Lily's hand and walked her to the door. "We can just get your chocolate and take it home if you want."

They passed through the door, and the vanilla scent of something delicious in the oven—cookies?—reminded him he hadn't eaten any lunch. Aiden pushed the door shut behind them, just as Mira appeared at the kitchen entrance. Her brows rose when she spotted them.

"Hi, Lily." Mira's warm smile crinkled the corners of her eyes. "I'm glad you stopped by."

"You're here!" Lily's voice rose. "We didn't see your van."

"It's getting an oil change. Tally picked me up today." She cast a glance at Aiden through lowered lashes.

"Good to see you, Mira." His words came out more stilted than a rookie's first day at a fire station. He swallowed and tried again in a more amiable tone. "We'd both like a hot chocolate and a couple of your croissants, please."

Mira beamed at him. "Are these to go?"

He nonchalantly let his gaze drop to her fingers. *Nope. No ring.* "I think we'll stay here to eat," he replied.

Mira nodded. "I'll be right back."

Aiden followed his daughter to the same table they'd sat at before. Lily settled Siggy into place and then swung her legs up and down in a flurry of restlessness. "I hope Mira remembers I like marshmallows and whipped cream."

One side of his mouth curved up. "I'll bet she does. You be sure to thank her."

"I will. My friends think it's cool that I go to a coffee shop and get chocolate coffee."

"You don't get coffee, Lily."

"I know that. But they don't." She bounced off the chair to explore items for sale on shelves mounted against the wall.

Aiden smiled benevolently. Hanging out at a coffee shop must make her feel grown-up. "Don't touch anything," he warned. "Some of that stuff might break."

Lily kept her hands at her sides until Mira emerged from the kitchen with a tray of drinks and chocolate croissants. Lily eyed the cream piled high atop her mug and giggled. "You remembered. Thank you."

Mira laughed. A winsome, musical sound. "You're quite welcome. I fixed your daddy's the same way as yours."

"It looks great." He wasn't sure when he'd last had a mug of hot chocolate, but the over-the-top concoction had such a steamy sweet aroma that he didn't wait to take a sip. "Fantastic," he said to Mira. "The best hot chocolate I ever tasted."

"Thanks, but it's hard to go wrong with *chocolat avec de la crème.*" She peeked at Lily, who busied herself with a spoon dipping out bite after bite of sweets. "Plus a little marshmallow, of course."

"Those French phrases roll off your tongue like butter. Are you fluent?"

She pushed out her lips, raised her shoulders, and turned out her palms. It was the most Gallic shrug he'd ever seen. "Only when it comes to the kitchen. The master chef I apprenticed with is from France. He opened a bakery in Key West. It was either pick up his phrases or find another place to work."

"I hear the Keys are impressive."

"They are. There are touristy areas and quieter ones, but all of them are amazing. I should know. I'm a conch."

"A what?"

"A conch. Born and raised in Key West. This may shock you, but my trip here is the first time I've ever been out of Florida. The Midwest sure has its own kind of beauty, especially now. Leaves turning color. Temperatures that require a shopping expedition for heavier clothes. And," she pointed at the table, "the need for hot chocolate to warm a body up."

"True." He fiddled with his napkin. "I'm curious about something. You told me you lost your mother. Do you have other family back in Key West?"

"No." She paused, and something drew her brows together. "I don't have family in the Keys, although there are friends who feel like family."

He knew he was asking too many questions, but he found himself consumed by an insatiable urge to know more. Everything about her, from the thick coppery red braid to the freckles across her nose to the leather clogs on her feet, tugged his desire to put together the puzzle pieces and figure this woman out, even if it meant asking a bold question. "Key West to KC is a long way to come. What kind of business brings you here?"

Her head jerked up, and she bit her lip as Tally burst from the kitchen and called, "I pulled out the last batch of croissants. They look wonderful. You sure do have a knack."

"I'm sorry. It's almost time for me to go home. I need to finish up in the kitchen."

She turned, but Aiden rose and took hold of her arm. Then he made an offer he hoped she wouldn't refuse. "You said your van is in the shop. Can Lily and I give you a ride home? We're not in any hurry to leave."

The suggestion had his daughter bouncing up and down in her seat. "Please, Mira? You don't need to be scared. Daddy's a good driver."

At that, Mira smiled and nodded.

By the time he and Lily had finished their drinks and eaten the last crumb of croissants, Mira walked from the kitchen with Tally, clearly in the middle of an animated discussion. "I like that thought. Let's talk more about it tomorrow," Tally said.

Mira leaned to hug the silver-haired woman—obviously, the two had become close—and then she headed toward their table. "I'm ready if you are."

"Let's go." He opened the front door. "Ladies first."

Mira and Lily exited ahead of him, and his heart lifted when he saw his daughter reach for Mira's hand. They strolled toward the pickup together. Aiden unlocked the doors and buckled Lily in her seat. He slid behind the wheel while Mira took the front passenger seat. "Nice truck," she said, fastening her seatbelt.

"I like it." He had more questions but didn't know how to ask them without sounding like a detective during an interrogation. Making small talk hadn't been a strength for him in the past. It still wasn't.

Luckily, Mira filled the silence by chatting with Lily, who seemed over the moon to make conversation. While she talked to his daughter, Mira motioned where Aiden should turn. When she pointed to the entrance of a gated community, he swallowed his surprise. She lived in a swanky golf club mansion? He could never have imagined it. Mira seemed too down-to-earth. He drove up the long and curved driveway toward a house that made him feel uncomfortable and completely out of place.

"Your house is pretty, Mira." His daughter didn't have the same qualms he did.

"Thanks, Lily, but it isn't mine. I'm only staying here for now."

The distinct feeling that he was hopelessly out of his league reappeared to haunt him. Why would she be staying in a palatial house? No, this wasn't a house. It was an estate. He braked near the entrance.

She placed her hand on his arm. "What can I say, Aiden? Once again, I am in your debt. I'll need to bake a mountain of croissants to thank you."

"That's not necessary." He squared his chin and decided to follow his heart, hoping against hope he wouldn't make himself look like a jackass. "But there is something I would like you to do."

She pinched her lips together quizzically before asking, "What is it?"

"Will you go to dinner with me?"

A twinkle sparked in her green eyes that made his mouth tip up. She didn't hesitate before giving the answer he'd hoped for. "I'd love to."

Chapter Eleven

Early morning sun blazed through the window near Mira's bed, spotlighting the effortless dance of dust motes. She yawned and stretched out her arms to find Louie burrowed under the comforter. Lifting the cover, she located him. "Hello, little guy." The pup raised his head, eyes bright, and tail thumping like a drum. "I must say, you make a perfect bedwarmer."

Mira scooted to the floor and donned a soft white robe that Elise had given her. Louie jumped down next to her and shook himself, his tags jangling. The night had brought a hard frost that chilled the room. She could have turned up the heat but decided a more attractive idea would be to grab an extra blanket and climb back into bed. The book she'd started reading sat temptingly on her bedside, and she couldn't wait to delve into it. Shivering a little, she pulled the warm robe tighter.

She had gone shopping with Elise only once, knowing she'd need something other than summer-weather wear. After Mira had chosen a few items, she took them to the cashier. Elise had pulled out her credit card, but Mira delicately refused the offer. Since then, Elise made it her business to go off on her own and pick up one thing or another for Mira. A pair of warm boots. A robe. A jacket.

"You're my niece," Elise told her, when Mira, worried over what Tom would think, protested the gifts. "Please indulge me. I enjoy spoiling my brother's daughter."

Mira leaned her head against the window casement and studied the beauty of grass and plants in the backyard, frosted like living sculptures. Key West never had frost or snow or sleet. The idea of experiencing the chill of late fall and early winter sounded appealing. What would it be like to stand outside during a snowfall? Should she stay long enough to find out?

Similar questions flitted into her head more often each day like determined ghosts. So far, life in Kansas City had been a captivating experience. Tally was friendly and fun to work with. When she lamented how business had slowed in recent years, Mira had suggested, as tactfully as she could, more updates to the menu with new offerings that appealed to a more health-conscious culture. Tally quickly embraced the ideas and even agreed to use the local Farmers' Market for fresher produce. The challenge of helping to rebuild a business transformed each day into a pleasant adventure, and Mira looked forward to doing more.

Overall, life had developed into a mellow routine. Mrs. Caldwell, with her quiet ways and continued kindness, made the Becker house feel like a home. Mira had even become adjusted to Elise's frenetic pace overseeing fundraisers for her favorite charities, along with her penchant for extravagance. She seemed to find the greatest pleasure in picking out and giving gifts, as though to prove her love.

Then there were the two Becker daughters who had moved far away. Mira wondered if she'd ever have the chance to meet them. The three girls had had one short, albeit stilted, conversation on the phone. They had been awkwardly polite with each other, but not one iota of warmth had developed between them. If only they would come to KC so they could meet in person. As a matter of fact, Mira figured a visit from Carolyn and Kat would do the entire family a world of good.

Loss and guilt. Mira understood it only too well. The ragged hole left by Pauline's death still ached. Some days it took more than one round of yoga poses and meditation to keep from breaking out in hives or bursting into tears.

Yet, all in all, remaining in KC had been an easy choice, despite the fact that Dinah called at least once a week to ask when she planned to come home. Mira hadn't even tried to give her an answer because she simply didn't know.

Tom, however, kept her at arm's length like he was still waiting for her to reveal the hidden reason for knocking on their door.

And then she considered Aiden and Neal. As far as she could tell, they were both pleasant enough guys, and each one of them appealed to her in a different way. But it was too soon to know whether a feeling with either one would ever amount to more than friendship.

A tap at the door caused Louie's tail to wag into a blur. "It's Elise," a soft voice called.

Mira turned away from the window. "Come in."

Elise stepped into the room with something in her hand. "I found more pictures of Jimmy." Louie raced over to greet his mistress, and she bent to pat him. "Mrs. Caldwell is on the way to take you outside, Louie. Hang on."

Mira took the photos Elise handed her and thumbed through the pile. She put her favorite one on the top. James Todd appeared to be of college age, wearing a pullover sweater, jeans, and an ear-to-ear grin. "Oh, look how young he is." Mira traced a finger over the image. "What a handsome man."

"He was quite good-looking." Elise's face softened. "When he was little, I took care of him while our mother worked. She wasn't really the nurturing type with her children, but she did love her career. I often felt Jimmy belonged to me more than her."

"Did you have any other siblings?"

"No, there was only the two of us. Our parents divorced when I was in college. Daddy found someone else in short order, and he disappeared from our lives. Mother went to work as a secretary at an aerospace company in St. Louis and stayed there until she retired. She passed away just before Tom and I were married." When Elise lifted her chin, her eyes were wet. She cleared her throat. "Did you notice anything else about that picture?"

Mira studied the image again, and her mouth curved. "I smile like him, don't I?"

"You certainly do. I said so early on, but it's even more pronounced in this photo where he's closer to your age. His smile and yours are identical."

Mira's heart skipped a beat at the realization. Could she actually have a family? Right here in Kansas City? It was a weirdly gratifying moment. Even if Tom didn't believe her story, it pleased her to be reminded that Elise did.

Mrs. Caldwell entered the room. "There you are," she said to Louie. "Let's go outside." The poodle perked up his ears and trotted toward her. She picked him up, and on the way out the door, said, "Breakfast is nearly ready."

Elise tucked a strand of hair behind her ear. "Why don't you hold on to these pictures until I can have copies made for you?"

Mira touched the top photo. "I'd like that."

"Consider it done. I'll see you downstairs for breakfast." Elise headed toward the door but stopped short of exiting. "By the way, I'm beyond pleased that you and Neal hit it off so well. Tom says he's a hard worker who's going to be a very successful lawyer one day. I think he's a perfect match for you."

"He is nice." *That starry look in her eyes. She all but has us walking down the aisle.* The thought amused her. "But, we barely know each other."

"Time will take care of that, darling." Elise smiled. "Speaking of time, we really need to make an effort to get better acquainted. Tom and I want to learn more about your life in Key West, but he's been so busy at the office, and I have three events coming up."

Mira recalled the strain she'd sensed between the couple. "You both seem a bit tense. I hope it's not because of me."

"Not at all," Elise answered too quickly. "This season is always our busiest time of year."

"I've been thinking. Maybe it would be better if I found a hotel to stay in until I head back home. I'm sure it doesn't help that I'm here like some uninvited guest who showed up but doesn't know when it's time to leave."

"This house could hold an army of guests without causing us any difficulty at all. And let me remind you. You are not just a guest. You're family."

"Then, as family, there's a little something I'd like to give to you and Tom." Mira picked up a small round box from the dresser and handed it to Elise. "I hope you like it."

Surprise and curiosity registered on Elise's face as she pulled off the box top and then stared inside. "Is it a humidifier?"

"No, it's a diffuser. I thought it might help you and Tom sleep a little better." She didn't add that she hoped if they felt more serene, it would ease the edginess between them. Edginess, she surmised, that had arrived the same day she knocked at their door. "It's simple to use. Put in water and then a few drops from the bottle of lavender oil you'll find in the box. Lavender is a calming scent. You'll get a much better night's rest."

"Thank you. That sounds lovely. I've always enjoyed the scent of lavender."

"Then I think you'll like using this." Mira gave Elise a hug.

"I'm sure we will."

"There's a meditation app I can help you download, too. It helps me whenever I get wound too tight."

Both of Elise's eyebrows shot upward.

Too much, Mira! She backpedaled as quickly as she could. "No big deal. I just thought you might be interested. Pauline and I had all sorts of little tricks to help us keep a peaceful frame of mind." She realized she sounded like an advertisement from the Water's Edge Healing Spa, even though her words were true.

Elise nodded, but her lips thinned. "I see."

"Okay, then." Mira decided it was good she hadn't suggested stargazing as another sure-fire remedy for tension. Elise didn't look like the stargazing type, although she—and Tom—would most certainly benefit from an evening doing not one single thing other than sitting quietly for a while gazing up at the sky. "I'll see you downstairs as soon as I change."

Elise left the room with a troubled expression. Mira chewed the inside of her cheek and raced to turn on the shower so she wouldn't hold up breakfast. She reached for lavender-scented—she practiced what she preached—soap and let the warm water run over her body before sudsing up in a soothing lather. Clearly, Elise had been pleased about Mira's openness to Neal but upset over the insinuation there was friction between Elise and her husband.

Mira decided one thing felt certain.

It was a blessing she'd fudged her plans and told Elise she had a meeting that evening with Tally rather than a dinner date with Aiden. A strong suspicion declared Elise wouldn't be pleased by the truth.

Mira and Aiden had planned to eat at the same restaurant where she'd run into him before. She didn't want any awkwardness with Aiden showing up at the Becker home to pick her up like they'd been transformed into a couple of high school kids. Besides, Elise meeting Aiden would only be upsetting for everyone.

As soon as she walked through the restaurant door, she spotted Aiden sitting on a bench in the lobby. He rose with an easy grace that sent her heart skipping into double rhythm. Now wasn't the proper moment to analyze her feelings.

"This is the first time I've seen you without a braid." His grin broadened. "I like your hair loose. It looks nice."

She unconsciously smoothed a thick curl away from her face. "Hair like mine is easier to deal with when twisted up in a tail." Her cheeks flamed at the compliment, which made her feel even more self-conscious. "Shall we find a table?"

Aiden held out his hand, and she let him lead her to an empty booth. He seemed uneasy, so she didn't say much. They each took a seat and placed their orders with almost no side-conversation. Yet the silence was a comfortable one, as if there wasn't any need for talk.

He handed her a napkin-rolled set of silverware. While she unwrapped it, she slanted a leisurely look at him. It was nice to study his features uninterrupted by her job at the café or in the middle of a crisis. Her memory had served her well. Aiden was broad-shouldered and almost too attractive, with the kind of face and physique that would be perfect on one of those charity calendars Dinah ordered every year where each month a shirtless firefighter held an adorable rescue puppy. Dinah would always show the calendar to Mira and Pauline with the same comment, "There are supposed to be puppies in here somewhere, but I sure don't see them."

Conversation from other tables drifted toward them. Mira placed the napkin across her lap and said, "Where's Lily?"

"My parents' house. They watch her when I'm working or when I have something going on." She could hear the smile in his voice when he talked about his family.

"She's so cute. Smart, too. You must be proud of her."

Aiden's face flushed to a deeper shade. "I can't imagine my life without Lily."

"I'll bet you're a great dad."

"I try, but I won't deny it's hard." He shook out his napkin. "What about you? How are things at the café?"

"We haven't had any more fires, if that's what you mean," she said wryly. "Actually, we're doing pretty well. We've made some changes to what we offer, and we're thinking up new ideas to bring in customers. Tally says if we get much busier, we'll need to hire extra help."

"I suspect Tally would be thrilled if you stayed longer than a month or so. Lily bends my ear all the time about going to the coffee house so she can see you. She'll be miserable when you go."

Mira sensed the question in his comments. "Who knows when that will be," she said softly. "I'm still not sure myself."

"I asked you before what business brought you to KC, but you didn't get a chance to answer. Is it something you can talk about?" He arranged his fork and knife neatly on the table instead of looking at her.

The back of Mira's neck itched. She had to clench her fingers together to keep from scratching it. "I came to tie up a few loose ends related to my mother, and the Beckers offered to let me stay with them." *Not complete honesty, but also not a total lie.*

"I hope you don't think I'm prying." He reached for her hand. "Sorry if it sounds that way."

"No worries." His calloused palm sent a small flare blazing up her arm. The zap of warmth caught her off guard. She concentrated on breathing in and out and caught sight of their server. To regain a hint of composure, she announced, "Here comes our food."

Aiden released her fingers, and the baffled look on his face made her wonder if he'd felt something too.

"It's a good thing," he said. "I'm so hungry, I could eat the north end of a southbound bear. How about you?"

He'd recovered himself enough to make a nonsensical comment—such a funny remark, Mira found herself easing into the same casual rhythm.

"So could I," she assured him with a smile.

Chapter Twelve

His cell phone jangled insistently from the dark granite counter. Aiden loaded another dirty plate into the dishwasher and glanced at the caller ID before picking up. "Mom?"

"You'll never guess what happened," she paused dramatically, "I won!"

He waited long enough to let her words sink in, but they still didn't make any sense. "What are you talking about?"

"I entered my cinnamon roll recipe in a contest, and it won first place. The prize is a weekend in Branson at a hotel right on the lake." She stopped to catch her breath. "Plus, they gave me tickets to several shows and gift cards to three restaurants. I can't believe it."

"What's not to believe? You make the best cinnamon rolls I've ever tasted. I'll bet you blew all the other entries away. So, when's your big trip?"

"It would be this weekend, but after your dad and I talked about it, we decided not to go."

"You're not going? Why?"

"Because I checked your schedule. You'll be working. We thought about taking Lily with us, but the shows aren't really geared toward a little girl."

"Mom, you and Dad haven't had a vacation in I don't remember how long. You're going, and I don't want to hear any argument."

"How can we? What will you do with Lily?"

"Don't worry about her. I'll rearrange my work schedule." He propped the cell phone between his shoulder and ear to wipe his hands on a towel.

She didn't say anything in response. Aiden figured she must be digesting the information. When she finally spoke, a veneer of doubt coated her voice. "Well, if you're sure."

"I'm positive. You and Dad need to have some fun. Go to Branson. You deserve it."

"If you think you can manage, I suppose we would enjoy a few days away. I had to chuckle at your dad's reaction when I told him. He went downstairs right away and started sorting through all his gear. I think he was daydreaming about the possibility of a new place to fish."

"I've heard a few of the guys say fishing in Branson is excellent. Dad won't be disappointed."

"Now that I know we're going, I can get excited. He can have all the fun he wants fishing while I shop. Thanks for rearranging your schedule, son."

"All the kudos belong to you and to Dad. You both help me out in a hundred different ways. I think you better start packing, Mrs. Award-Winning Baker. And congratulations."

He ended the call with a grin. His mom was as pumped up as if she had been given an Olympic gold medal. His chest expanded a little with pride. She had always brushed off compliments about her culinary talents, but now his mom had iron-clad proof of her expertise.

Aiden punched in the number for the fire station and leaned against the counter while the phone rang. With any luck, Zamp wouldn't be in a lousy mood. The captain disliked rearranging work schedules on short notice. Five minutes later, Aiden had his answer. He hung up with a shake of his head. Zamp had barely allowed him to utter one sentence before proceeding to give him an earful. According to the captain, there were already two guys scheduled to be off. Giving anyone else time off was not only a breach of policy but out of the question.

Aiden hated to ask Chrissy. According to Puno, she was scrambling to get ready for their vacation trip planned to begin right after shift change.

What am I supposed to do now? Ruin Mom and Dad's trip or be a jerk and call in sick at work?

Lily wandered into the kitchen, rubbing her eyes. "Can I have some juice?"

Ordinarily, he wouldn't give her sugary stuff so close to bedtime, but Aiden grabbed a fruit punch juice box and jammed—much harder than necessary—a tiny straw into a tiny opening. His daughter took the box and sat at the table.

She gulped a large slurp. "What's the matter, Daddy? Your face is frowny."

"Is it?" Aiden smoothed his features. "Sorry about that. I was hoping to trade my days off, but the captain said no."

"Why do you want to do that?" She scratched an itch on her arm before her skinny little legs went into motion, swinging forward and back. *Oh, man. The sugar was already kicking in.*

"Memaw and Papa wanted to go out of town." He sat in the chair next to her. "I was going to change my schedule so they'd be free to do it." He made his eyes big. "Guess why? Memaw called to say she entered her cinnamon rolls in a contest, and she won a trip! Isn't that cool?"

Lily squealed. "I love Memaw's rolls."

"Who doesn't? The judge must have loved them, too."

The little legs stopped swinging. "Are you mad because they have to watch me instead of going on a trip?"

Man, his little girl was way too clever for her age. "I'm not mad, Lily-Lou. I was only thinking how it would be fun for them to have some time away. It's not every day a person wins a prize, you know."

Lily scrunched her small forehead and took another long pull from the straw. Her face brightened. "I know what. Ask Mira if I can stay with her. You said she's your friend now. She's my friend, too."

He considered the idea for about three seconds. "That's a really big favor to ask. Mira's busy, and I don't want to inconvenience her."

"But it would be fun—like going to a sleepover. Just ask her, Daddy." Lily's eyes sparkled. "Please?"

He wasn't so sure having a sleepover with an eight-year-old guest could be described as fun for anybody. Mira might have plans with what's-his-name. Or she might prefer a quiet evening all to herself. "Let me think about it." He glanced at the wall clock. "Look how late it is. Time for you to start getting ready for bed."

Aiden ran warm water into the tub and poured in enough soap for a foamy bubble bath. Lily soaked in the suds, swirling around the bubbles and dunking her floating toys until the water cooled, and her fingertips resembled raisins. He helped her put on her pink unicorn pajamas and told her to brush her teeth while he turned down the bed and gathered the four storybooks she had chosen—one more than the usual three.

When Lily jumped into bed with Siggy in her arms, Aiden tucked the covers around them. He sat close enough that she could lean against his chest and see the pictures while he read. For some time now, he knew his daughter recognized many of the words on each page, but she still clung to the habit of having him read to her each evening, a task he'd taken over once Rose had become too ill to do so. Truth was, he really didn't mind. The calming ritual helped shift the chaotic pace of a long day into a peaceful night.

When Aiden closed the final storybook, he kissed a drowsy Lily goodnight before turning off the light. His daughter's idea teased at his brain. Would it be too bold to ask Mira? Too presumptuous? Rather than answer his own questions, he decided to seek out an unbiased opinion. Not from his parents, though. They'd cancel their trip for sure if they knew he couldn't get off work. He thought a few moments and then called Puno's number.

"Hello, Stewart. Keith's sound asleep. He wasn't feeling well." Chrissy had picked up her husband's cell.

"I'm sorry to hear that. Hope he's better tomorrow."

"I imagine he will. He's got tickets for us to see the Chiefs play a charity game and the next day is vacation."

"You're right. He wouldn't miss football for anything. Or lounging on the beach either." Then it occurred to him that Chrissy's opinion might be even better than Puno's. He gave her the short version of his dilemma and waited.

"Keith told me about this girl who works at the coffee shop. If Lily brought up the idea of staying with her, I'd say that's a good sign."

"Lily does like Mira, but this is a big favor. It's not like I'm asking her to give me a cup of coffee. How do you think she'd feel about it?"

"Oh, this is fun. You're worried about what she thinks." Chrissy didn't bother to smother her giggle.

"Why shouldn't I be?"

"Well, it says one thing loud and clear. There is no point whatsoever in me trying to fix you up with any of my friends. I believe you've already found someone who interests you."

"That's ridiculous." *Or is it?* "Look, I'm just trying to work it out so Mom and Dad can enjoy the trip she won."

"Okay, pal, here's what you need to do. Go ahead and ask her. It's a simple question, and the worst that can happen is she says she can't do it. No big deal."

He rubbed his forehead. "I don't know. For some reason, it *feels* like a big deal."

"This gets more fascinating by the minute." She snorted into a chuckle. "Aiden Stewart, I'm telling you to stop procrastinating and call her, or I'll tell Keith you're scared to death of the girl in the coffee shop. Can you imagine what he'll say to the other guys?"

"You wouldn't."

"Oh, wouldn't I?"

Chrissy got the same joy out of pranking people that Puno did. It made them a dangerous—albeit entertaining—couple. "Okay, you're right. I'm turning a simple question into a thing. I'm going to ask her. If she won't do it, maybe I'll call in sick. Who knows? I might really get sick if Mom and Dad ditch their trip because of me."

"Way to man up, Stewart. I'm proud of you. Now get on it before you change your mind."

"Will do, Mrs. Puno."

"And Stewart," she added, "you better report back to me on what Mira says."

He put his phone down and grabbed a beer from the refrigerator. By the time he drained the bottle, he felt daring enough to go for it. He dialed the number Mira had given him and she picked up on the first ring. "Hi, Aiden."

"Did I get you at a bad time?"

"I've got an excellent book in my lap, but that's okay. What's going on?"

"Well," he cleared away a frog from his throat, "a funny thing happened today. My mother called to say she won a contest for her cinnamon roll recipe."

Silence. In a bewildered tone, she said, "Good for her. That's great."

"She won an all-expense-paid trip for herself and Dad. A weekend in Branson."

"Branson? Where's that?"

"It's in southern Missouri. Kind of like—" *How to describe Branson?* He continued, "the Midwest's version of Vegas, with shows and restaurants and shopping places, plus a big lake."

"Well, that sounds like fun. I hope they have a great time."

"This brings me to the reason I'm calling."

"Oh?" More silence, as she most likely waited to discover exactly what his mom's trip had to do with her.

"It's like this, they're planning to go this weekend, but I have to work. I tried to rearrange my schedule, but the captain said it wasn't possible. Too many other people were off. I think I mentioned to you my parents are the ones who watch Lily when I'm working."

"Would your parents be able to take their trip some other weekend?"

"Their plans are all set, and I don't think they can change the date. I'm afraid if I ask them to reschedule, they'll just decide not to go at all. They do so much for Lily and me that I really want them to have a chance to get away and enjoy themselves. I'd hate to be the reason they miss out on the opportunity."

"I'm going to guess there's no one else who can take care of Lily."

Aiden swallowed uncomfortably. "Not anyone who's available Saturday during the day and overnight. I'll be off Sunday morning."

"You should have told me what you wanted from the beginning. Interesting as your story is, you had me wondering. As it turns out, I am available this weekend, and I'd love to spend time with Lily." She paused. "That is, if you're okay with me watching her."

The long list of persuasive points he had meticulously constructed in his head to convince her dissolved like sugar in a cup of industrial-strength firehouse coffee.

"You bet I'm okay with it. Why else would I have called you?"

Chapter Thirteen

Could anything on earth compare to the aroma of bread baking? Mira inhaled the earthy and slightly sweet scent as she pulled a tray from the oven.

"I can't wait to try it." Tally peeked around Mira to admire the golden-brown focaccia. "Do you know three customers asked what we were baking? When I told them, they wanted to order some. If this tastes half as good as it smells, you've got another winner on your hands."

Mira smiled. "I guess we'll soon find out."

The feta and fire-roasted tomato focaccia bread had been an experiment—a recipe she'd spent a couple of days thinking about. Focaccia was a favorite of hers, and she'd decided to play with the proportion of fresh herbs. She inhaled another whiff of her creation. It smelled divine.

Mira poked the bread with a knife. It looked good and had the right texture, but a taste test would reveal whether a new item would be added to the café's ever-expanding menu. She busied herself cleaning up while the bread cooled for fifteen minutes and then she sliced it into neat portions. Before she had finished, Tally grabbed the end piece and popped the morsel into her mouth.

"Ummm." Tally closed her eyes in rapture. "This is exquisite. It's going on next week's menu for sure."

"As soon as we get all the ingredients in stock. I don't want to promote until we can produce." Mira took a bite and savored the taste. "Rosemary, parsley, thyme, basil, and sea salt. I was worried about how the herbs would come together, but this seems to work."

"I'll say it works." Tally settled on a stool near the workspace. "Customers will love it. Mira, you have a real talent for baking. Sometimes I wish I could just come here, place my order, and take it home to eat while I watch TV. Business has picked up so much that I'm tuckered all the time."

"Why don't you have a cup of tea and another slice of focaccia? I'll watch the counter."

Tally helped herself to more of the warm bread. "You know, lately, I've been thinking about visiting my daughter and grandkids."

"Any time you need a vacation, all you have to do is let me know. I'd be happy to handle the café for you."

"Actually," Tally picked at a piece of feta on the bread, "my daughter's called every night this week. She's worried about me living all alone. Guess she's afraid I'll fall down one of these days and not be able to get back up. A couple of times, she's mentioned the idea of me being closer to her. She suggested I move to Colorado."

Mira's eyes rounded. "I didn't know you were thinking about moving."

Tally gave a one-shouldered shrug. "I'd like to see more of my family. My grandson plays football for his high school team. Can you believe I've never been to a single one of his games? And my granddaughter is getting ready to start middle school. She takes dance classes, but I've missed all her recitals. I haven't been there for them, and I'd like to be a part of their lives while I still have my wits about me."

Mira dropped onto the other counter stool. "Are you serious? That would mean you'd have to close the café."

"Maybe, but I'd rather find the right person to buy this place than close it down. Someone who'd love it the way I do. Maybe somebody like…you?" Tally eyed Mira expectantly.

"Wow. That's a bolt out of the blue. I don't know what to say."

"You told me you always wanted to have your own bakery. You could build this place into whatever you want it to be."

"That's an interesting idea." A rush of excitement bubbled in Mira until reality set in. "But I don't have the money to start my own business right now. My mother left me a small inheritance, but it's not nearly enough to support a venture this enormous."

"Oh, well. It was just an idea." Tally deflated a little. "The workload gets to me sometimes, and the thought of you taking over seemed like an inspiration, and the perfect solution."

"I'm flattered you think so. If my circumstances were different, I'd jump on the chance. This is a wonderful place."

"It is. One of these days, I'm afraid I'll have to make a hard decision." She rose slowly from the stool, as though her back ached. "Hey, let me know what ingredients we need for the focaccia bread. I want to put in a supply order so we can be ready."

"Sure. Let me check on things out front while you take a break." Mira walked from the kitchen to the café floor, her head spinning.

Sunshine gleamed through the windows, showcasing the fact that half of the tables seated customers. Tally's endorsement and the quiet hum of conversation sent Mira's dreams climbing toward the stratosphere. The café did have a lot of potential. Mira hadn't done much more than orchestrate a few menu changes and rearrange the goods Tally displayed for sale. The minor tweaks had increased business by at least a third, but a lot more could be done.

If they maximized Wi-Fi capability, completed a remodel to add more space, and created a small meeting room for groups to use, Mira was confident it would help boost sales even more. She could even envision the addition of a few tables in front of the building for customers to dine outside on balmy days. But all of that took money. Mira leaned her elbows on the counter, resting her chin on her palm. What was the point of dreaming up changes? The shop didn't belong to her, and from what

Tally had said, who knew how much longer it would even be around?

The front door squeaked open, and Mira's gaze flicked to the entrance. She straightened up in a hurry. Aiden was holding the door for a middle-aged couple to step inside. He lifted a hand to wave at her, and the trio proceeded toward the counter.

"Mom and Dad," Aiden said, "this is Mira. Mira, these are my parents, Bob and Betty Stewart."

The woman broke into a friendly smile. "I am so glad to finally meet you. You're as pretty as Lily and our son said you were."

Aiden's face flushed. "All right, Mom, you don't need to tell her all our secrets."

The unexpected compliment pleased Mira enough to take pity on Aiden and change the subject. "Congratulations, Betty. I hear you won a contest. As one baker to another, I'd love to taste those cinnamon rolls some time."

"I'll make a batch for you as soon as I can." Betty's face lit up with pleasure. "Aiden tells us you're going to watch Lily while we're in Branson."

"Yes. Lily's so sweet. We'll have a great time. By the way, where is she?"

"She's at school," Aiden said. "We stopped by because I wanted to introduce you to my parents since they'll be dropping her off at my house on their way out of town Saturday morning."

"Yep, we'll be on the road bright and early." Bob looked like he was ready to leave right away. "I already have my fishing gear packed. I'm gonna catch me a whopper or two."

Bob's grin reminded Mira of Aiden's. "I'm sure you will. Where I come from, fishing is a big part of life. A nice easy rhythm and a perfect way to kick back and relax. Unless you're reeling in a monster, of course."

Betty nudged her son. "Aiden told us you're from Key West. I looked it up on the Internet, and the pictures are amazing. I told Bob, one of these days, we need to go there and visit."

"You'd love it." Mira warmed with pride as she always did when someone praised her hometown. "And Bob, when you go, you should try deep-sea fishing. Talk about catching whoppers. In the Keys, you could hook one of those 'we're going to need a bigger boat' types of fish."

His eyebrows lifted. "You just put Key West on my bucket list."

Betty glanced at her watch. "I'd love to stay and chat longer, but we need to run. It's almost time to pick up Lily. Before we go, could we get a half dozen of your chocolate croissants to take with us? Lily loves them, and I'm dying to taste one myself."

"Absolutely." Mira stepped to the case and picked out six croissants, placing them into a box.

Aiden got out his credit card and handed it to her. "Lily is so excited she's practically bouncing off the walls. I appreciate you agreeing to stay at my house. I know it's not as convenient for you."

"No worries. I figured that would probably work out best since I'm not sure if the people I'm staying with have plans for the weekend. Tell Lily I can't wait to see her."

Aiden took the box of croissants from Mira, and the crinkles deepened around his eyes. "I owe you big time for this."

"Don't be silly. I'm happy to help."

He regarded her steadily, and it appeared he was about to say something when Bob interrupted. "If we don't get going, we'll be at the tail end of the pick-up line at school. You know what a pain in the posterior that is."

Aiden nodded and said to Mira, "I'll talk to you later." He swiveled away from her toward the door. His parents waved and then followed their son. The three of them disappeared from the café almost as quickly as they'd arrived.

"When the good Lord made that man, He sure knew what he was doing." Tally came up behind her from the kitchen. "Who were those people with him?"

"His parents," Mira replied, her brows creased in thought.

"Get outta town. He brought them in to meet you?"

"I told you I'd be watching Lily this weekend. Since they'll be the ones dropping her off, Aiden thought he ought to introduce us."

Tally huffed out a breath. "Oh, come on. He could have made the arrangements without any introductions. It's not like Lily doesn't know who you are."

A young man in a faded college sweatshirt strolled to the counter for a coffee refill. Taking his cup gave Mira a minute to think about what Tally said. Was this meeting with Aiden's parents more than a casual part of the favor he'd asked? She topped off the man's mug and handed it back to him with a distracted smile.

"I don't know, Tally. Maybe Aiden was being considerate because his parents were concerned. He and I haven't known each other very long. After all, he's entrusting me with his daughter. They probably wanted to be sure I didn't look like a wild-eyed kidnapper."

"Take it from me, whenever a man wants a woman to meet his parents, there's something more than politeness involved. I don't think you realize the way he looks at you. His eyes go gooey as melted caramel. It reminds me of the way Jamie rivets his eyes on Claire during a love scene on the *Outlander* series. Come to think of it," Tally eyeballed the ceiling, "I bet Aiden would look great in a kilt."

Mira chuffed into laughter. "I've never seen *Outlander*, but you created an image I won't soon forget."

"Maybe you better savor the thought the next time you see that young man."

"Tally, you've given me a lot to think about today." She wiped her hands on her apron. "But I need to go back to the kitchen and work on some bread dough. There's nothing like a round of kneading to help a person sort through thoughts."

She left Tally at the counter, staring at the door with an unabashedly sappy smile on her face.

Mira washed her hands, sprinkled flour on the breadboard, and turned out a bowl of dough. She folded and pushed and rolled. The kneading machine sat nearby, but the feel of the smooth dough under her hands and the steady repetitive motions felt more like therapy than work. By the time the dough became smooth and springy, she felt much more mindful than before. Her thoughts, too, had consolidated into several interesting conclusions.

The idea of buying Tally's café appealed to her more than she wanted to admit, but the revelation came as a surprise. Ever since Tally had suggested the sale, ideas about what she could do with it whirled around in her head at hurricane speed. Even though she knew she couldn't afford the purchase, an odd longing to take control of the café and make it her own caught her up short. What propelled such a strong urge to start a business in KC, when all along she had planned on a return to the Keys?

A less welcome thought pushed its way in. The Beckers. She'd noticed the chill between them had deepened. Elise accepted Mira wholeheartedly, in a "love me, love my dog" kind of way, almost daring her husband to say anything to the contrary, yet Tom stayed courteously aloof. She couldn't help thinking again that it might be better if she left. Yet the thread of connection between her and Elise hadn't frayed. Besides, if James Todd was indeed her father, she'd be forever linked with the family, whether Tom liked it or not.

Mira held back a sigh. As if all those matters weren't enough to consider, Tally had planted another notion in her head. Aiden dressed in a kilt, standing beside a fire truck. Now Mira couldn't shake the picture. This disconcerting—or should she say provocative?—visualization left her worrying there might be a reason she hadn't originally counted on that made her want to stick around.

Chapter Fourteen

Arms loaded high with cupcake-filled boxes, Mira backed out the café door. A chilly breeze lifted wisps of hair that had come loose from her braid as she trekked outside. She caught a glimpse of her beloved van and smiled. Not only did the VW come in handy for delivery purposes, but it also provided a memorable accent to any event, an accent which helped highlight their most recently introduced service—catering. The new undertaking already had bookings at several small venues.

She tightened her hold on the boxes and edged forward. Since she couldn't see in front of her, she cut her eyes from side to side, hoping she wouldn't bang head-on into anything. The longer she kept the boxes clutched to her chest, the more her arm muscles burned. Stacked up, the containers were a lot heavier than she thought they would be. *Cha. Why didn't I pull the van closer to the entrance?*

"Can I give you a hand?"

She recognized Aiden's voice and came to a stop. "If you could take some of these boxes before I drop them all over the place, it would be great."

"My pleasure, ma'am." He took all but one. "Don't you think you ought to get a cart before you hurt your back and end up in traction?"

Her shoulders relaxed at the lightened load and the roguish expression on his face. "Tally's going to add a cart to her list. Catering is something new for us."

"Always the busy bee, aren't you? Seems like every time I see you, you're rushing from one place to another. It makes me wonder. Do you ever take time for yourself?"

She balanced the box she held with one arm and reached to open the van door with the other. "With business picking up at the café, daytime is my busy time." She carefully arranged the box in the back of the VW so it wouldn't slide around. "I'm putting in more hours than I thought I would, but I don't mind. I like being busy. Evening is my time to relax."

"I'm not talking about sitting in your room reading." He placed the other boxes into the van. "When do you do anything that's only for you?"

She paused to think about it. "Reading *is* something I do for myself. I also meditate, and I practice yoga. In the Keys, I used to go out in the evening and sit by the ocean. Hearing the waves roll in is heaven."

"Sounds like you miss Key West."

He stared at her so intently, she squirmed. "It's hard not to miss a place you've lived all your life."

Aiden lowered his gaze to examine the asphalt. "You told me you were here to take care of things for your mother. Have you tied up the loose ends yet?"

"A few things are still up in the air. I honestly don't have a definite plan. I wish I did. It might make some decisions easier."

His eyes returned to hers with a searching look. "I hope you don't take offense at me saying so, but as far as I'm concerned, the longer you stay, the better. We'd—Lily and I, that is—we'd miss you if you left."

Another cool gust of wind ruffled her hair, but Aiden's remark warmed her so much, she didn't feel the chill. "I know I need to figure out my next move, but for the moment, it's easier to tread water. I think I'm still trying to get used to the fact that Pauline is gone. Sometimes it's hard to wrap my head around the truth. One thing is for sure. Nothing so far has lit a fire under me to pack up and leave. Kansas City is a nice place, and the people I've met have been good to me."

"What about the friends you're living with? Do they care how long you're here?"

Her hand prickled, and Mira scratched it absent-mindedly. "They said I could stay as long as I want. It's a different world with them. We could go a whole week without seeing each other in that enormous house of theirs. It's the total opposite of my place in the Keys." She slammed the van door shut. "I am sorry, but I need to rush if I'm going to get these cupcakes to a baby shower before the expectant mom goes into labor."

Aiden's lop-sided grin appeared the tiniest bit vulnerable. "Guess I got off track. I didn't mean to keep you. I stopped by to say my parents will be at the house tomorrow when you get there. I might see you for a minute or so before I have to leave for work, but they'll tell you about Lily's routine. Is around seven o'clock okay?"

"Oh, my gosh, what's wrong with me?" Mira's hand flew to her cheek. "I forgot to ask you something. Would you mind if Lily comes to the house where I'm staying instead of me going to your house? When I told the Beckers I was going to watch your daughter, Elise came up with a great idea. She suggested Lily stay at their house. They have so many fun things for a kid to do. A theatre room where we could stream movies. A game room I know she'd enjoy. There's even an adorable little dog for her to play with. But if you're not comfortable with it, I understand."

"Elise Becker?" Aiden's forehead wrinkled in thought. "Isn't she married to Tom Becker?"

"Yes." Mira's eyebrow arched up. "Do you know them?"

"I should have realized it when I saw their house. Who hasn't heard of the Beckers? He's the most well-known lawyer in town, and she's in charge of practically every big charity gig."

He sounded more incredulous than annoyed, but clarification was in order. "Does this mean you approve of the change in plans, or is the answer no?"

"It's fine with me. Given everything I've ever heard about them, I don't see any problem. And you'll be there. It's not like Lily will be alone with strangers."

"I know she'll have a good time. Elise is thrilled about the idea of having a little girl around to spoil."

"I'll give my folks the address. Mom will freak out over meeting them."

"They're just people, like you and me."

"They might be people, and they might be like you, but they're not like me." He chuckled.

Mira's phone buzzed. "That's probably the woman who arranged the shower wondering where the cupcakes are. I'd better run. Thanks, Aiden."

"No, thank *you*. My shift is over Sunday morning, so plan on seeing me around eight-thirty."

Mira smiled and gave him a thumbs up. She climbed into her van and put the cell to her ear without bothering to look at the caller ID.

"Darling, this is Elise." Her voice sounded low and tight.

The need to swallow stuck in Mira's throat. "Is something wrong?"

"It's Tom. He set an appointment for you to take a DNA test this afternoon. I can't help feeling frustrated with him. My husband is simply adamant that you go through this ridiculous procedure. I told him if you don't want to do it, he'll just have to cancel. I certainly don't need any proof that you are who you say you are."

The itch on Mira's hand traveled up her arm. The fact that Tom felt it necessary to analyze her honesty proved one thing beyond any doubt. In spite of all she'd done to show him the kind of person she was, he didn't trust her. He still insisted on proof that she wasn't a liar. Breathing in and out twice to reduce her level of disappointment, Mira said, "What time, and where do I need to go?"

Aiden pointed his pickup in the direction of his parents' house. Filling them in on the change in plans required an in-person visit, before he picked up Lily from school. His thumb tapped the steering wheel, and he shook his head in bewilderment. Tom and Elise Becker. The most prominent couple in the entire city. Mira said they were her friends, but how in the world had she connected with them? Mira, in far-off Key West, and the Beckers, here in the Midwest. The facts didn't add up. Come to think of it, Mira seemed determined to avoid a discussion on the reason for her pilgrimage. Bringing up the subject only resulted in vague answers and a swift shift to another topic. Something more was happening here than she let on. He'd bet his last dime on it. But what?

He pulled the truck into his parents' driveway and fisted the keys before strolling toward the door. As soon as he opened it, the enticing aroma of cinnamon rolls hit him full force. He followed the scent to his mom's kitchen, where she stood, wearing her serious baker apron and a determined expression. The counter had a dusting of flour scattered over it with measuring cups and spoons cluttered every which way. Her arms were wrist-deep in dough.

"Why are you in baking mode? You guys are leaving tomorrow."

"I wanted to give Mira some of my rolls and see what she thinks. I'd love to get her opinion."

"Didn't you already get a judge's opinion? Anyway, it looks like you've got enough dough to feed thirty people."

"Yet my rolls always get eaten, don't they?" She rubbed the back of her hand against her cheek, leaving a smudge of flour on her face. "I've got one more batch to get in the oven, and then I can pack."

"Since you're baking so many, feel free to send a few of those my way, if they're not already spoken for."

"I'll see what I can do." She flattened the dough and brushed it with melted butter. "Is there something you need?"

"I stopped by to tell you there's been a slight change in plans for tomorrow."

She paused to look at him, her brush in the air. "What do you mean?"

"Instead of staying at my house, Lily's going to stay at the place where Mira's been living since she came to KC."

"Where's that?"

"I'll text the address to you so you can GPS it. All I need you to do is pick up Lily from my house before I leave for work and take her to Mira's."

She narrowed her eyes at him. "What kind of place is that? This isn't in some shady part of town is it?"

"I've seen the house. From the outside, anyway. It looks like a perfectly nice place to me." He looked at the ceiling to keep from smiling.

"These days, you can't be too careful. Mira seems like a wonderful girl, but what if the house is a death trap? She doesn't have any children—at least not that you've told me about. Whose idea was it to change where Lily stays?"

"The people Mira lives with." He studiously avoided eye contact with his mom, afraid he'd burst into laughter.

"I don't like this, Aiden. I don't like it at all. Who are these people? Have you met them?"

A spoon on the counter had some cream cheese frosting on it. He swiped a finger across the spoon and then tasted the sample, letting his mom stew. "As a matter of fact, I know several things about them. You do, too."

"I don't have time for riddles." Her hands went to her hips. "Who are they?"

"No big deal. Only Tom and Elise Becker."

She jerked her chin toward him. "Who?"

"You heard me, Mom. Tom and Elise Becker. Lily's going to spend the night at their tiny little shack. From what Mira described, it'll be more like staying at Disneyland." His mother's eyes went wide, and her mouth gaped open. "Well, what do you think? Is the Becker home an acceptable place for your granddaughter to stay?"

When she apparently regained her ability to speak, she sputtered, "I'm glad I made plenty of rolls."

"What do rolls have to do with any of this?"

"I'll bring this entire batch to the Beckers. Enough for everybody in the house. They'll sample my very own cinnamon rolls. Can you imagine what my bridge club will say when they hear about this?"

Aiden moved toward the oven and peeked in. "Don't forget to spare a few for me. If there's enough left over, I'll take some to the guys."

"Don't even suggest it. Every single one is going with Lily to Mr. and Mrs. Becker. Who knows how many people they have in that huge house of theirs? I'll have enough to feed them all."

"So you're freezing me out, huh, Mom? Come on." He reached for an iced roll sitting on the counter.

She slapped his hand away. "After I get back from the trip, I'll make a batch for the station. Now you get out of here and let me finish."

He held up his hands. "Guess I know how I rate. I'll see you tomorrow. Have fun on the trip."

His mom didn't answer. Tongue between her teeth, she brushed the dough again in loving strokes with renewed effort, like an inspired artist placing paint on canvas.

Women who loved to bake. Was it one of those secret sisterhood things?

Chapter Fifteen

Her blood hummed, and her pulse hammered. Why in the universe did she feel in such a dither? Mira peeked at Elise, who sat at the breakfast table as unflappable as ever. Her elegant white cashmere sweater and navy slacks screamed high-end couture.

Tom lounged at the table in a golf shirt and khakis, a more casual outfit than his regular Saturday uniform. He made painfully polite chit-chat to Mira, even though she knew he'd been annoyed when the golf-powers-that-be decided to close the course. She supposed that when winds gusted frigid blasts strong enough to bite through a heavy jacket, golf wasn't deemed possible—even for die-hards like Tom.

The temperature today had dropped to one of the coldest she'd experienced so far. She picked at her food, hyper-aware of the conditions outside, nervous over Lily's pending arrival, and harboring a slight resentment over Tom's insistence she take a DNA test. At least the cotton sweater she had on felt like a warm hug.

Before a sliced strawberry made it half-way to Mira's mouth, the front doorbell chimed. Her fork clattered to the table, and she popped from her chair.

Elise waved a hand. "Darling, Mrs. Caldwell will get the door."

"I need to be there. Lily is probably scared." Mira tugged the hem of her sweater to smooth it and left the table. She reached the foyer at the same time as Mrs. Caldwell, who encouraged her with a smile before she opened the door.

Lily stepped cautiously inside, followed by Bob and Betty Stewart. The child's face went from woeful to bright-eyed elation. With one hand tightly clutching Siggy, she raced toward Mira, who squatted to welcome her with a hug. "I'm glad you're here," Mira whispered. "We're going to have a great time."

"You won't believe this, but she was a chatterbox until we got into the car." Betty's gaze swept the foyer. "Her daddy was a wreck, all worried about imposing on you."

"No one is imposing. We're delighted to have Lily as our guest." Elise joined them, with Tom following behind.

Mira made swift introductions and then nibbled her lip since everyone appeared too ill at ease for comfort.

Tom broke the ice. "I'm looking forward to this." His tone was surprisingly genial. "We haven't had a youngster around since our girls were little. It will be good practice for whenever we become grandparents." He flashed an engaging grin at Lily. "It's nice to meet you, young lady."

"You aren't grandparents yet?" Bob extended a hand and eyed Tom in disbelief. "I can testify it's the best job the good Lord ever invented."

"Someday, we hope to have the pleasure." Tom shook Bob's hand. "Neither of our daughters seems to be in much of a hurry, though."

"I understand you won a contest and are on the way to Branson." Elise broke into the conversation evenly. "It sounds like a delightful trip."

"We're looking forward to it." Betty handed Elise the large box she carried. "These are for you. My cinnamon rolls. The winning recipe. I brought enough for everybody."

Elise appeared to stagger under the weight of the box. "Thank you. We look forward to trying them."

"Come on; we need to hit the road." Bob must have had his fill of the awkward gabfest. "Here's Lily's suitcase. Aiden will be here first thing in the morning to pick her up. He said to call him if you have any questions."

Betty bent to kiss Lily. "Be good and have fun, sweetheart. We'll see you when we get back."

"She'll be fine. Travel safe and enjoy your time away." Mira straightened. "I can't wait to taste the rolls. They smell heavenly."

A short chorus of goodbyes later, Mira and Lily stood on the porch to watch Bob and Betty climb into their SUV. Containers and bags were stacked high enough in the vehicle to be visible through the windows. Several fishing poles were piled on top of the jumbled items. Clearly, the Stewarts intended to be ready for anything. Mira and Lily waved as the vehicle pulled away and then Mira hurried the little girl inside to warm up.

"Mira." Elise's soft voice caught her attention. "Why don't you and Mrs. Caldwell show Lily to her bedroom? If you need us, we'll be in the dining room. Please join us if you're hungry."

"Follow me." Mrs. Caldwell started up the steps.

"Come on, Lily. Let's get you settled in." Mira took charge of a small rolling suitcase decorated with a rainbow of brightly colored unicorns. The case thumped on each step.

Mrs. Caldwell led them to the bedroom next to Mira's. "Mrs. Becker thought this would be the most convenient. It's good to have you here, Lily. Please let me know if I can get you anything."

Lily and Mira crossed into the bedroom. The child looked overwhelmed. "This is a big place."

"It is; isn't it?" Mira remembered her own reaction to a Becker-sized bedroom. "But, I'll be right next door, so there's nothing to worry about."

"What will we do today?" Lily hugged the sloth against her chest.

Mira had researched possible child activities for inspiration. "I have a few ideas. But first, let's get unpacked."

She hung up Lily's coat and arranged the things from her suitcase, including three new books Aiden had bought her. "Sometimes, Daddy and I walk to the bookstore, but he said that's only for times when we aren't in a hurry."

"That sounds like fun." Mira set the books on the nightstand by Lily's bed.

"The lady at the desk helps me find stuff to read. She said I'd 'specially like the mermaid story. Will you read it to me?"

"I can do that," Mira said. "But first, would you like some breakfast?"

Lily shook her head. "Memaw brought me breakfast."

"Well then, how do you feel about making a batch of…slime?" The expression on Lily's face was worth every hour Mira had spent finding the right recipe.

"Yes!" The child appeared to forget her nervousness. She hopped up and down with barely contained enthusiasm.

"Making slime is messy, so that's a kitchen job. You might want to let Siggy rest in bed while we work."

"Okay." Lily placed the sloth on a pillow. "See you later, Siggy."

They skirted around the dining room, where Elise and Tom were finishing breakfast, and used the back entrance to the kitchen.

Mira had bought sheets of sturdy clear plastic to cover the granite countertop. She laid them out and then draped herself and Lily in old shirts she had found at a thrift shop. Once she placed all the ingredients on the counter, they set to work.

At one point, Elise poked her head in, but she exited right away. Who could blame her? In the pristine kitchen, bottles of glue and food coloring must have looked like a disaster waiting to happen. But nearly two hours later, no catastrophe marred the area. They had created, played with, and stuffed four plastic bags with slime tinted in Lily's favorite colors: purple, red, green, and pink.

"Can I take them home?"

"Let's see." Mira scrunched her brows together. "I don't think I have any use for slime. Mrs. Becker doesn't and neither does Mrs. Caldwell. I guess they belong to you. We'll store them in the fridge until you go home, but first we'll need to clean up."

They set to work, restoring the kitchen to its neat, pre-slime condition. Mira pulled over a stool for Lily to stand on near the sink and helped her wash off bits of slime and color. As they dried their hands, a tap of nails announced Louie's entrance into the kitchen. His nose twitched as if he hoped to catch the aroma of food.

"Lily, meet Louie." Mira laughed. "Your names almost sound alike."

The child backed up a step, her eyes large.

"He's friendly. Just hold out your hand and let him sniff it. That's how dogs get to know you." Since her arrival at the Beckers', Mira felt like she'd become a semi-expert in how to deal with canines.

Lily's narrow shoulders were stiff, but as soon as the poodle gave her fingers a loving slurp, she visibly relaxed and rubbed the dog's back with growing enthusiasm. "He likes me."

"He sure does. Shall we take him outside for a walk?"

Lily nodded. "I'm going to pretend like he's mine. Daddy says I can't have a dog yet."

"I bet Louie will love pretending to be your dog."

They bundled up and set out to explore the perimeter of the back yard. Lily held on to the pup's leash, proud as a new mother. While they walked, Mira pointed out a cardinal sitting in a tree and a squirrel scampering across the yard. The sight wound up Louie into a chorus of sharp yaps that made Lily giggle. When Mira realized her own cheeks were beginning to grow numb, she cut short the long walk she'd planned. They strolled back to the house, where Mira warmed up hot chocolate prepared according to Lily's precise instructions. Louie parked himself near the girl's feet and watched her expectantly. The occasional bite of mini-marshmallow Lily tossed to him kept the dog glued to her side. Mira glanced toward the clock and couldn't believe how fast the morning had flown.

The rest of the afternoon passed as quickly, with a blanket picnic in the game room, after which they used the same blanket to create a fort. Mira turned out the lights and used a flashlight she had commandeered from Mrs. Caldwell to read the mermaid story. She even embellished the tale by telling Lily about a mermaid festival in Key West, where mermaids from all over the country gathered to celebrate.

But the best part of the day, the one Mira enjoyed most, was when she told Mrs. Caldwell and Elise that she and Lily would prepare dinner for the family.

They surprised the Beckers with pigs in a blanket served with an herb-based dipping sauce Mira had created. Air-fried French potatoes seasoned with paprika, garlic, and onion powder, plus a simple tossed salad, completed the meal. Betty's cinnamon rolls provided the perfectly-decadent dessert. Mira held her breath, waiting for a reaction from Tom and Elise regarding the unorthodox dinner. She hoped for Lily's sake they'd at least pretend to like it.

"I haven't eaten anything like this in a long time." Tom patted his stomach and warmly announced, "It was delicious. You ladies did a great job."

"I'll have to spend extra hours working off all the calories, but I must admit I enjoyed it myself. And the rolls. I can understand why Betty won a contest for them. They're buttery and quite exquisite."

Lily beamed as Mira, dazed with shock—and possibly carb overload—said, "It does no harm to splurge occasionally. Variety is what keeps life interesting, don't you think?"

"We made the best dinner ever." Lily pronounced her opinion as she reached down to pet Louie's head. "Mira, will you help me cook this for my daddy sometime? He always has to make dinner by himself."

Mira's heart gave a little tug. "Sure we can, honey. I think he'd appreciate it."

Elise raised an artfully-manicured brow. "Darling, did I mention Neal is coming by in the morning for breakfast? He and Tom have a case they need to discuss. He told me he's eager to see you again."

Astonished, Mira looked at her. "No, you didn't say anything about it."

"I must have forgotten. It was one of those last-minute things. You know how meetings are."

Mira didn't miss the moment of surprise on Tom's face before a silent look from Elise wiped it away. The nonverbal communication said it all. Mira would bet money that not even Neal knew he was coming over for a meeting…yet.

"Okay, Lily." Mira picked up her plate and rose. "We don't want to leave a messy kitchen for Mrs. Caldwell. Let's get to work, and then we'll go to the game room and play for a while. After that, we'll watch whatever Disney movie you want."

"Can we make popcorn?"

How Lily could think about popcorn after all she'd eaten came as a surprise, but Mira looked over at Elise, who responded with a nod. "You certainly can. Mrs. Caldwell will show you how to use the popcorn machine. We've had it for years, but I never quite figured it out."

"Popcorn and a movie? It's been a long time, Elise." Tom shrugged and crossed his arms. "Maybe you and I should join them. It would be almost like old times."

"Well…I do need to make a quick phone call. After that, I thought I'd prepare for my next committee meeting." Elise's gaze went to Lily, and her face softened. "But, I suppose I could wait until tomorrow to make plans."

"It's settled then. Mira, when you two are ready to start the movie, call us. There's no need to bother Mrs. Caldwell. I remember how to work the machine."

Mira had to clamp her lips together to keep them from dropping into open-mouthed disbelief.

Chapter Sixteen

The pain of an elbow jab to the ribs captured Aiden's attention in a hurry. "Ooof," he said. "Why did you do that?"

Puno slammed his locker door shut. "I've asked you the same thing twice, and you didn't so much as grunt. Where's your head today? I know we had a busy shift, but we've had a lot worse."

"Sorry. What did you say?"

"I said," Puno sighed heavily, "Chrissy wants to know how the arrangement with Mira worked out. I need an answer, or she'll give me holy hell on the way to the airport. That's what happens when you get advice from her instead of me."

"I already told you. Mira watched Lily last night."

"Uh-uh. Not what I mean, and you know it. Chrissy doesn't want the basics; she wants the female details. You know, stuff like does Mira laugh at your lame jokes? Have you kissed her? Did you give her the key to your house?"

"Hold on. First off, Mira and I do *not* have a hot and heavy relationship. We're just getting to know each other. Why would I give her the key to my house? Anyway, as it turns out, Mira watched Lily at her place, not mine."

"Her place? I thought you said she was staying with friends."

"She is. My folks dropped Lily off on their way out of town, and as soon as you quit hounding me, I'm leaving here to pick her up."

"You let your daughter stay at a stranger's house?" Puno grabbed his duffle. "You've never even let her go to a sleepover. This doesn't fit with what I know about somebody as uptight, upright, and overprotective as you."

"Point taken. I need to loosen up and start giving Lily a little more rein. But Mira's friends, the people who own the house, aren't exactly strangers."

"You met them?"

"No, I didn't meet them. But," Aiden's shoulder bunched, "I know who they are."

"Are you being obscure on purpose? Or just to tick me off? Chrissy won't take a lack of information lying down, and I'm the one who's gonna pay."

Aiden huffed out a breath. "All right then, here it is. Mira is staying with Tom and Elise Becker."

Puno's eyes grew a size bigger. "Huh? From what you've told me about her, I can't imagine how she got hooked up with them."

"Yet, that's the way it is." Aiden wished Puno would drop the line of questioning.

"Weird. Why would somebody show up out of the blue from the Keys to live in a mansion and go to work in a coffee shop? I don't get it."

Aiden shrugged. "You know as much as I do."

"Good Lord. When I tell Chrissy, she'll go nuts. I bet you'll get a call from my wife as soon as we get back from vacation. She won't like it when I can't answer the ten thousand questions she's going to ask."

"Tell her not to waste her time. There's nothing else to report, and I don't know anything more than what I told you." Aiden grabbed his bag. "I need to go. See you later, man. Have fun on the beach."

As he walked to his truck, it irritated Aiden to admit the questions Puno raised had given additional fuel to his own. The situation *was* weird. And exactly his kind of luck. He hadn't thought it possible. For the first time since Rose's death, he felt a pull—a reawakening—of his soul. But Mira obviously had a secret she wasn't willing to share. Maybe more than one. If he let her into his life, would he live to regret it? Could getting involved with her become the biggest mistake he'd ever made?

By the time he stopped his truck in front of the Becker home, Aiden had talked himself off the ledge with sensible self-advice. Mira wasn't under any obligation to reveal her life story. He ticked off the things he did know about her. She was attractive and kind. She was thoughtful to his daughter. Not once had she hesitated to lend a hand when he needed one. Tally certainly appeared to appreciate having her at the café. And as for the Beckers, he doubted they would allow Mira to move in with them if she had a heinous past. Why not let what he felt develop and see where it led?

Feeling slightly less off-kilter, he got out of his vehicle and adjusted his jacket. A glance around the neighborhood was an eye-opener. Golf course in the backyard. Perfectly manicured lawn. A generous amount of property between the Becker home and the mansion on either side. What did people like this do for a living? They certainly weren't fire-fighters. Or policemen. Or teachers. He shoved his hands in his pockets and hiked to the door. A video camera mounted on the wall and aimed in his direction caught his eye. He swallowed and touched the doorbell.

Chimes pealed out a tune he didn't recognize. Some-thing classical, he bet, waiting for a few long minutes before the door swung open. A woman who appeared to be middle-aged nodded pleasantly at him. "You must be Aiden. Please come in."

He stepped inside. "Thank you."

"Lily and Mira are at breakfast. I'll let them know you're here."

The spacious foyer left him tongue-tied. He cleared his throat. "I'd appreciate it," he said. *Good Lord. I sound like my father.* Aiden ventured into other territory. "Are you Mrs. Becker?"

"No, I'm Mrs. Caldwell, the household manager. Have a seat if you like." She indicated a leather chair near the door and turned away.

He had no desire to sit. Feeling like a yokel, Aiden pulled at his earlobe absently. *What made me think the household manager was Mrs. Becker?* In a place like this, Elise

Becker wouldn't answer the front door. She'd be more likely to have a uniformed butler or aproned maid as they did in the movies. He took in the high ceiling and marbled floor, and a smile played at his lips. Mom must have been thrilled to get a first-hand glimpse of such over-the-top splendor. Another story for the bridge club. But as for him, the opulence felt strangely uncomfortable.

"Daddy!" Aiden's heart melted as it always did when he heard the excitement in his daughter's voice. She raced to him, and he lifted her into a tight hug.

"I missed you, Lily-Lou. Did you have a good time?"

"Uh-huh. We took Louie on a walk and had a picnic and cooked dinner and watched a princess movie."

Aiden chuckled at the stream of words and rubbed her back. His gaze moved from his daughter's shiny hair to an arched entryway that framed Mira and a man. A familiar-looking man. *The guy she had dinner with. What was his name? Neal.* He placed Lily back on the floor and a muscle in his jaw jumped. "I hope Lily wasn't any trouble," he finally said.

"Not at all," Mira replied. "She's wonderful. We had so much fun."

We? As in Mira, Neal, and Lily? "Well, I appreciate your help. So do my folks."

"It was no problem at all. And tell your mom we loved the rolls. It's not hard to figure out why her recipe took first place. I might have to see if we can steal it for the shop. They'd be a big hit with our customers." Mira was jabbering almost as fast as Lily had.

The too-frequent use of the word *we* grated on him. "Mom's never given her recipe out before, but she says it'll be published in a magazine since she won the contest. I guess that means whoever wants the recipe is free to have it."

He knew his tone had gone colder than last week's leftovers, and he saw two deep grooves appear between Mira's eyes.

"All the same, I'll ask Betty if it's okay."

Lily, oblivious to the suddenly glacial atmosphere, bounced up and down on her toes. "Mira and me are going to make you a special dinner. You'll like it, Daddy."

"That sounds nice, sweetie."

Neal took Mira's arm in what struck Aiden as a not-very-subtle message and said, "It's good to see you again, Aiden. If you'll excuse us, we're in the middle of breakfast, and I'd hate it if Mrs. Caldwell had to reheat the food."

Mira glanced from one man to the other uneasily. "Lily had some fruit and toast and scrambled eggs. I set her suitcase over there next to the door." It looked like she was going to say more when she paused and turned her attention to Lily. "I hope you come visit me again soon."

"I will," chirped Lily. Aiden reached for the suitcase handle, but his daughter got there first. "I can do it myself, Daddy. Bye, Mira."

He opened the door, and she rolled the suitcase outside. Aiden gave an abrupt nod toward Mira's perplexed face before following Lily. He walked his daughter to the truck, and she started to chatter again so fast that all he caught from her commentary was something about slime in her suitcase. He didn't want to think what she meant by that.

"Mira's nice. She taught me how to make dinner, and she tells me stories like Mama used to do." She giggled. "Have you tasted pigs in a blanket? They are super good. We are gonna cook them for you sometime."

He'd never heard of a dish called pigs in a blanket. Maybe Lily had it confused with a story. *The Three Little Pigs?* "I don't know about that, Lily. Mira's busy with her job and…everything. We'll talk about this some other time."

"I know what. When we make dinner for you, let's invite Memaw and Papa to come over. You've never fixed them dinner before."

It was as though she'd tuned out what he said. "Let's wait and see what happens." His heart shriveled to the size of a prune. Lily liked Mira far too much, and it scared him. He'd convinced himself Neal was no more to Mira than a casual dinner date, but obviously he'd been wrong. Who knows? Maybe the hot-shot lawyer had spent the night with her. Why else would he be at the Beckers for breakfast? He imagined them sitting around the table like a family while Mrs. Caldwell poured coffee from some fancy silver pitcher.

He could see it now. Mira, so wrapped up in Neal and her work at the coffee shop that she'd have no time for anything or anyone else. In an equally dismal vision of a worst-case scenario, he reminded himself she could pack up and head back to Key West at any moment. Either option meant the same result. Mira would be out of his daughter's life. His, too.

They had both already been through enough. Lily had lost her mother. He had lost his wife. Neither one of them needed this. Getting attached to Mira was nothing less than a potential invitation to disaster.

An ache throbbed at his temple, and he massaged it. Navigating his way through a fresh round of pain reminded him how he felt before when his heart had been splintered into a sorry mixed-up jumble of pieces.

Chapter Seventeen

Mira inspected a vivid work of art that covered the entire portion of the museum's wall. She wasn't quite sure what to say, but the light gleaming from Neal's eyes told her he expected a response. "It has a lot of energy," she finally offered. "And the colors take my breath away."

It was the most charitable comment she could muster since the piece didn't look to her like anything but a crazy quilt of faces, hands, and assorted body parts. Each segment had been placed randomly together with little regard for where they belonged on the human form.

"This is one of the museum's most prized acquisitions," Neal informed her. "I helped to negotiate the contract after I joined the board."

"It certainly is…interesting. Was it hard to secure?"

"A small museum owned it, and the directors needed to liquidate some assets. We came to an agreement on price, and then Elise stepped in to work her fundraising magic. It was quite a coup for us. This is an important work."

"That's great, Neal." She wondered what time it was but hesitated to peek at her phone. "Thanks for showing me around. I didn't realize you knew so much about art."

"Modern art is stimulating. I'm glad to see you appreciate it, too."

Appreciation wasn't the word she would use, but if she dared to admit the pictures on the museum walls only confused her, Neal might feel compelled to explain, and she didn't have time to listen.

"This has been educational, but I really do need to go. I promised Tally I'd be at the café by one o'clock, and I don't want to be late. Could you take me back to the Beckers' house, so I have time to change?"

"My apologies. I must have lost track of time." He took her arm and guided her toward the exit. "When do you get off? Maybe we can grab a bite for dinner and talk more about the museum."

"You're sweet to invite me, but I'm exhausted. Lily had trouble falling asleep last night. I guess she was nervous about being in a strange place, so I let her crawl in bed with me. Having an eight-year-old toss and turn next to you isn't very restful. Poor thing. She was missing her daddy and grandparents." Mira chose not to add that the long breakfast meal and the last-minute trip Neal suggested to the museum had further taxed her energy level. By the time her workday ended, she'd be lucky if she could keep her eyes open long enough to drive home.

"I understand. Let's get together another day." Regret dulled his words to a pale shade of gray.

"Absolutely," she replied in a twinge of self-reproach. There wasn't any reason to dampen his previously good-natured spirit. "Sounds like fun."

Mira let Neal handle the conversation on the ride home, trying not to nod off. Luckily, he had mastered the ability to both ask and answer questions. All she needed to do was give him an occasional "Uh-huh," and he would forge ahead. This worked out well since a clamp had started to squeeze an ache at the back of her head. Nerves and lack of rest had a way of creating havoc with her peace of mind. At least she hadn't gotten lightheaded or broken out in hives.

Mira imagined that Lily must be in an equally sleepy state and hoped Aiden would be patient. He'd seemed so odd when he had come to pick up his daughter, his eyes hard and flat as stones. He didn't try to tease her or even flirt a little—something that she had found surprisingly appealing.

Neal pulled his car to a stop in front of the Becker home. "Here you are. I hope you get some rest this evening. I'll call you tomorrow."

Mira rewarded his comment with a grateful smile. "If I hadn't been so tired, I'd have enjoyed the tour more."

She got out and lifted a hand to wave as he drove away. *He is a thoughtful man. And he makes me feel…*Hard as she tried to complete the sentence, no fitting mood or sensation came to mind.

Cutting around to the side of the house, Mira decided to enter through the back door rather than the front. A short walk in the brisk air couldn't help but perk her up. As she approached the garage, Mrs. Caldwell opened the door to her bungalow, attached to the garage by a walkway, where she had her own private quarters.

"I thought you planned to work today," she said. "Should I set another place for lunch?"

"I'm only here long enough to change clothes and grab my van. I'll be here for dinner, though."

They walked together toward the kitchen entrance, startling a gray squirrel. The animal scampered from the yard toward a tree covered with bright red leaves. Mira watched him scurry up the tree and disappear. "Squirrels are kind of cute," she observed.

"Cute, but they can be terrible pests. They are rodents, you know. A few years ago, one gnawed its way into the attic over the garage. Mr. Becker had to have wildlife control trap him."

"Cha. I hope this guy behaves himself. I kind of like him."

Mrs. Caldwell chuckled. "Don't tell anyone, but so do I."

Mira studied the woman's face. "I get the feeling you've been with the Beckers for a long time."

"Over twenty years now. It's much quieter with the girls out on their own. There was always something going on when they were here."

"Why don't they come to visit?"

"They do occasionally, but life gets hectic. They both have jobs and their own busy lives. The youngest one, Kat, also goes to school."

Mira's eyes prickled. "If my mother was still alive, I'd see her as often as I could."

Mrs. Caldwell touched her arm. "That's because you know how losing someone you love feels. I'm not sure the girls have figured that out yet. It is a shame. Even when people come from different perspectives, removing a loved one from your life isn't a recipe for happiness."

Mira opened the door to the kitchen for Mrs. Caldwell and followed her inside. She was too worn out to process what she'd heard, although the idea made perfect sense. "Hopefully, it will all work out soon. I can tell how much Elise misses her daughters."

"I suppose Mrs. Becker made her share of mistakes. But, then again, haven't we all?"

The wall clock showed eleven-thirty, and Mira inhaled sharply. "I've got to run, or I'll be late. See you this evening."

Mrs. Caldwell's voice rose slightly to slow Mira's exit. "I found Lily's little stuffed animal. She left it on your bed."

"Uh-oh. She loves Siggy. I'll take him with me. Maybe I can drop him off at Aiden's after work."

Mira moved into a sprint as she headed up the stairs to her room. She changed from her sweatshirt and leggings into a nice pair of jeans and a long-sleeved t-shirt bearing the coffee cup logo of Steamin' Mugs. With no time to brush and redo her hair, Mira tucked loose curls back into place, pulled on her coat, and grabbed Siggy.

She nearly ran into Elise in the hallway. "Sorry. I'm late for the coffee shop."

Elise pursed her lips. "I do wish you'd consider working for Tom. The firm could use your talents, and you'd have your weekends off."

"I don't think legal work is right for me. Besides, I love what I'm doing. It's why I went to culinary school."

Elise expelled a quiet breath. "Did you and Neal have a good time?"

"We did, even though I wasn't the best company. I'm completely whipped after last night."

"Lily is a lovely little girl. She reminds me of my oldest. Carolyn was always on the quiet side. Shy, but quite firm with whatever she wanted. Kathryn tends to be a bit stubborn, too. I think I see that same characteristic in you, Mira."

"I hadn't thought about it, but maybe so." The backhanded compliment pleased her even though she knew it shouldn't. "Thanks again for letting Lily spend the night. She had a good time."

"Having a little girl in the house again made me feel fifteen years younger."

Elise's pensive expression prompted Mira to pull the woman into a quick hug. "I've got to run. I'll see you at dinner."

The low temperature chilled her, so she fired up the van's heater and pushed the speed limit as much as she dared, hoping she wouldn't be late. Ahead of her lay an afternoon of baking—muffins?—and she welcomed the opportunity to soothe herself with prep work in a kitchen warmed by oven heat, alive with the scent of comfort food. As she parked her van in the lot, her guilt level rose. There were many more cars than usual. Tally must be frazzled indeed.

Inside the shop, most of the tables were occupied. Tally stood behind the counter, looking like her feet hurt.

"Sorry I'm late." Mira joined her.

"It's okay. The day hasn't been too bad. Mostly, people were craving lattes and baked goods. It's typical when the weather turns cold. I wonder if it might be a good idea to hire some extra help for a while. With the additional business, it's getting to be a lot for just the two of us."

"Sounds good to me. One or two part-time people would help, especially with the holidays coming up and us catering more events." Mira put on an apron and tied it at the waist.

"We need to talk about a few other things, too." Tally rubbed the side of her face. "My daughter called again last night. We talked for over an hour. I was awake for most of the night, thinking everything over, and I finally came to a decision. I'm putting the café up for sale."

Mira stood rooted to the floor. She stared at Tally, who had apparently found something interesting on the wall to look at. "I don't understand. I thought you were happy with the way things were going. You just mentioned hiring more people. Yet you've made up your mind to sell?"

"I'm afraid so." Tally glanced around the room, and then her gaze strayed reluctantly to Mira's. "Last night, my daughter texted pictures of the perfect little condo she found for me. It's less than a mile from where she lives. We talked about putting a contract on it because property sells so fast there. I really don't want to postpone this any longer. You said you didn't have the funds to buy the shop, but if you really want this place, maybe we can find a way to make it happen."

"You think so?" Mira perched on the apex of a fence between disappointment over Tally's decision and gratification that her employer thought she had the pluck to take it over.

"The café needs someone with your energy and imagination to freshen it into a new concept. Something young people would love as much as older customers."

Mira let the idea sink in and cogitate. Owning a café had been her dream since the day she started culinary school. A place where she could fully expand on her ideas and the practices she'd gleaned from her own research, as well as the things she'd learned from Pauline. Opportunities didn't come around every day. Why not take this one?

An internal voice answered the question. *Money and timing.*

Mira sighed. "I truly wish I could. The trouble is, I don't have the cash, and I don't have the credit history or collateral to borrow the kind of money it would take."

"I have confidence in you, Mira. Maybe I can lend you enough to help with the down payment. I love this place, and I know you'd take good care of it. If we can work the details out, the café wouldn't need to go on the market."

"I could never ask you to take such a gamble."

"With the economy the way it is, I'm not sure how long it'll take to sell. I don't have time to wait around forever, and I want the right person to have it." Tally sprayed the counter and wiped it with fierce strokes. "A fellow from a development company called me a few weeks ago. He's interested in turning the shop into one of those chain pizza joints. I'm not crazy about the idea, but if you're not interested, I guess I could call him back."

"Another pizza place? I don't like that idea either. Look, I need to get the baking started. Before you call this guy back, can you give me a little time to decide whether or not I can find a way to manage taking this on? There's so much to think about."

The clouds on Tally's face cleared. "I can—as long as you don't take too long. My daughter needs an answer soon."

Chapter Eighteen

Apitch akin to the sound of fingernails scraping slowly down a chalkboard entered Lily's voice. She was on the verge of a major meltdown, and Aiden's patience had already been stretched so tight he feared it might snap. "Come on. Stop whining, Lily."

The sharp command only intensified her distress. "I want Siggy." Her breath huffed in and out faster and faster until she began to cry in deep, gulping sobs.

Aiden swiped his hand across his forehead. He hadn't seen her so wound up in months. Maybe he shouldn't have let her stay with people she barely knew. Even though Lily told him on the way home how much fun she'd had, her red-rimmed eyelids confirmed she hadn't slept well. To keep his response even, he counted to ten—plus a little beyond—before he spoke. "Lily, you need to settle down. I'm sure Siggy is at Mira's house. I tried calling her, but she didn't pick up. She's probably busy at work or… something. I'll try again later."

He had no intention of imagining what Mira might be busy doing. When he recalled the possessive way Neal had taken her arm—as though she'd given him the right to do so—an unmistakable meaning lodged in his brain. She had feelings for Neal. Not the best message to receive when he'd begun to think he might have a chance with the beguiling young redhead from the Keys.

Damn. This was worse than maneuvering around an obstacle course during training. Romantic terrain flummoxed him, but this time Aiden wasn't about to call Puno or Chrissy for advice. Anyway, even if he wanted to, they were on some exotic island in the Bahamas. He could, however, fix Lily her dinner. As he prepared the food, he realized how badly he needed someone who'd let him vent his frustration. But who? By the time he filled Lily's plate, Aiden had made up his mind. He'd interrupt his parents' trip and call his mom.

While Lily picked at the food on her plate, he punched in the number. His mom picked up and listened to him gripe as intently as Aiden knew she would. Then the questions came. Aiden spit out each answer. No, Mira never said she had a relationship with Neal. No, he hadn't called her to ask. Yes, the situation could be business-related since Neal worked for Tom Becker. Yes, he supposed he could be reading too much into what he saw. No, he didn't think calling Mira tomorrow would be the best idea.

But even after his mom had finished minimizing his concerns, Aiden found he couldn't shake the certainty Neal had designs on Mira. And if Neal made Mira happy, who was he to interfere? He walked to the table and absent-mindedly patted Lily's back since she'd turned on the tears all over again.

"I can't sleep without Siggy."

"We'll get him tomorrow. Just one night. You can go one night without Siggy."

"No, I can't." She sniffled.

"Tell you what. I'm going to fix you a nice warm bath with as many bubbles as you want. After that, I'll make some hot chocolate. Not fancy, like at the coffee house, but with lots of marshmallows. Then I'll read you not one, not two, but three stories. You'll fall asleep in no time."

She glanced toward the window. "But it's still light outside, Daddy."

"That's okay. When a person is really, really tired, going to bed early is a good idea. You'll feel much better tomor-row. First thing in the morning, we'll drive over and get Siggy."

"Before we eat breakfast?"

"If that's what you want, we'll go before breakfast." *What if she wakes up at five in the morning?* He hoped the Beckers—and Mira—would understand.

Aiden let her stay in the tub until the water cooled. Then he made a game of buttoning her—she didn't ask to do it by herself this time—into her favorite flannel pajamas. The red ones printed with smiling sloths. Finally, he tucked her into bed with two plush toys, a puppy on one side of her, and a unicorn on the other. She looked so woebegone that his heart felt heavy, but he opened the first book and plowed into it. When he finished the third story, he closed the cover and glanced toward his daughter. Her eyelids were drooping. She could barely keep them open. Aiden leaned over to kiss her forehead. "Good night, Lily-Lou," he whispered. "I love you."

"Night, Daddy," a small, sleep-muffled voice replied.

Bedtime crisis averted. Aiden left his daughter's room and plodded toward the bathroom, turning the shower on full force. While he waited for the water to get hot, he stared at his reflection in the mirror. The strain of the day showed in the dark stubble on his face, hair mussed every which way, and a hint of purple under his eyes. He ought to turn in early, too. At the moment, he looked—and felt—like roadkill. "So much for romance," he announced to his likeness. When condensation clouded the mirror, he turned away and stepped into the shower. The water pounding against his back released the tight muscles in his neck and shoulders. He breathed in the steam and raised his head until the water ran over it, erasing any other sound. If only he could numb his mind as easily.

Consider the things you're grateful for. Rose had often counseled him to do so when his determination faltered. She'd even practiced the art herself, right up until the day she died. *Well, why not?* Like a comforting childhood prayer, he counted them off. He had Lily, a true gem of a daughter. A job he loved, and one that made a difference in other people's lives. His parents, of course, who never failed him or their granddaughter. Good friends and colleagues. No major money worries. When it came right down to it, what did he have to complain about?

Aiden shut off the shower and toweled himself dry. Crumpling the damp terry cloth, he wiped off moisture from the mirror. Whether it was the hot shower, Rose's calming words filling his subconscious, or a combination of both, he looked and felt one hundred and ten percent better than he had only moments before. No more roadkill, thankfully.

He pulled on an old sweatshirt and a pair of training pants. Tonight might be a good time to start reading the biography his dad had loaned him. He couldn't remember who it was about, but the man had been a World War II general that his dad swore was a genius at plotting strategy. Aiden figured he could use a little expertise in plotting strategy. It might help him get one over on Puno. He tossed the book onto his bed. Before he laid down, he decided to check on Lily and make sure she hadn't kicked off the covers.

Yawning, he headed toward his daughter's bedroom. The hall light burned brightly. Strange. He could have sworn he turned it off. Aiden opened the door a crack, peeked inside, and then flung it wide open. Lily's bed was empty.

"Lily," he called. "Where are you?"

No answer. He checked each possible hiding spot in her bedroom. Nothing. Expanding the search, he peered behind the couch in the great room, checked the kitchen pantry, looked into the bathroom near her room, and scrutinized every corner of the basement. His mouth dried up, and his stomach turned over with the same squeamish sensation he had when en route to a call at work. The sinking feeling of not knowing what might lie ahead.

The yard. He glanced at the foyer closet and noticed the door wasn't shut all the way. When he opened it, an empty hanger proclaimed that Lily's bright yellow jacket wasn't where he'd hung it. His gaze shot to the front door. It was unlocked, though it hadn't been earlier. Aiden's heart banged hard against his chest, but he schooled himself to remain logical. There was no sign of a break-in, so she hadn't been kidnapped. It wasn't dark yet. The sun still sat on the horizon. She had probably gone outside to…what? Aiden yanked the door open and raced to the front porch.

A breeze set the leaves on the ground into swirls of motion. Scanning the yard, he saw no sign of his daughter. He hurried to the backyard. She wasn't on the swing set or near the wooden playhouse he'd built for her. The only other thing he saw was one lone soccer ball in the middle of the yard. He pivoted toward the house and spied the bright blue rock she'd painted for him shining in a flower bed. A lump formed in his throat.

He cursed softly to himself. *Lily, where can you be?*

Dashing back to the house, he grabbed his cell phone. Maybe she'd gone to see one of her neighborhood friends. Aiden dialed three different sets of parents and felt his blood pressure rise with each conversation. Not one of them had seen Lily, but all offered to scout around the nearby yards and playgrounds. Desperate to talk to some-one he trusted, Aiden cracked his knuckles. Puno and Chrissy were thousands of miles away. He could call his parents, but they were most likely on the road returning home from Branson. At this point, he didn't want to scare them into feeling as frantic as he did.

Only one thing left to do. Hands shaking, Aiden inhaled a deep breath and dialed 911. He explained with a growing sense of panic what had happened. An intake officer asked him questions about Lily—questions that brought him from a numbed state of shock to a horrifying awareness that his daughter had truly gone missing. When the officer told him someone would be dispatched to his house to take a full report, Aiden put down his cell and contemplated whether the time had come to call his parents.

He raked a nervous hand through his hair as he stared out the window. He knew only too well how easily fear could paralyze a person and inaction always multiplied fear. There had to be something he could do. Or someone who could keep him from feeling so helpless and utterly alone. An idea materialized. His daughter had been with Mira yesterday. Maybe Lily said something to her that would provide a clue. The police would likely end up talking to Mira and the Beckers anyway since he told the officer she'd spent last night with them. He had no desire to debate whether calling Mira was right or wrong. He picked up his cell, praying this time she'd answer her phone.

"Hello?"

Her soft voice moored him. "This is Aiden."

"I'm sorry I didn't return your call earlier. I've been baking for an event."

"It's Lily. She's gone missing."

Mira's breath caught. "Missing? What do you mean?"

"I put her to bed early and then took a shower. When I went to check on her, she was gone. I've looked all over the house and yard. The neighbors are searching for her, too."

"Oh, no. Do you have any idea where she might be?"

"None. I was hoping she said something to you last night that might help me find her."

A long moment passed. "I can't think of a thing. She seemed fine, though she did have trouble falling asleep. She got homesick for you and her grandparents. Have you called the police?"

"I'm waiting now for an officer to get here."

"This is foolish for me to say, but try not to worry. I feel sure she's safe, and I know you'll find her."

The gentle lift and fall of her voice soothed him like honey eased a raw throat. "I hope you're right."

"What can I do to help?"

"The police will probably want to talk to you and maybe even the Beckers." Aiden rubbed the back of his neck. "I think I told you an officer is coming. I can't remember what I've said." He needed a lifeline. Someone to chase away the horrible images running through his head. "Are you free to come over?"

"Give me a few minutes. I'll be right there."

"I'm about half out of my mind. Lily's too young to be wandering around by herself. It's cold outside, and it's getting dark. If anything happens to her…"

"Listen to me. She's going to be all right. Don't let any other thought into your head. Promise?"

Aiden swallowed. "I promise." He ended the call and dropped his phone on the table. Pacing across the room, he realized the dark shadows were growing longer. A spate of nervous energy kept him on his feet, fear gnawing deeper into his gut. In a single stroke, he axed the promise he'd made to Mira. The haunting thoughts returned, and even when he tried to shake them from his head, they wouldn't leave. He attempted to steady himself.

She must have fallen asleep somewhere in the house. I haven't been thorough enough.

And even though he knew it was a foolhardy nail to hang his hopes on, Aiden returned to Lily's room, intent on finding her, searching in all the places he'd already hunted.

Chapter Nineteen

Mira gripped the phone tighter so she wouldn't drop it. *If I'm unnerved by this, how must Aiden feel?* Her advice to him now seemed beyond arrogant. She closed her eyes and waited for her skin to prickle with the tell-tale sign of hives. But nothing happened. Breathing in and out as mindfully as she could, a semblance of sanity returned.

"What's wrong? You look like a ghoul is sitting on your shoulder." Tally's voice ended any further self-talk.

"That was Aiden. Lily is missing."

"Missing? As in, she wandered off? Or somebody took her?"

"I don't know. He said he put her to bed, but now she's gone, and he can't find her anywhere." Mira amazed herself at how composed and normal her voice sounded.

"I can't believe it." Tally's eyes grew enormous with horror. "Did he call the police?"

"An officer is on the way to his house." Mira untied her apron and put it on the counter. "The baking is finished. I hate to leave you such a mess, but I need to see what I can do to help."

"You go to Aiden. He needs you. I'll take care of the cleanup. When I think of all the awful news stories I've heard, this makes my stomach sick. I never thought anything like this would happen to somebody I know."

Tally's comments chilled Mira to the center of her bones. "I'll call you later." Mira grabbed her coat and rushed toward the door.

"You tell Aiden I'm pulling for him," Tally called after her.

Mira picked up her pace to a jog. She reached the VW, parked at the far end of the lot, and climbed inside. As she buckled her seat belt, she realized Elise and Tom deserved to be notified, especially since the police might contact them. She held her phone with one hand and steered her van from the lot with the other. Elise picked up, and Mira filled her in on what Aiden had told her.

A minute of silence followed, as though Elise had been too stunned to respond. She finally said, "Dear God. What do you suppose happened?"

"I've told you as much as I know. Since she was at our house last night, the police will most likely want to speak to you. I'm on my way to Aiden's now. I'll let you know if I find out anything new."

"Oh, that poor little girl. I'll talk to Tom. He may have suggestions on what to do." She took a hasty breath. "We'll help in any way we can. Tell Aiden that if the police can't find Lily, we'll hire a detective who will."

"Thanks." Mira ended the call. She'd been afraid Elise would react with resentment over a situation that could have a uniformed officer knocking on their front door. Yet she'd been concerned and caring, expressing nothing but support. It was anyone's guess, however, what Tom would say about the situation Mira had gotten the family snarled in. She wasn't sure she wanted to find out, but there were more important worries at the moment.

Lily. Where could she be? Mira culled through her memory, considering every conversation they'd ever had. Betty and Bob spent a lot of time caring for Lily. Could the child have missed them so much she tried to go to their house? No. Too far away, from what Aiden once told her. On top of that, Lily knew her grandparents were out of town. It made sense she might go to see one of her neighborhood friends, but apparently, Aiden had already checked into that possibility.

Mira glanced at Siggy, sitting on the passenger seat, and her throat tightened. She'd once read that the first seventy-two hours were the most important in locating a missing person. Three minutes missing was unimaginable, let alone the thought of a child being lost for three days. She wished she could find an instruction book or someone who could advise her. She needed concrete steps and a reliable game plan.

Wait a minute. Books? Yes, a bookstore. Lily told her about one she loved to visit, but didn't give a name. All Mira remembered was that Lily and Aiden sometimes walked to a bookstore near their house. She knew it was a long shot, but she pulled the van over anyway to run a Google search on her phone. The online hunt brought up two places worth investigating. A used bookstore a few blocks away, and what appeared to be a small bookshop. She drove to Jerri's Used Books first.

The store was tucked next to a large office supply chain store, but its lights were turned off. Mira slowed to a crawl and saw a "Closed" sign hanging from the door. A boatload of disappointment hit. If only Lily had been sitting in front of the store, waiting for someone to find her. She steered the van away and headed for the remaining bookstore, her hopes fading with the sun.

Within a short drive, she arrived at The Novel Idea. Mira pulled over; her hands clamped on the steering wheel. The lights in the store were on, but suddenly her inspiration felt foolish. Aiden was waiting for her, no doubt wondering if she'd ever arrive. The officer would probably be sitting there, too. She ran her tongue across the inside of her cheek and turned off the ignition. As long as she was there, she might as well check out the lead. Mira opened the shop door and a bell jangled. She hurried inside.

"May I help you?" A woman wearing glasses and a bright smile greeted her.

"I hope so. By any chance, did a little girl come in? She has brown hair and stands about so tall." Mira used her hand to indicate Lily's height.

"My clerk said there is a little girl upstairs. I wondered about her being here by herself, but apparently she's waiting for her father to pick her up."

"Thanks." Mira didn't wait to hear more. She raced up old wooden steps that groaned with each footfall. At the top of the stairs, she glanced to the right, where a sofa had been placed near a wall of books. There she found Lily, sound asleep, her brown hair splayed loose, and her head resting on the arm of the sofa. Sagging with relief, Mira crept toward the sleeping child, afraid she might startle her.

"Lily," she called softly.

Lily blinked, and her eyes fluttered open. She sat up and rubbed the back of her hand across her face. "Where's Daddy?"

"He's at home, and he's worried sick about you."

"I wanted Siggy." Her lower lip quivered. "Daddy said we couldn't get him 'til in the morning. Siggy gets lonesome without me. I wanted to come to your house and get him myself."

Mira gathered Lily into her arms for a comforting hug. She figured it wasn't the time to mention the Becker house was miles away. "How did you end up here?"

"My legs got tired. I fell asleep waiting for Daddy to come get me."

"But he didn't know where to find you."

Her eyes went from slotted with sleep to wide open. "He knows we always come to this bookstore. Is he mad at me?"

"No, Lily. He's not mad." Mira blinked through tears that blurred her line of vision. She pulled out her phone. "I'll call him right now and let him know I'm bringing you home."

As soon as Aiden heard she'd found Lily, his frantic voice cracked with emotion. Tears pooled again in Mira's eyes. This time they overflowed. She had to talk Aiden down from making an immediate trip to the bookshop. "Lily's fine," she said. "You stay with the officer, and I'll bring her home." For good measure, she added in a stage whisper, "She's worried about you being mad, so try to stay calm," and then ended the call.

"Can we get Siggy first?" Lily looked at Mira with a pitiful expression.

Mira wiped away the damp streaks on her face and smiled. "Guess what? Siggy's in my van waiting for you."

The little girl's smile lit the room. She took Mira's hand, and they descended the creaky steps together. Mira thanked the clerk, and Lily waved goodbye to the woman on the way out the door.

In the van, Mira buckled Lily into the back seat and handed Siggy to her. The girl's arms wrapped tight around the plush animal.

"I know you're supposed to be in a safety seat, but this is the best I can do. Don't tell on me, okay?"

"I won't," Lily said solemnly.

Mira tried to keep the ride home lighthearted by prattling about anything she could think of during the short drive to Aiden's. With each moment, responses from the back seat grew shorter and drowsier. The poor thing had to be wiped out. Mira shut her mouth and let Lily sleep, shuddering at the thought of a child wandering around alone in the dark.

When they reached Aiden's neighborhood, the front floodlights were on, reflecting off a black and white squad car parked in the street. She pulled around the police vehicle and into the driveway. The van hadn't even come to a complete stop before Aiden burst from his house and sprinted toward them. Mira pointed toward the rear of her VW, and he wrenched the door open.

"Lily." Relief softened his voice to a near whisper. He pulled his daughter from the seat and cradled her in his arms.

"Hi, Daddy," she said sleepily, the words slightly muffled against his chest.

Mira had to turn her head and swallow before she got out of the van. An officer trooped from the house. A short man who looked like he was ready to go home.

"Are you Mira Gordon?"

"I am."

"Would you mind filling out a statement so I can close the case?"

She nodded and followed Aiden inside. After going through the story a second time, Mira reduced it to writing on an official affidavit and signed the document.

The officer took it from her and grinned. "I'm glad everything worked out. Thankfully, most of these cases do. If you ever need anything, feel free to call me." He gave Aiden his business card and lifted a hand in farewell.

"Give me a minute, Mira. I'm going to put her to bed." Lily had drifted off again, her head resting on her father's shoulder, Siggy tucked tightly in her arms.

Mira hadn't realized how weak her knees had suddenly gone. She crept toward the sofa and dropped into the seat, releasing a huge cleansing breath. During her years in the Keys, she'd been through several hurricanes, but nothing came as close as this ordeal had for scaring the wits out of her. The commitment it took to be responsible for a child brought a whole new level of fear, unlike anything else. She wondered if Pauline had ever experienced such stomach-churning terror. If so, she'd never let on.

Aiden returned to the living room, his face gray and drawn.

"You better sit down before you fall down," she told him.

He positioned himself next to her. "I don't know how to thank you. When I think about how this could have turned out…"

"It was a lucky guess. At least Lily knew enough to go somewhere she'd been before instead of blundering down the street and getting lost."

"We'll definitely have a talk tomorrow about the rules on leaving the house."

"Maybe you should wait a while, Aiden. You don't want to upset her."

"Don't worry; I'll stay calm. This is all my fault. I've been thinking about installing a security system, but I kept putting it off. What kind of father am I?"

"You're a hard-working one who goes above and beyond. Do you know how much Lily talks about her daddy? She loves you so much."

"I try, but I'm an imperfect man. And an even less perfect father." His eyes were suspiciously shiny, and he blinked a few times.

"Stop beating yourself up. You just had a terrifying experience. Enough to upset anyone."

His gaze held hers for a moment, and he gave her a crooked grin. "Once again, the voice of reason. I could get used to having you around." He took her hand and squeezed it.

Mira's cheeks warmed when he didn't let go. She started to pull her hand away, but Aiden threaded his fingers through hers. Then he lowered his head closer until their lips touched. A seismic ripple rolled from the back of her neck down her spine. The kiss went from gentle to searching as he explored the curve of her mouth. Her arms wound around his neck, and her heart swelled so fully that it felt like it could jump right out of her chest.

Aiden was the first to break the kiss. He rested his forehead against hers, his breath uneven. "I didn't plan to do that, although, the fact is, I've been wanting to kiss you for a while."

His admission sent a tidal wave of sensation coursing through her. She traced a finger from his cheek to his jaw. "Would it be wrong for me to say I'm glad you did?"

"Not in my book."

He held her a minute longer, then let go of her to stand and stretch his neck from side to side. She felt a second of profound disappointment.

"I'm sorry, Mira. I need to call the neighbors and let them know Lily's safe. I'm sure they saw the squad car and assumed the worst."

"You're right. I have calls to make, too." She knew the Beckers and Tally must be beside themselves with worry. She rose and smoothed her hair. "It may sound trite, but I am incredibly relieved everything worked out the way it did."

"Me, too," he replied fervently. His hand cupped her cheek. "Would it be okay if I call you after this settles down?"

"I wish you would," she said, her mouth tipping up at the quiet hint of sweet possibilities in his voice.

Chapter Twenty

Louie slurped a damp line across her cheek. "Now? Are you sure?" Mira opened her eyes and squinted at the poodle, whose eager expression indicated he was not willing to retract the I-need-to-go-out signal. "All right. Just a minute."

She rolled out of bed and stretched. Her day off, and it was six o'clock in the morning. Ever since Louie had become accustomed to sleeping in Mira's bed each night, he'd gotten used to her taking him outside first thing in the morning. Tempting as it was to ask Mrs. Caldwell to do it so she could slip back into sleep, Mira denied herself the luxury. She knew how much Mrs. Caldwell valued her early morning solitude—a chance to sort out her day before the family came down for breakfast.

Mira changed into a pair of flannel jogging pants and pulled a jacket over her ancient t-shirt. "Okay, little man," she grumbled, "let's go." Louie trotted behind her down the hallway. She softened her step past the Beckers' bedroom when something stopped her. Did she detect a whiff of lavender? She sniffed again and held back a giggle as she continued downstairs to the kitchen.

"Good morning," she said to Mrs. Caldwell, who was busy chopping veggies near the sink.

"Would you like me to take the dog out?" The woman set her paring knife on the counter.

"No, we're fine. Go ahead with what you're doing. Come on, Louie."

Mira stepped outside to the patio, and Louie scampered around the pool—now covered for the season—to an area designated as his personal lavatory. While she waited, Mira hugged the jacket tighter around herself and exhaled a puff of air. The puff turned into a faint cloud of fog. Fascinated, she did it again. In the Keys, she'd be in shorts and a sleeveless top this time of year. A nice thought, but something about the brisk temperature in KC captivated her. How delightful it would be to grab a cup of hot tea and turn on the fireplace in her room to read and relax. Especially after all that had happened yesterday. Tally's news about selling the café. Lily's disappearance. The tender moment she'd shared with Aiden. Too tired to process any of it when she'd gotten home last night, she'd fallen sound asleep as soon as her head touched the pillow.

Today would be soon enough to try and make sense of it all.

Louie finished his morning business and bounded back to Mira, his tail swishing. He sat on his haunches in front of her and raised his front paws, eyes trained on her face. She laughed out loud. "You know the routine, don't you? Bathroom and then breakfast."

The poodle barked once and hopped up and down like a canine track star. She grabbed the lively little dog and carried him inside. His nose immediately twitched toward the corner, and he wriggled to get down. Mira put him on the floor, and he raced toward his food bowl.

"For such a small dog, he sure is a glutton." Mira shook her head at the gusto with which Louie attacked his food. "Can I help you with breakfast?"

"Thank you, but I'm nearly finished with prep. Would you like a cup of tea?"

"That would be wonderful." Mira perched on a high stool near the counter.

"You're up early. I thought Monday was your day off." Mrs. Caldwell filled a cup with hot water and gave it to Mira, along with a teabag.

Mira took the cup gratefully, wrapping her chilly hands around the mug's warm surface. "It is, but I'm more awake by the minute." Her gaze traveled to the oven. "I know everyone counts calories around here, but what do you think about me making chocolate croissants for breakfast one day next week?"

Faint lines appeared at the corners of Mrs. Caldwell's eyes. "As long as we don't do it often, I think your croissants would be well received."

"Good." Mira took a sip of tea. "Do you enjoy working for the Beckers?"

"How could I not? In the early days, before they moved to this house, I came in once a week to clean. Things were different back then. Mr. Becker had just started to build his career."

"What do you mean by different?"

"I mean different in the way things are for most young couples starting out. They counted pennies and shopped bargains. Then, shortly after Mr. Becker's career took off, my husband died. The family moved to this house, and Mrs. Becker offered me not only a full-time job, but a place to live. I'm not sure how I'd have gotten by without them."

Mira pictured a time when Tom and Elise shopped discount stores and worried about money. The unexpected notion prompted more questions. "Did you know Elise's brother?" It seemed presumptuous to identify James Todd as her father, even though Mrs. Caldwell knew the story.

"I did," she replied. "He was a kind-hearted young man. Smart, too. A little bit spoiled, if you ask me, although he never let it go to his head. Mrs. Becker doted on him."

"She must have been distraught after the accident."

Mrs. Caldwell paused in thought. "When the news came, it broke her into a thousand pieces. First, she blamed herself for not insisting he fly to the conference rather than drive. Then, after the tears finally stopped, she separated herself from everything except clouds of worry over her family." She sighed deeply. "As time moved on, life settled back into place, but she had changed. It was like she built a wall around herself. Her way of coping, I suppose."

"Nothing feels normal after you've lost someone you love."

"You're so right about that, my dear." Mrs. Caldwell patted Mira's arm. "But enough chatting. I need to get back to work, or breakfast will be late."

"Thanks for the tea." Mira lifted her cup toward Mrs. Caldwell and then turned away, mulling over what she'd heard. The journey through grief took an untold number of forms. Could anyone say which path was right or wrong? Her heart pulled with sympathy for Elise as well as for Mrs. Caldwell.

I wonder if anyone can ever fully heal?

As Mira climbed the stairs, she glanced down at her grubby attire and decided she ought to change into something less casual. Tom and Elise always came to the table picture-perfect—they would never dress in a ratty old t-shirt—as if they expected a photographer to show up any minute. Sometimes Mira longed for the less fussy atmosphere of Key West, a place that focused more on celebrating life every day than on what to wear.

She reached the Beckers' door and tiptoed past—yes, definitely a lavender scent—and hustled into her own room for a long hot shower. Afterward, Mira plaited her wet hair into a loose fishtail braid and abandoned her t-shirt and flannel pants for a sweater and the nicest pair of jeans she owned. A rap sounded at the door. Elise opened it to peek inside.

"I'm going down for breakfast. Would you like to join me?" Mira nodded. Elise came into the room and took her arm. "Tom has an early meeting with his staff, so it will be just the two of us this morning."

They strolled to the dining room, arms linked. Mira listened as Elise chatted amiably about her latest charity function, a light flush tinting her cheeks as she spoke. There wasn't any doubt she had a passion for what she did.

From women working in underdeveloped countries to museums to scholarship funds, Mira had witnessed the amount of time and energy Elise channeled into causes she cared about. The same energy she poured out on her loved ones.

By the time they reached the table, Mrs. Caldwell, through whatever mysterious radar she possessed, had already poured coffee. She had a fresh cup of tea brewing for Mira.

Elise laid a napkin on her lap. "I'm glad you're in good spirits today. After what happened with Lily, I was concerned for you."

"I'm fine. I only hope Aiden is." Her belly fluttered when she spoke his name, and Elise eyed her curiously. "He was frantic," Mira added.

"I imagine so. What a frightening experience for everyone. Thank heaven it all turned out well."

Mrs. Caldwell served them each a slice of quiche that smelled divinely of mushrooms and sausage and spinach, alongside a bowl of mixed fruit. Mira picked up her fork. "Yesterday was a day filled with surprises. Tally even handed me one. She's decided to sell the café."

"Oh?" Elise's eyes widened. "I'm sure the news disappointed you, but in my view, it's fortuitous timing. I wanted to tell you this when Tom was here, but since you shared the news about the café, there's something we'd like to do for you. How would you like to go back to school? Graduate school or whatever else might interest you."

Mira took a tighter grip on her fork. "But I did finish school. Culinary school. I also did an apprenticeship. There's really nothing else I'm interested in."

"Darling, if you're saying this because you think Tom isn't on board with taking care of your school expense, I can assure you he is."

"I appreciate your generosity. You've both been kind, but at this point, I'm not going back to school. I want to pursue the career I've already chosen."

"But if Tally sells the café, you'll be out of a job, won't you?"

She considered telling Elise about Tally's offer but squelched the impulse. She wasn't inclined to make it sound like she was fishing for money—especially coming on the heels of Elise's proposal. "There are other shops in the area. I can find something else for the time being."

"I wish you'd think about our offer before you make up your mind."

Mira shoveled a bite of quiche in her mouth so she wouldn't need to answer right away.

Elise chased a blueberry with her spoon and finally broke the silence. "I talked to Carolyn and Kathryn yesterday. They're both planning to work out their schedules so they can be here for Thanksgiving this year. It will be the perfect time for you to meet them, and what a treat to have the entire family together for the holiday."

"That sounds nice." The idea rose goosebumps on Mira's arms. She had looked forward to meeting her cousins, but with reality close enough to touch, her nerves jumped to full attention. Would Carolyn and Kat be as skeptical of her as their father? Mira wasn't sure she could deal with staying in a house where three people, instead of one, didn't believe what Pauline had told her. Which brought up another topic. "The DNA test Tom wanted me to take. Have the results come back yet?"

Spots of color bloomed on Elise's cheeks. "Not yet. He said something about the lab being backed up. I apologize again for my husband's insistence. His line of work lends itself to a belief in the folly of misplaced trust."

Mira decided it best to be charitable about Tom's request. "I get where he's coming from. One person looking like another isn't proof. According to what I've been told, most everyone eventually runs across a face that resembles theirs. It doesn't make them blood relations." She lifted her cup for another calming sip of tea. "If I'm honest about it, I wouldn't mind seeing evidence myself. I'd love to know beyond any shadow of a doubt if I truly belong here."

"Oh, darling, of course, you belong here." Elise squeezed her hand gently. "There is no question whatso-ever in my mind that you're Jimmy's daughter."

"Well," Mira said. "I guess we'll find out soon enough."

Chapter Twenty-One

The night had brought Aiden more agitation than rest. He'd drop off into sleep until the house creaked or the furnace kicked on, and then his eyelids would fly open. Each time it had happened, he'd felt compelled to get up and check on his daughter, just to be sure she was still safely tucked in her bed.

The brief periods of sleep he'd managed to catch had given him the most vivid dreams he'd ever had. In one, he kissed Mira long and searchingly, pushing the limits of decency. He'd awakened out of breath and with an impatient hunger deep in his belly.

A good while later, he fell asleep again to dream about his daughter's empty bed. This time, the pounding of his heart awakened him, his forehead so slick with perspiration that he needed to get up and wipe it off. *A post-traumatic stress nightmare.* He had red-penciled a diagnosis for himself and then climbed back under the covers, staring toward the ceiling to pick apart his dream about Mira. That scenario must have been hatched from wishful thinking after the kiss they'd shared—passion tinged with a touch of something that made his heart heavy.

When the friendly light of morning finally arrived, Aiden watched through bleary eyes as his daughter ate her cereal. She seemed unaffected, keeping her attention riveted on a cartoon video. He'd decided to keep her home from school, worried the weekend events might have affected her, but so far, she seemed surprisingly cheerful. With Siggy sitting next to her, she looked much better than he did. Still, he kept a vigilant eye on her, searching for any sign that the previous night's misadventure might slither in and distress her.

"Lily-Lou," he said, keeping his tone light, "will you promise me something?"

She turned her gaze toward his, her eyes wide and trustful. "What, Daddy?"

"If you have a problem or you get upset, will you come to me instead of trying to take care of it all by yourself?"

She wrinkled her small forehead and pondered his question for a minute before she answered. "All right." With no other reaction than a smile, she spooned another bite of cereal into her mouth and went back to the cartoon.

Talk about anticlimactic. Kids. Aiden shook his head ruefully. "Don't get too wrapped up in your video. I promised Memaw and Papa we'd visit today and hear about their trip."

With his gentle nudge, Lily finished the last few bites of her breakfast. "Memaw promised to bring me something."

"That wouldn't surprise me a bit. Let's go and see."

Not long after scrambling around to load the dishwasher and then change clothes, they arrived at his parents' house. Aiden realized the return to a sense of normalcy had soothed his spirit, but it hadn't done much to add pep to his step. He unbuckled Lily from her safety seat and let her gallop toward the front porch, plodding resolutely behind her.

"Lily!" His mom opened the door, and his daughter all but vanished in her grandma's embrace. "Don't you ever run off by yourself again."

Aiden didn't want to belabor the issue, so he gave his mom a warning glance to slow her down. "It's fine, Mom. She understands."

They stepped inside, and the familiar aroma of cinnamon wafted through the air. "Since you didn't get any rolls before we left, this batch is for you to take to the station."

"That's perfect. It's my turn to do meals, and thanks to you, breakfast is now covered. I'll be the man of the hour."

His dad put down the newspaper and then enfolded Lily into his arms. "We brought you something."

"What?" She danced in excitement. "What is it?"

"Go ahead and show her, Bob," his mom said. "I've got rolls almost ready to come out of the oven."

His dad took Lily's hand, and they left the room.

"You two spoil her rotten," Aiden rolled his eyes with a mock sigh.

"Why shouldn't we? We're her grandparents. Spoiling her is our job. Besides, it's only a t-shirt and a little game. She is our only grandchild, you know."

He let the implication slide. "Sounds like you had a great time."

"It was nice to get away." She narrowed her eyes at him. "But you should have told us what happened with Lily right way instead of waiting until afterwards. We would have driven straight to your house if we'd known."

"Since Mira found her, there wasn't any need to scare you. Believe me; I would have called if she'd been missing much longer."

"Thank the good Lord for Mira, but don't you dare hold such things back again."

He'd expected this. His mom would fuss and cluck over what had happened to cover her own alarm. "All right," he replied meekly, sounding exactly like Lily had when she was eating breakfast. "Hey, have you got a minute to give me your opinion about something?"

"What?" She pulled a baking sheet from the oven and slid another pan of rolls inside.

"It's about Mira."

She placed the hot pan on a cooling rack and settled into the chair next to him at the table. "What about Mira? Tell me more."

"We had a…moment." Aiden shifted uncomfortably.

"What exactly does that mean?"

"Yesterday, I kissed her."

His mom's mouth dropped open. "You did what?"

"You heard me. I wonder if it was a good idea, though. After all that happened, we were like a couple of train wrecks. I don't want her to think I took advantage of the situation."

"Did she seem upset?"

He reviewed his memory for clues. "No. She told me she was glad I kissed her."

"Sounds like that answers your question. Aiden Stewart, I've been waiting months for you to open up to the idea of having a woman in your life again. If you don't go after this girl, I swear I'll…I'll never bake another batch of rolls for you again."

"Believe me, Mom, I am more than a little interested, but I'm also worried. Am I moving too fast? All I know about Mira is she's pretty and sweet and a good person to have on your side. She grew up in Key West. She's friendly enough with the likes of Tom and Elise Becker to move in with them, and she's got some hot-shot lawyer chasing after her. It all works out to one big question. What do I have to offer? Maybe she's out of my league."

"Don't be ridiculous. You've got a great career. And a good head on your shoulders. You're a gentleman and *almost* as handsome as your father. Any girl would be lucky to have you."

"Wait a minute," he said. "Look at this again without the mom filter. I'm a widower with a child. I work crazy shifts as a first responder and deal with situations that are physically and mentally demanding. It's tough to forget some of the things that happen on the job, and sometimes I carry them home with me. That's a lot for another person to take on."

"Right here and now, I want you to stop trying to talk yourself out of what could be one of the best things to happen to you since Rose." Her tone softened the scolding words.

Aiden's heart grew heavier. "That's another subject eating into me. Rose. Before we got married, I promised that I would always love her. Now Mira's come along and made me think I could love her, too. Is it disloyal for me to develop feelings for someone else?"

She took hold of his hand. "Son, this isn't an either-or proposition. I would never suggest you stop loving Rose. I only want you to keep in mind that your heart is big enough to love someone else, too. Instead of turning yourself inside out, talk to Mira."

"Look at this, Daddy." Lily skipped into the room toward her father. "See what Memaw and Papa gave me?"

"Nice," Aiden said. He eyed a neon pink t-shirt labeled "Branson" and what looked like a board game. "What do you say to Memaw?"

"Thank you." Lily hugged her grandma.

"You are so welcome, sweetheart." She returned Lily's hug and then scrubbed a hand across her eyes. Her gaze moved toward the oven as if pulled there. "I've lost track of the schedule. Will Lily be with us tomorrow?"

"Nope, I've got one more day off."

"Oh, shoot. I should have waited to bake these." Her hands went to her hips. "The rolls won't be as fresh the day after tomorrow."

"Mom, I can promise you they won't last more than ten minutes once the box has been opened."

"Hmm," she replied, obviously distracted.

Lily handed the new treasures to her father and scuffed her shoes on the floor at the less-than-scintillating discussion. "I'm going downstairs to help Papa put away his stuff. He's going to let me practice with his fishing rod."

Aiden nodded his approval, and she left the kitchen like a missile.

His mom had the grace to wait until Lily was out of earshot. "Getting back to our discussion, can I ask you a question? Are you going to take my advice and see Mira today?"

"I doubt it, Mom. I have an appointment to set up a security system, and Lily's with me. Besides, Mira's shop is closed on Mondays."

"You do have a phone, dear," she chided him.

"I'll see how the day pans out."

"Honestly, you never used to be so bashful. For a big tough guy, you certainly are a Nervous Ned when it comes to this woman."

It bothered him to be so defamed, but he couldn't think of a fitting rebuttal. "In my line of work, we're trained to be cautious. Besides, don't you think I ought to find out more about Mira—and tell her more about me—before I try to jumpstart anything important between us? There's nothing wrong with being careful."

"Handling a fire in a safe way is one thing, but this is different. If you have feelings for a person, you shouldn't waste precious time. Don't be afraid to stand up and tell her."

"I'm not afraid, only on my guard. It's best for everyone's sake. Lily's, Mira's, and mine."

She shook her head at him. "Faint heart never won fair lady."

He held up his hands, only half-kiddingly. "Okay, okay. I get your drift. You think I'm a coward. Thanks a bunch for the helpful advice, Mom."

"Anytime, dear." She smacked his arm lightly and flashed an unrepentant smile. "And that ends my observations—at least until I think of something else to convince you that you need a loving woman in your life. You get on downstairs now and help your dad while I finish my baking. On the way, you can decide whether or not to listen to your mother's advice."

"I think my ego will be a lot safer in the basement." Aiden slinked away from his mother's outspoken opinions. Sometimes, he wished she were a little less bold, but the idea of a meek Betty Stewart did not compute. He did feel a slight sense of relief. It lightened the load to speak out loud the concerns colliding against each other in his head. Despite her candid viewpoint, she had helped him see better through the dense smog of doubt.

From the top of the stairs, he heard his dad holler to his mom, "Honey, remember to save me one of those rolls."

Without missing a beat, she chuckled and yelled back, "Will do, dear."

The banter between his parents triggered a deep longing for what he had lost—and what he knew they still had after so many years. His throat constricted, and he coughed once to clear it. Maybe his mom was right. What could it hurt to see Mira and be upfront enough to tell her how he felt? For all he knew, she might have the same doubts and fears as him. And if they both had similar feelings, maybe, just maybe, the two of them could work this out.

A fresh stream of conversation laced with laughter floated from the basement. Sighing, he shoved his hands into his pockets and ambled down the steps.

Chapter Twenty-Two

Mira shifted restlessly in her seat and glanced again toward the bistro's lobby. She'd already finished studying the entire menu and had decided what to order. Now she scanned the faces of new customers filing in as others strolled out. She didn't see any sign of Aiden.

He had called her early in the day, asking her to meet him at a restaurant near the café. The urgency in his voice promptly kindled a pins-and-needles impatience to see him, piqued with curiosity over what he had to say. Maybe Aiden had more news about Lily, although Mira had to admit a part of her hoped their meeting was about more than that.

As the waiter approached her for the second time—she felt sure he would ask her if she wanted to go ahead and order—Aiden stepped through the entrance. He nodded in her direction and wended his way to the table.

Her heart slammed against her ribs as he approached. It seemed strange she could feel so captivated merely watching him walk toward her. She couldn't remember anything generating a similar effect on her—unless she counted the soulful yearning that surfaced whenever the sun dipped into the sea at day's end.

"Sorry to keep you waiting," he said. "I had to stop by my parents' house, and Mom nearly talked my ears off. She always has a lot to say."

Mira read the amusement in his eyes and smiled. "How's Lily?"

The server moved to the table and handed Aiden a menu. "Do you need a few minutes to look this over?" He waited for an answer.

"Please," Aiden replied.

The server's order pad sank lower, and he pivoted away impatiently.

"I already decided on a salad," Mira quickly offered. "I have a feeling our waiter's ready to get the order turned in. I know where he's coming from. A table where people sit around without eating or drinking isn't making money for anybody."

"I never thought about it before." Aiden waved the waiter back to the table, who took their orders with an unabashed grin.

As soon as he left, Aiden leaned forward and folded his hands. "Here's an example of how fuzzy my mind's been. I've already forgotten what you asked me. What was it again?"

"How's Lily?" She repeated her question. Aiden certainly did seem preoccupied.

"Fine. Acting no different than she does every day."

"I want to apologize for not bringing Siggy back to her right away. I had him in my car and planned to stop by your place after I got off work. If I'd come over before I went to the café, she wouldn't have wandered off."

"Stop it. None of this is your fault. I had a talk with her. Lily understands she shouldn't have left the house without me knowing it. And just in case she ever forgets, I'm now the proud owner of a system loaded and armed to alert me if anyone opens a door or window."

"Impressive, Mr. Stewart." The corner of her mouth curled up. "Now, let's talk about how *you're* doing. No wonder you feel fuzzy. This whole situation had to scare you to death."

"I feel a lot better since I have a game plan in place. You know what? Not a day goes by where it doesn't cross my mind that parenting isn't for wimps."

She laughed softly. "Pauline didn't get down in the dumps very often, but when she did, she'd say, 'My bucket is empty today.' Then one or another of her friends—our friends—would pick up the slack and give her a break. Kind of like your parents do for you."

"I couldn't function one day without them." Aiden's eyebrows bunched together. "I've never heard you speak of your father. Tell me about him."

The potential of dangerous territory constricted the muscles in her neck. "My father wasn't around," she said carefully. "It was always just the two of us, Pauline and Mira."

"I like your name. It's pretty but not common. Is Mira short for Miranda?"

She breathed a sigh of relief. He'd changed the subject. Maybe he had sensed her anxiety. "People often think I'm a Miranda, but I'm not. To give you a little perspective, my mother had a lot of female problems when she was young. It turned out she needed surgery and her doctor told her she'd never be able to have children. I'm living proof he was wrong. Pauline was so thrilled when she got pregnant that she named me Miracle—Mira for short."

"Do you have younger brothers or sisters?"

"Nope. There's only me. Any siblings for you?"

"One older sister. She lives in Montana. We get together whenever we can."

"I always wished for a brother or sister. But Pauline and I were so close that sometimes she seemed more like a sister than a mom. I miss her so much." Mira cleared her throat. "If I stay busy, I can almost forget she's gone."

Aiden's glance held a sense of empathy. "I know what you mean. There are times when I go into the house and expect to hear Rose's voice."

She played with the edge of her napkin. "If you don't mind my asking, what happened to your wife?"

His expression shadowed. "Cancer. She passed away a few months after she was diagnosed."

"I'm sorry. Cancer is purgatory on earth. That's what got Pauline, too. It must be a comfort to have Lily."

"It is. You sure made an impression on her. She talks about you all the time."

"I'd love to have her over again. The Beckers feel the same way."

He paused a moment, watching her long enough to make her squirm. "Exactly how did you get to know Tom and Elise Becker?"

Mira rubbed her lips together while she thought. Should she use the vague fiction the Beckers invented to explain her presence, or should she tell the truth? "It's a little strange," she finally said.

"If you don't want to talk about it, I understand." Keen interest sparked in his expression, but it was gentled by compassion.

All at once, the things she'd kept silent for so long pushed out like a wave to shore. "As I said before, it was always Pauline and me. When I was little, I'd ask her about my father, but she'd never answer. It didn't take me long to figure out it hurt her too much to discuss."

A comforting hand reached out and took hers. Bolstered by the kindness in his eyes, she continued.

"Before Pauline died, she gave me a letter she'd written. She said not to open it until after she was gone. Long story short, the letter informed me that a man named James Todd was my father. Pauline had met him at a conference in the Keys, and they had fallen in love. They had planned to make a future together. He said he needed to go home to his family in Kansas City first to make arrangements, and then he'd come back. But he never did. After I read the letter, I hunted for him online and discovered he was Elise Becker's brother." As soon as the words left her mouth, she felt ten pounds lighter. It felt good to tell the truth instead of dancing around it.

Aiden's eyebrows shot upward, and his grip on her hand tightened. Her news had obviously left him speechless, so she continued. "The reason I came to KC was to find my father. I wanted to meet him, and to tell you the truth, I guess I also wanted to find out why he abandoned my mother."

He finally found his voice. "Have your questions been answered?"

She shook her head. "Not as I'd hoped. I found out James Todd died in a car accident on his way home after he left the Keys. That's the reason Pauline never heard from him again."

"Mira, I'm so sorry." He paused, apparently intent on choosing his next words with care. "I guess this makes you the Beckers' niece."

"Depends on how you look at it. Elise believes I am, but Tom asked for a DNA test."

"He did?" Aiden's back straightened indignantly. "How did you feel about that?"

"I took the test, but we're still waiting for the results. It's weird how things work out. When I decided to come here, I felt sure about everything. Now I'm not as confident. I guess the DNA test will confirm the truth once and for all."

"To come all this way, hoping to find your father and getting news like that instead. I don't know what to say." He brushed his thumb across her knuckles.

"The Beckers are keeping it all low key. Tom decided it best we tell people I'm a friend of the family until we're sure. Consider yourself special. You got the unvarnished truth."

"It seems to me you've got a lot hanging over your head."

Mira smiled weakly. "It would be nice to know I found family here, but no matter what happens, I still have family in Key West."

"Your friends?"

"Yes. They've always been there for Pauline and me. I was just on the phone to Dinah—my mother's best friend—last night. She's like a second mother to me. Dinah wants me to come home. She found a small place she thinks would be perfect for me to set up my own bakery. A great location not too far out of the way and at a decent price. She's talked to our other friends, and they want to pitch in and help me buy it."

His brows dipped. "Sounds like you're giving serious thought to this."

"I'm not sure. So many things are up in the air. If the DNA test tells me that I'm not who I thought I was, there's no reason for me to stay. What else can I do but head back to the Keys?"

He released her hand. "What about your job? If you leave, I'd be willing to bet Tally would miss you."

"I doubt it. She's putting the café up for sale."

"She is?"

"Tally plans to retire and move to Colorado, where her daughter lives."

"Why don't you buy *her* shop," he said, a little too quickly.

"I love the café, but her asking price is too steep. I don't have the collateral for a loan large enough to buy her place, plus do the updates it needs to be successful. She says there are a couple of developers interested, and they can offer her top dollar. This is Tally's retirement money, so she can't just give her café away. I've thought about trying to work something out, but I haven't come up with any ideas."

His features darkened. "You're going back to Key West, aren't you?"

The server arrived with their orders, saving her the pressure of a reply since she hadn't a clue how to answer. A somber mood settled in the space between them. Mira drizzled dressing on her salad and used her fork to rearrange the lettuce. She desperately wanted to say something to lighten the unsettled mood. "Here I am, dominating the conversation. When you called, I got the impression you wanted to talk about something. Seems like we got off track with all these other things."

"I, uh, mostly wanted to thank you again for your help with Lily." He propelled his words out so fast they ran together. "My folks send their thanks, too."

His demeanor had grown stiff and awkward, nothing like the way he'd been earlier.

"There's no need to thank me. I'm glad she's okay." Mira put down her fork. "I guess I'm not as hungry as I thought."

"Me either. Maybe we should just go." He waved to the server. "I'll get this. I owe you."

She wished Aiden would smile again. "I'm not kidding about seeing Lily. Maybe you can bring her by the café sometime soon for another hot chocolate."

"I'll see if we can work something out before you leave."

Mira winced. She hadn't said for sure she was going. Aiden avoided glancing her way as he gave the cashier his card, processed the transaction, and then opened the front door for her. A blast of cold air greeted her, and she clutched the edges of her coat together. They walked silently toward Mira's VW.

An older couple got out of their car and gave the van an appreciative once-over. The man grinned and lifted a thumbs-up in Mira and Aiden's direction.

The couple's gesture slightly thawed Aiden's demeanor. "Your van sure does attract a lot of attention."

"It's an eye-catcher, isn't it? The van used to be Pauline's conversation piece, and now it's mine." She stopped at the VW and smiled up at him. "You didn't need to buy dinner for me, but it was really sweet of you."

He rested one shoulder against the van and looked at her thoughtfully. It seemed like he might be balanced on the edge of a revelation. "Want to know something?" he finally said. "If I had any right to an opinion, I'd ask you to stay in Kansas City."

Encouraged by the note of longing in his voice, she tilted her face upward. She was so certain another kiss was imminent that her heartbeat zoomed up like a jackrabbit's, and her eyes drifted to half-mast. Waiting, she hoped he'd make her body tingle as thoroughly this time as he had on the evening she brought Lily home.

Aiden leaned toward her, and then he paused, like he'd thought better about putting his mouth against hers. A breath later, to her great dismay, he pushed away from the van, pasting a crooked smile on his face before he nodded a silent good-bye.

Chapter Twenty-Three

After everyone finished eating, Puno scraped bowls and emptied drips of water from glasses, which Aiden then piled into the dishwasher. They had teamed up to fix dinner, inventing a creation they dubbed Everything-But-The-Kitchen-Sink chili. The meal had been served alongside stacks of Saltine crackers and a mountain of shredded cheese. Aiden had been surprised how well the dish turned out, even if it may have been on the somewhat spicy side.

He'd hidden a grin as more than a few of the guys grabbed for their drinks and guzzled water in between each bite. Aiden could have told them they were fortunate. If Puno had been given a free hand, somebody would have called for the fire extinguisher instead of water. Nevertheless, the new recipe did what they wanted it to, namely use up every stray vegetable in the refrigerator, along with three extra-large cans of chili beans. The pot holding chili had been scraped clean, without a single dab left over.

Puno handed Aiden a bowl. "I have a feeling this meal may come back to haunt us later."

"Heartburn?"

"Actually, I was thinking more about the aftereffects of beans."

"Well," Aiden replied philosophically, "look on the bright side. Maybe the gas will go up and not down."

Puno snorted. "In your dreams. Hey, speaking of dreams, how's it going with the red-headed stunner? What's her name again? Oh yeah, Mira."

"I'm not sure it's going anywhere." Aiden dodged the question.

"What are you talking about? The last time you mentioned her, you sounded just this side of love-sick, especially after she tracked down Lily for you. C'mon, man. Tell me you're not getting cold feet again."

"This isn't about cold feet. Here's the problem. I'm pretty sure she's not planning to stick around much longer. She wants to start her own bakery, and apparently, there's a place in Key West she's interested in. On top of that, she's…all wrapped up with the Beckers and people who travel in their orbit." *Like a certain hot-shot lawyer. Talk about a completely unfair advantage.*

"Really? I thought she liked it here, working at that little coffee shop. The one with the oven fire."

"Mira says the owner is planning to sell. She'd like to buy it, but she can't jump through all the hoops to take out a loan."

"If she's tight with the Beckers, why doesn't she ask them for help? Judging by the castle they live in, they must have more money than God."

"I don't think she'd consider asking them." He stopped short of explaining the weird reason Mira came to KC in the first place. Mira's story wasn't his to share—at least not with Puno, who would be sure to tell Chrissy. "Anyway, she has people she considers to be family in the Keys. They want her to come back."

Puno playfully shoved Aiden's arm, but his eyes were solemn. "Hey, man. If you're serious about this girl, then don't roll over. Do something about it. Let me think." He scratched his chin. "Here's an idea. Why don't you offer to co-sign a loan so she can buy the café? That'll keep her here."

"Don't you think that's a little premature—and manipulative?"

"You're not manipulating. You're offering her an opportunity. If she stays, you've got time to win her over. If she says no and decides to leave, then you'll know it isn't meant to be. Either way, the choice is up to her."

Did the idea make sense? Before Aiden had an opportunity to hash through Puno's suggestion, Brody stuck his head into the kitchen. "We're playing cards, and the guys want coffee. Will you fix us a pot, Puno?"

"When did I become your minion?" Puno grumbled under his breath, but he stretched his arm up to grab a filter from the top shelf of the cabinet. He pulled, and a brown cloud dumped on his head and his shoulders.

One of the oldest pranks in the book. A filter stuffed almost to the brim with dry ground coffee. Aiden bit back a chuckle. He had to admit the look on Puno's face was priceless as he spewed a string of expletives.

Brody slapped his knee and guffawed. From the other room, the guys hooted and roared with laughter. At the firehouse, revenge usually arrived in unexpected and often disgusting ways. Puno lucked out. Payback could have involved the garbage disposal, the shower, or his bed.

"Very amusing." Puno wiped his face. "Now, I've got coffee inside my shirt, and it itches like hell."

Aiden pointed. "It's in your hair, too. Well, at least you guys are even now."

"Don't be so sure," Puno said as he brushed coffee from his head onto the floor.

The comment had barely left his mouth when the alarm buzzed. An emotionless voice on the intercom informed them of a structure fire. A big one. Aiden and Puno locked gazes. Pranks and dirty dishes and revenge were swiftly dismissed as they raced to grab their gear and join the others. Aiden, Puno, and Captain Zampella leaped aboard the first truck and were out of the station within sixty seconds, tearing down the street with the siren wailing.

No sooner than they arrived on the scene, Aiden's breath caught. The first-floor windows glowed with flames, and smoke rolled from the rooftop of a two-story home. Bystanders on the street were gathered in bunches, their hands moving with excitement as they talked. Zamp barked out orders, while Aiden and Puno began to lay a supply line. Aiden kept the crowd within his side vision. At least they were staying out of the way. Not all crowds were so cooperative. The scream of another siren grew closer. The second pumper.

"Interior attack through the front door," Zamp hollered.

Aiden went toward the home's front entrance carrying the business end of the hose. He turned the knob, which thankfully was unlocked, and shoved the door wide open. A plume of thick dark smoke poured out. Aiden motioned toward Puno to start the stream, and the blessing of cool water squirted from the hose into the room. The other pumper pulled up as Puno joined Aiden on the porch.

"The owners just got here," Puno shouted. "Nobody inside but the family dog. The wife is hysterical."

Aiden nodded. "Take the hose. I'll go in."

"Shit," Puno replied, but he didn't argue. "Zamp isn't gonna like you doing this without orders. If you don't see the dog right away, get your ass back out here."

Aiden nodded and stepped inside. The smoke was so thick he couldn't see a thing. He turned on his flashlight and dropped to his hands and knees to crawl forward. Lower to the ground, his vision improved while smoke hovered above him like an ominous thunderhead. It stood to reason that his best chance of finding the animal would be to feel along the floor while Puno kept a steady stream of water pumping in his direction. The moisture hissed and steamed as it fell around him.

He moved his gloved hands to the right and then to the left. Nothing. He crept farther inside and repeated the exercise. Still nothing. He could no longer hear Puno, but he figured his partner would be cursing like a sailor by now, screaming for him to get out. Just a few more feet. If he didn't find the dog, he'd give up.

His hand slid forward and brushed against something. Inching closer, he saw it. A small black and white dog, lying prone on the floor. Aiden couldn't tell if the animal was breathing or not, but he grabbed the limp body with one hand and then turned to crawl back. When he caught sight of the front door, he rose to a knees-bent crouch and quickened his pace as best he could, feeling more than seeing his way out.

The threshold was just in front of him, almost within reach, when a flash lit the home's foyer like a lightning strike. He heard a sharp crack, and the floor gave way. Aiden's feet broke through the hole, and he sank to his knees. Balance gone haywire, he dropped his flashlight, desperately trying to hang onto the dog, when he pitched forward. Burning debris rained down on him. Flailing his free arm to find support, an image of Lily barreled through his brain.

Please don't let me leave her alone.

Heat waves shimmered around him, and his helmet crashed against something hard. Fire and smoke faded to black.

When he woke up, Aiden was on his back in the front yard. His helmet was gone, and he felt the scratch of wool against his neck. Someone had folded a blanket and placed it under his head. He blinked a few times, and Zamp's face came into focus. Deep lines on the captain's face smoothed.

"Don't try to get up. An ambulance is on the way."

Aiden's head ached like a hammer had bludgeoned his brain, and his ears were ringing. He groaned. "What happened?"

"Flashover. Somehow you broke through the sub-floor and hit hard enough to put one helluva dent in your helmet. Looks like you also have scrapes and burns, though they seem to be minor. You're going to the hospital to get checked out."

Aiden weighed the information and then lifted his head up from the blanket. "Anybody else hurt?"

Zamp put a restraining hand on Aiden's chest. "Puno has a few burns. He pulled you out."

"Will he be okay?"

"His injuries look minor, too. You guys were lucky." Zamp took a deep breath. "Thank God we've got the fire nearly under control, but I'd like to know what the hell got into you? Why did you go inside without permission?"

"A dog. I was looking for a dog."

"That's what Puno told me," Zamp grumbled.

Aiden coughed. "Did the dog make it?"

"We weren't sure at first, but Brody gave her oxygen, and she finally came around. You know the rules, Stewart. We'll discuss this later."

"Yes, sir." He decided not to think any more about what Zamp would have to say. Faced with a similar situation, Aiden figured he'd probably have made the same choice.

Another siren announced the approach of an ambulance. Puno showed up next to Zamp, his face smudged, and his forehead shiny with perspiration. Zamp gave both men a pointed glare before he left. Aiden turned his head toward Puno, and the dull throb in his head made him wince.

"You okay?" Puno eyebrows were crimped together.

"I've got a headache that won't quit. What about you?"

"I smell like a pot of brewed coffee. Other than that, only a scorch or two, but the captain says I have to get checked out anyway. Policy."

"Swell. Looks like I'm on Zamp's bad side again."

"He'll get over it. You rescued a dog. The owner is now gushing with goodwill and claims she's gonna write a letter to the city council about how thankful she is that you risked your life to save little Fluffy. Trust me. You'll come out of this looking like a hero."

"Well, Zamp will put an end to that."

"It's his job to keep egos in check." Puno chuckled and then sobered. "Want me to call your folks?"

"I guess you better. My cell's in my locker. When you call them, be sure to relay this as gently as possible so you don't freak them out. Say going to the hospital is only a precaution and there's no need for them to show up."

"You know me. I can be tactful when necessary. I have to call Chrissy, too."

"Well, don't freak her out either."

"Got it. While I'm waiting for my own ride to the ER, I'll make the calls. Any more orders, boss-man?"

The ear-piercing screech of the ambulance paused their conversation. Lights flashing, the vehicle stopped in the street near where Aiden lay. Attendants snapped a gurney into position and rolled it toward them.

"Looks like I'm about to go. No more orders, Puno. Only my thanks."

"It's all part of the job, man. You'd do the same for me."

Aiden reached for Puno's forearm and held on to it for a moment. "Thanks for having my back."

"That's what firefighters do, buddy," Puno replied.

Chapter Twenty-Four

Mira picked up a novel from her nightstand, ready to forget her own dilemmas through the portal of a fictional world. If she got lucky, maybe she'd find answers to the questions bobbing up and down in her head like a ship in stormy seas. *Am I really James Todd's daughter, or do I only wish it were so? Would I be happier back in Key West? What in the universe makes Aiden so moody?* She shook her head, took a sip of hot tea to settle herself, and opened the book to Chapter One. Ten minutes later, the story about an old woman remembering a long life had drawn her in. She hunkered against Louie, who snuffled, and turned another page, more absorbed with every word.

Somebody outside her bedroom door knocked, and the spell was broken. Elise came in. "I hope I'm not disturbing you, darling."

"Of course not," Mira replied and reluctantly put her book down. Louie jumped to attention, his tail wagging a frenzied welcome.

Elise sat on the edge of the bed and rubbed the pup's ears. "I was wondering if you've heard from Neal lately. He told me he was going to call you."

"No, it's been a few days since we last talked."

"Since he said he'll call you, I'm sure he will. Neal is a very dependable man."

"He seems to be." Mira wondered where the conversation was heading.

"I've been thinking about Thanksgiving. It's only two weeks away, and the girls are both so excited about meeting you. Carolyn will be here with her husband, and Kathryn is bringing her young man, so I thought it might be a good idea to invite Neal to join us. We'd have an even number of guests seated around the dinner table."

"But Neal isn't my young man. He's only a friend."

"I know. But there isn't anything wrong with inviting a friend to dinner, is there?"

"I guess not." *Inviting a man to Thanksgiving dinner. What better way to make him think I have notions that go beyond friendship?* She recognized the hope in Elise's face and cautiously selected the best way to phrase her response. "Here's the thing, though. Since I'll be meeting Carolyn and Kat for the first time, I'd like to focus on them. If Neal is here, I'd have to make small talk with him. I would much rather spend time getting to know the girls."

"Oh. I see what you mean." Elise's forehead creased in thought. "In that case, we won't worry about it. I'm sure the two of you will see each other again soon. And darling," she squeezed Mira's hand, "don't worry about what Carolyn and Kathryn will think. They'll love you, just as I do."

She knew Elise wasn't showy about expressing emotion, so the endearing comment warmed Mira's heart. "I hope so."

Elise dropped her gaze to Louie and fussed with the dog's fur. The phone on the nightstand jangled, breaking the silence. Mira picked it up.

"This is Betty Stewart." Betty's voice sounded like she was coming down with a cold. "There's an emergency. We have to go to the hospital. I hate to ask a last-minute favor, but Lily's in bed asleep. It would be best if we didn't have to wake her up. Can you come over and stay with her until we get back?"

Mira's heart banged. "Is something wrong with Bob?"

"No. It's…Aiden. They were working a fire, and he got hurt. Puno called to tell us."

She bolted upright in bed. "Is he okay?"

"Puno made a few of his corny jokes when he called, but I could tell he was downplaying the situation. He said an ambulance took Aiden to the hospital. I need to see for myself what's going on with my son. If you can stay with Lily, I'll text you our address."

"I'll be there as soon as I get dressed." Mira ended the call and jumped out of bed. Her hands shook as she tore across the room to grab her clothes.

Elise rose, with Louie in her arms. "What in the world is wrong?"

"Aiden's been hurt fighting a fire. He's at the hospital now. Bob and Betty need to go to him, and they asked me to watch Lily."

Elise's fingers covered her mouth in horror. "How bad is it?"

"They don't know any details yet." Mira pulled on a sweatshirt and yoga pants and then grabbed her keys. "I'm not sure how long I'll be."

"Please call me when you have any information. I know Aiden is a good friend to you, and he is poor little Lily's father. I'll pray for him."

Not trusting herself to speak, Mira nodded as she raced to the stairs.

The minute she pulled her van in front of the Stewarts' home, she noticed their vehicle in the driveway. Bob was behind the wheel of the car, the exhaust pipe pouring steam into the cold night air. Betty stood at the door. When Mira loped toward her, she breathed a swift "Thank you" and then raced toward the vehicle. Betty climbed inside, and as soon as the car door slammed shut, Bob sped away.

Mira stepped into the house and took a few breaths to steady herself. A thought occurred to her. *I have no idea where Lily is.* Betty hadn't told her anything other than that Lily was asleep. But where? She'd never been inside the Stewart house before and tiptoed from room to room on the first floor, where she found only a kitchen, dining room, living room, and bathroom. She eyed the staircase and sighed. Intrusive as it felt, she tiptoed up the steps and turned on the hall light. Bathroom. Master bedroom. Another bedroom. The final door at the end of the hallway was closed. Mira took a deep breath and nudged it open. She peeked inside.

Lily slept peacefully, her arm slung around Siggy. Mira blew out a breath of relief and pulled the door shut gently. *Please, oh please, let her stay asleep.* The last thing she wanted to do was explain to Lily what was going on. She backed away and trod as softly as she could down the stairs, wincing when the bottom step squeaked. A mirror on the wall reflected her wide, frightened eyes—and a complexion even paler than usual. Worry lines puckered her features. Not even her breathing exercises could smooth the lines into anything approaching calmness or serenity.

Pacing around the living room, she looked for something to do. Turning on the television might wake up Lily. But if she didn't find a way to occupy herself, she'd go out of her mind with worry. A stack of *Taste of Home* magazines on the coffee table caught her eye. She seated herself on the sofa and picked up a magazine, flipping through the pages. The recipes weren't like anything she'd find in *Pastry Arts*, but the photos were attractive enough to occupy her mind. At least for a while.

After Mira plopped the final magazine back on the table, she got up to peer out the front window. No cars. She glanced at her phone. No messages. She'd been there for nearly two hours without a word from the Stewarts. Surely, they would call her, unless…Her thumbs poised over the phone, ready to send a text message to Betty— lower-key than a call—but changed her mind. If there was bad news, they didn't need her curious questions. She put down her cell and paced some more. If only she could go and see for herself that Aiden was okay.

Her shoulders ached with tension, and an itch started on her neck. Not a good time for a panic attack. She went back to the sofa and closed her eyes. Deep inhale of cool air. Exhale warm air. Focus on the rise and fall of the chest. She remembered Pauline's soft voice. *Live in the moment.* Following four yoga breaths, her body had softened, and the tingle subsided. She opened her eyes and sent herself a message. *I can handle whatever comes. I WILL handle whatever comes.*

The sound of a vehicle from the street drew her to the window like a shot. The Stewarts were pulling into the driveway. She hurried to the front door and opened it, welcoming the fresh, frosty air. Betty trudged up the walk while Bob pulled the car into the garage. Worry lined Betty's face, but her mouth lifted in a frail smile when she saw Mira.

"He has a concussion and some minor scrapes and burns. They're keeping him overnight as a precaution, but they expect to release him in the morning."

The sharp edge of terror left Mira. She put her arm around Betty. "Thank the universe. You look wrung out."

"I'm always a little scared whenever he goes to work. I keep thinking anything could happen. We've been lucky so far."

"Worrying that something could happen doesn't mean it will." Mira hugged her. "All you can do is try not to let what-ifs swallow you up."

"I can't thank you enough for coming over. You must be exhausted, too."

"Now that I know Aiden's going to be all right, I'm fine. And Lily didn't stir the whole time I was here."

Bob joined them, looking a few years older than when she'd last seen him. "Aiden sends his thanks, Mira."

"Is it for sure he'll be out of the hospital tomorrow?"

"That's the way it looks," Bob said.

Mira turned to Betty. "Will you call me in the morning and let me know? I'd like to stop by and see him when he gets home—if you think it would be okay."

Betty's eyes crinkled at the corners. "You know what? That would be the best medicine any doctor could prescribe."

In the morning, Betty phoned to let Mira know Aiden had been discharged. "We picked him up from the hospital. I offered to stay and help out, but he says he's fine. Have you noticed my son can be stubborn? He claims all the doctor wants him to do is take it easy, so he insisted on keeping Lily with him instead of sending her to our house."

Mira couldn't resist asking, "Did you tell him I planned to stop by?"

"No," Betty chuckled. "I didn't say a word."

Mira had already boxed up a half a dozen of the chocolate croissants she'd baked, and on the way to Aiden's, she stopped by the grocery store for more supplies. It was nearly noon before she pulled into the driveway at his house. Balancing the box and a grocery bag, she went to the front door and knocked.

Lily peered out the window and then opened the door. Her mouth broadened into a huge grin. "Hi, Mira."

"I came by to see you and your dad. Is he sleeping?"

"He's on the couch watching television." She opened the door and eyed the parcels Mira held. "What did you bring me?"

"Something you'll like. You haven't eaten lunch yet, have you?"

Lily shook her head.

"Good. Help me take this stuff to the kitchen." She handed the box to Lily.

"Who is it?" Aiden's voice came from another room.

"It's Mira," Lily called back to him.

Mira didn't want Aiden to get up, so she shouted, "Stay where you are. I brought a few things for you."

He didn't respond, so she walked with Lily to the kitchen. Mira hoped her presence would please him rather than set him to scowling. She whispered to Lily, "Remember when we talked about making dinner for your dad? I brought everything we need. We'll just do it for lunch instead. Shh. Don't tell him."

Lily's eyes grew enormous, and she danced around the kitchen. Mira dimpled as she put away the groceries.

Aiden, obviously ignoring her request for him to stay put, appeared at the doorway wearing athletic shorts and a t-shirt. His face showed off cuts and red patches. His hands were bandaged. It didn't escape Mira's notice that he leaned a muscled shoulder against the wall as if he needed it for support. "What's going on here?"

"We're gonna make lunch for you." Lily paused. "After I go to the bathroom." She hustled from the kitchen.

"Aiden, why don't you go back to the sofa and lay down? You look like a stiff breeze could blow you over."

"It was a rough night, but I'll be fine."

She bit her lip. "I'm so glad you're okay. I was worried about you."

He shrugged. "Stuff happens. It's what you sign up for when you decide to be a firefighter."

His face had lost enough of its normal color that it made her nervous. "Will you at least sit down? Please?" She motioned to a chair by the table.

For a change he listened and eased into the chair. "My folks told me you watched Lily last night so they could come to the hospital. You're mighty handy to have around."

"Gee, thanks. Seriously, I didn't mind at all. I'm only sorry you got hurt."

He shifted in the chair and breathed in like his chest bothered him. "It wasn't only me. My partner Puno got injured, too, when he pulled me out of the flashfire. Luckily, he'll be fine. But me? I had to get a concussion on top of burns. That's why they made me stay overnight."

"What happened?"

He managed a smile. "It's extremely dramatic. I went into a burning house—to save a dog."

Mira fought the urge to hug him. "I think that's about the sweetest thing anyone's ever told me."

"Most firefighters don't like to be described as sweet. Hot, maybe. Strong enough to carry a two-hundred-pound victim, for sure. Not sweet."

"But a dog, Aiden? No matter what anybody says, that's sweet."

Lily returned to the kitchen, gabbling a mile a minute. "Daddy, Memaw said you have to rest. Go to bed while we fix lunch."

"Your daughter's right. Don't make us rough you up."

"I think I'm roughed up enough. Not going to bed, but I'll take my place on the couch," he said. "Call me when lunch is ready." He winked at Lily. "I'm looking forward to food that doesn't come from a hospital cafeteria."

He inched his way from the room while Mira and Lily got to work wrapping cocktail-size hot dogs in biscuit dough. When the cookie sheet went into the oven, Mira let Lily measure out ingredients for a dipping sauce. While the hot dogs baked, they put the finishing touches on a light fruit compote. When the oven timer buzzed, Mira held up her forefinger. "We did well. Part of being a good chef is having everything come together at the same time." Her hand opened to give Lily a high five, and then they arranged the meal on the table.

Lily ran to get her father and led him to a chair. He moved so slowly, Mira knew he must be hurting.

"Looks great," he whispered, so unlike his normal voice her heart pinched.

"We made pigs in a blanket," Lily giggled. "And they're my favorite."

"So I see." He smiled at her.

Conversation evaporated as they began to eat. Mira watched the interaction between Aiden and his daughter. He said all the right things to her about how good the food tasted and gently smoothed her hair with a bandaged hand. *Like it or not, Aiden. You are sweet.*

They finished the rather absurd meal, and she noticed Aiden flinch when he turned his head to look at Lily. He needed to be in bed, but she knew he wouldn't lay down without persuasion.

"All right, you two, out of the kitchen. Go watch television. Shoo."

Mira sent them back to the couch while she got busy on the dishes. Once she'd dried the final plate and placed it on the counter with the others—not bothering to try and figure out where they belonged—she wiped her hands on a towel and tiptoed out. She hoped to find Aiden sound asleep.

Instead, Lily stared, completely absorbed in a cartoon. Aiden was splayed flat on the sofa, his face turned toward the kitchen door. His grin reached clear up to his eyes when he saw her.

"I left croissants for you in the refrigerator. Now, is there anything else I can do before I go?"

Lily waved her hand in a vague goodbye, and then went back to intently staring at her video. Aiden hauled himself into a sitting position, hesitating as if to gather enough strength to rise.

"Please don't get up," she said.

Of course, he ignored her. Once on his feet, he moved toward Mira until he was so close that his arm brushed against hers. One corner of his mouth lifted wryly. "Let me walk you to the door."

His scent of cedar-citrus soap felt as bracing as a walk in the park. "If I can help you in any way, please call me."

At that, he took her arm. In a subdued tone, his said, "I understand you have a lot of things to figure out, but there's something I need to know. And don't answer out of pity, just because I'm a little busted up at the moment. I can take the truth." They stopped short at the door, and she lifted her eyes to his, waiting. "Ever since I lost Rose, I had no idea if I could love anyone as much as I loved her. Truth is, I didn't even want to try. You're the first woman to make me think it's possible. But before I forge into something you may not want, or if you have plans that won't ever include me, I need you to say so."

For such a strong and capable man, she knew it must have been difficult for him to expose his fears so openly. Mira peeked around him to be sure Lily wasn't watching. She'd love to throw her arms around his neck and hang on tight, but despite the attraction she felt for Aiden, until she knew what path lay before her, the thought of even unintentionally hurting him reined in her impulse.

Shoving aside decisions and uncertainties, she answered in the most truthful way possible. Mira placed her palm against his cheek, pushed up on her toes, and touched her lips gently against his for an instant. "I love it that you're ready to make space for whatever or whoever you want in your life. But remember. You and I are new to each other. We need to test what we feel and see how things grow between us first."

She knew she had disappointed him, but she kissed him again anyway before she left the house. He was still standing at the door when she started the van and backed it out of his driveway.

Chapter Twenty-Five

Not a single drop of milk spotted the table or floor. Aiden had checked as soon as he came into the kitchen, where he found Lily at the table devouring a bowl of cereal. She had noticed him at the doorway and cheerfully informed him, "I fixed my own breakfast."

He'd slept so hard, he hadn't heard her rattle around in the kitchen. A bittersweet pang of pride pulled his heart. "You did a good job. You're growing up, Lily-Lou, but don't be in too much of a hurry."

"Mira told me you'd get well faster if I help you."

"Did she?" The idea of Mira looking out for him plumped up his pillows of hope.

Lily nodded and then placed her empty bowl and spoon on the counter. "I know what. Let's go see Mira today and get some hot chocolate."

"I'm not cleared to drive yet, Lily. Memaw is on her way over now to help me since you're on fall break. Maybe you can ask her to take you to the café later." Not that convincing his mom to do something Lily wanted would be hard. She doted on her grandchild. "Tell me what video you'd like to watch, and I'll put it on."

He set up the television set for Lily, and she settled on the couch to watch. The front door banged open and his mom called out a cheery "Hello" as she strolled into the house, puffing a little, her arms loaded down with bags.

"Hi," Lily and Aiden greeted her simultaneously.

Aiden shuffled over to his mom and tried to grab some of the bags. She held on to them and scolded, "Why are you wandering around? Sit and rest while I fix you and Lily something to eat."

"I already had cereal," Lily said. "I made it all by myself."

"You did? Great job, sweetie." His mom bustled toward the kitchen. It looked like she had enough food to last an entire week. Par for the course. He'd long ago realized that if Betty Stewart needed to feed two people, she'd prepare enough for ten, just in case.

Aiden followed her. "Let me give you a hand."

"Sit down. Now!" She shook her finger at him. "You're not supposed to be in action yet."

Rather than argue, he took a chair. "Look, I appreciate you coming over, but you don't need to do all this. Between watching Lily while I'm at work, and now with me laid up, your time is spent taking care of us instead of doing the things you like to do."

"What else do I have to do? Sit at home twiddling my thumbs until the next bridge meeting? Bake more cinnamon rolls? I've gained too much weight eating them as it is. Don't be obstinate. Family takes care of family. That's the way it works."

"I just don't want you to wear yourself out."

She turned on the oven. "Do I look worn out? I'm not exactly a fossil, you know." She gestured toward a pan. "I threw together your favorite breakfast casserole. It will only take a few minutes to heat."

"The one you make at Christmas? With bacon and cheese and mushrooms?"

"What else?"

"Oh, man. Lily will want a slice of that."

"I figured as much." Her gaze drew to the plant sitting on the floor near the window. "Dry as a bone. Don't you ever water this poor thing?" She filled a glass to moisturize the hard-packed dirt.

"I'm not much of a plant person. I keep forgetting about it."

She put down the glass and sat next to him. "How are you feeling today?"

"Sore. Aches and pains everywhere. If I get up too fast, I get lightheaded."

"Uh-huh. How long will you be on sick leave?"

"After the doc clears me, I'll need to do physical therapy to show I can handle coming back to work. Once the therapist and the doc both give me a thumbs up, I'll get to listen to Zamp lecture me about following orders, and then I'll be good to go."

"Your health is what's important, so don't try to rush things. How's Puno doing?" She got up to slide the casserole pan into the oven.

"He'll be back at work next week, but Chrissy's been worried sick about Lily and me. Puno called with a heads up that she's coming over tomorrow to deliver a meal. If this continues, I won't have to cook for a month."

"There's nothing wrong with being spoiled occasionally. Did Mira stop by yesterday?"

"Yep. She and Lily fixed lunch for me. Something special they made for the Beckers when Lily spent the night."

"Really?" Her eyes expanded with interest. "Some kind of fancy dish, I'll bet."

"Fanciest meal I've had in a long time. I think she called it—pigs in a blanket." The expression on his mom's face made him laugh out loud which set off a throb in his head. He rubbed the dull ache surreptitiously.

Luckily, his mom didn't appear to notice. "They served Tom and Elise Becker pigs in a blanket? I can't believe it."

"I'm told the dish was a hit."

"Well, I never. Maybe the Beckers are more down to earth than I thought."

"Maybe," he ventured cautiously, thinking about what he knew of their reaction to a recently discovered relative. He hadn't even met the man, but Tom Becker had already rubbed Aiden the wrong way. Mira was kind, honest, and unpretentious. How could he doubt her?

"It's nice seeing how fond Lily is of Mira. I'm not trying to tell you what to do, but I hope you won't let that girl slip away."

"Mom, this isn't the Wild West. I can't rope and hog-tie her."

"You can charm her, though. Show her what you're made of. That should be more than enough."

"I'd like to think so, but I can't know for sure. From what she says, there's a strong possibility she might move back to Key West."

"Then you better start thinking of a way to keep her here."

"You sound like Puno. When I talked to him, he suggested I co-sign a loan for her."

His mom's eyes narrowed fast. "Why does Mira need a loan?"

"She wants to open her own bakery. Apparently, it's been her dream. The woman who owns the shop she's working at now plans to sell, but Mira doesn't have the resources to buy it. She told me there's a place in Key West where she could set up a business, so she's thinking about going back home."

"Aiden," she murmured, "I know you're hurting now, but I see a light flickering in that face of yours that I haven't seen in a long time. I think you may have fallen in love again. Am I right?"

"I don't even begin to know how to answer you. Maybe?" It was a wishy-washy response, but still, he surprised himself by admitting as much. "The only thing I know for sure is that I'd like to find out."

"Do you trust Mira?"

He didn't need to mull over his answer. "Absolutely."

"Then why don't you go ahead and take the chance? Offer to co-sign."

"Just like that?"

"Just like that. If she's someone who has the potential of becoming your lifetime friend, partner, and lover, then you need to do whatever it takes to make it happen."

His brows bunched. "Yesterday, I tried to see where I stood. She kissed me, but almost the way a friend would. I flat out asked her if there's a chance for us, but she stopped short of committing herself one way or the other. There might be more to this than a possible move to the Keys. Her hesitation could be because of the lawyer. What if she has feelings for us both, and she can't make up her mind between the two of us?"

"My dearest son." She took his bandaged hand gently. "If you think you love this girl, do something about it. We both know how short life is. What in the world are you waiting for?"

He swallowed hard. There were all types of fear. He wasn't afraid to enter a burning house. If you followed rules and procedures, chances were good you'd stay safe. Love, on the other hand, was a much riskier business. No guidelines and no safety net. If he offered to co-sign a loan, it wouldn't leave any doubt how he felt about her. Did he have the guts to expose his desire in such an obvious way?

Aiden rubbed the whiskers on his jaw. Mira wasn't exactly the enemy. She had never hesitated to help him or his family. Maybe he was looking at this all wrong. Whether they had a future together or not, why shouldn't he be willing to help her out? If he offered something like the loan—a grand gesture—it might be enough to overshadow everything else on her plate and prove how much he cared. Hell, even if they were never destined to be more than friends, he'd still be happier if she stuck around. The more he considered the idea, the better it sounded.

"I smell bacon." Lily joined them in the kitchen.

"It's my breakfast casserole, almost ready to eat. Will you have some with Daddy and me?"

"Yummy," she said. "And Memaw, can we get my special hot chocolate from Mira's coffee shop later?"

"That sounds like fun. We can give your daddy some alone time so he can relax and do a little thinking without any distractions."

Lily turned her eyes toward Aiden. "Do you have stuff to think about, Daddy?"

"Yes," he replied. "I guess I do."

Chapter Twenty-Six

Most of the tables in the café were full. Mira found herself darting from the kitchen to the customers to the register as she tried to help Tally keep up with the ebb and flow of diners. She stifled a yawn brought on by getting up extra early so she could cut apples, roll out dough, and measure ingredients to fill holiday orders. The pumpkin and pecan pies were already finished, and now the scent of apple filled the café. They had decided to offer only three flavors of pie for Thanksgiving, which was only days away, and the new addition to the café's catering menu had proven to be another popular experiment—for all the good it did.

Tally had announced she planned to scale back on catering after Thanksgiving or they'd need to hire a helper. She didn't want to put on a new employee with the future of the café in limbo. An understandable but disappointing decision. Even though her boss had gushed over the number of pie orders, it obviously hadn't changed her mind about selling. Mira could almost picture a "Coming

Soon—Pizza" sign taped to the front door. Tally had gone so far as to plan a second meeting with the developer who was pushing hard to buy the shop. The idea of the cute little café turned into yet another pizza joint nearly brought Mira to tears.

She tucked a lock of red hair behind her ear and surveyed the customers on the main floor. With the sun lowering into late afternoon, most of them would soon begin to drift away. There were bills to ring up and tables to be cleared, but the pre-closing slowdown brought more time for her to think; not necessarily a good thing. Automatically, she focused her attention on calming breaths while she wiped a rag across the counter.

When Tally's voice chirped from behind her, Mira jumped. "I pulled the pies from the oven. Lordy, they smell as good as they look. If you'll stick around in front, I'll box them and attach the order forms." Mira nodded, and Tally turned to barrel back into the kitchen.

Glancing toward the clock, Mira leaned her elbows on the counter, grateful for a moment to herself. If only she knew what to do. She had considered calling Dinah but cast the idea aside because there wasn't any doubt what Dinah would say. "Come back home, lovie."

Oh, Pauline, I could sure use your advice.

The entry door squeaked, and in a start of surprise, Mira recognized the new customer as Neal. He'd never come to the café before. Once she thought about it, she realized with a pang of guilt it had been at least a week since she'd given him any thought at all.

"Good to see you again." He approached the counter with a wide smile. "Elise told me you were working today."

"I am, but we're closing in about half an hour. Can I get you anything? Coffee? Tea? A sweet treat?"

"You're a temptress. Just one mocha latte, please."

"Coming right up." She grabbed a mug, and the steamer hissed as she prepared the drink. Once she finished, she handed it to Neal.

"Thanks," he said. "If you're not too busy, will you sit with me for a few minutes? I'd like to talk to you."

She looked around the room and, since no one appeared to be in need of attention, said, "All right," curious about what topic he could possibly want to discuss.

They settled at a table near the door. Neal placed his cup in front of him and fidgeted with it for a few seconds before he finally took a sip. "I don't mean to put you in an awkward position, but I have a question. A while back, not long after you came to town, Elise asked me to join them for Thanksgiving dinner. Now she tells me you'd rather I didn't come."

Heat rushed into her face. Elise hadn't mentioned she'd already invited him. "It wasn't anything against you. I only thought it would be easier for me to meet Carolyn and Kat if no one but family was there. I'm sure we'll have a lot to talk about."

He leaned back, clearly astonished. "You've never met Tom and Elise's daughters?"

"No, I haven't." She bit her tongue to keep from saying why.

"I thought you were close to the family."

"Well," she cleared her throat, searching wildly for an explanation that wouldn't involve an outright lie. "I've talked to the girls on the phone, but I've never actually met them in person."

"You don't need to be nervous about them. Trust me; I've met Carolyn and Kat. Why don't you reconsider the idea of me joining the family for Thanksgiving? I could give you moral support. And," his mouth lifted in a hopeful grin, "it would give us time to get to know each other better in a relaxed atmosphere."

Her gaze dropped and then rose again to meet his. Neal deserved honesty, not the notion she wanted to start something between them. "I think you're a wonderful person, and I like you a lot. It's only that I'm…" Her voice drifted off.

"Not interested in a relationship?" His smile faded as he finished her sentence.

She nodded gravely. "I just don't see us as being anything other than friends, and leading you to believe anything else isn't fair."

Neal half shrugged in an abrupt motion. "I guess it's better to know where I stand than to think I might have a chance. I'm not blind to the fact that getting us together was Elise's idea. I had hoped it was because you might feel the same."

"Neal, I'm sorry."

"There's no need to apologize. When you go into law, you develop a thick skin. It's called survival." He took her hand in both of his and held on. "All I ask is one favor. If you ever change your mind, let me know, and we'll give it another shot."

She smiled at him as the entry door squeaked again. Neal's words had touched her. "You just made me feel incredibly special."

Her peripheral vision caught sight of a new customer. She glanced toward the door, and her back went arrow straight. *Aiden?* He stared at her as if studying a vignette on display and then pressed his lips together in a straight line. She didn't have time to say a word before he turned around and closed the door quietly behind him.

Aiden's expression made her heart hurt. She pulled her hand from Neal's. "I'm glad you came in so we could straighten this out, but I do need to get back to work."

He fumbled at his pocket. "Sure. What do I owe you for the latte?"

"Nothing. You don't owe me a thing." She smiled at him. "Take care, Neal."

He stood, regarding her for a moment, before he left. When the door closed, Mira trailed her finger through a smudge of coffee on the table. What awful timing. Her mind replayed the scene. Neal, holding her hand. Her, gazing up at him with a smile. She'd bet anything Aiden heard what she said—without the context of what came before. The look on his face told her so.

Cha. What must he be thinking?

She rose and paced to the window. Pauline's reliable VW van in all its colorful glory caught her eye. What if she put to the side any questions she had about her father? Didn't allow the past to interfere with the future. Forgot for a while, the notion of pleasing anyone but herself. If she did all those things, would she know what she wanted to do with her life? Mira weighed her options as she cleared tables, and before long the decisions she'd been wrestling with became clear.

Aiden moved as quickly as he could from the café to his truck and drove from the lot. He clutched the steering wheel so tight that the still-healing burns on his hands ached. Maybe it was good he hadn't waited for formal permission from the doc to drive. If he had waited around for a medical okay, he might have missed witnessing what had been going on right beneath his nose.

He'd been kidding himself about Mira, projecting his own feelings on her, and jumping to the conclusion he wanted. She'd been decent to him. She probably even cared a little. But a little wasn't enough when somebody else—a man with much more to offer—was in the running. The big-shot lawyer. He could probably write a check to buy the café for Mira without blinking an eye. And if that's what it took to make her happy, Aiden wasn't about to stand in the way. If anyone deserved to be happy, it was Mira.

By the time he pulled into the driveway at his house, he'd come to terms with the facts. Maybe someday—if she stuck around—they could be friends. But for the time being, better to step away than say anything that might muddy the water. It was the only decent thing to do. What he wasn't sure about, though, was how he'd explain to Lily why they couldn't see Mira anymore. Aiden stepped inside and found his dad in the living room, engrossed in a football game.

His dad looked up and frowned. "Whoa, son. Maybe you better sit down. You look paler than when you left. Did your headache come back?"

"I guess I'm not as well as I thought."

His dad patted the couch. "Why don't you sit down and watch the game with me? It's a good one. The score's tied."

"Maybe later. Is Lily in the kitchen?"

"Yep. She's helping your mom. They're working on something for Thanksgiving. I don't remember what." A player crossed the goal line to score a touchdown, and the crowd roared. The announcer's voice grew louder. His dad muttered something unintelligible and then returned his attention to the game.

In the kitchen, Lily and his mom were seated at the table. Dozens of red, yellow, orange, and green construction paper leaves were spread around in front of them. Lily's tongue peeked from the corner of her mouth as she used her marker to write on a red leaf. Despite how he felt, he couldn't help smiling. His mom looked up first.

"We're making gratitude wreaths." She squinted at him. "You look exhausted. I knew it was too soon for you to be out and about. Sit down this minute."

Aiden dropped into a chair. "What's a gratitude wreath?"

"We're writing all the things we're thankful for," Lily announced. "We're gonna glue them to paper plates with the middle cut out to make a wreath. Memaw says we can hang them up for Thanksgiving."

He looked at a small stack of completed leaves next to her. "Did you do all these by yourself?"

She nodded, her eyes shining. "Memaw helped me spell the words I don't know."

"Let's see what you have." He picked up the stack. Each leaf had a word written on it. He thumbed through them, reading aloud. "Cake pops. Siggy. My house. Memaw and Papa. Puppies. Peanut butter and jelly. Sparkles. Daddy. Mermaids. Hot chocolate. Mira." He swallowed and put the handful of leaves down.

"I want you to know," his mom said, "the leaves got a little mixed up while she worked on them. You were first on her list."

"I see," he replied.

Before speaking again, she scrutinized him. "Lily, I'm sure Papa is lonely out there by himself. Why don't you take a break and bring him some cookies? You can have a couple of them, too."

"Okay." Lured from her chair, she grabbed a plate of chocolate chip cookies from the counter.

As soon as she left the room, the question he'd expected came. "Tell me what happened."

"Nothing happened."

"Did you ask her to join us for Thanksgiving? I'm sure the Beckers will do an enormous feast, but surely she could come by for a short while."

"I didn't invite her."

"Did you forget to ask her after you told her you'd co-sign the loan?"

"We didn't discuss the loan either."

"For heaven's sake. You were so pumped up about talking to her when you asked us to watch Lily. Now it's like you've run out of gas. Did you or did you not see Mira?"

"I saw her. And I saw someone else, too."

"Who?"

"The lawyer I told you about. I walked into the café, and they were sitting together at a table, holding hands. I don't know what he said to her, but her face turned red, and I overheard her tell him how special he made her feel. I wasn't about to interrupt them with offers or invitations. No one's fault but my own. I misinterpreted how she felt."

"Are you sure? I hate to see you give up without fighting for what you want."

"What should I do, Mom? Challenge him to a duel?" He idly pushed the unmarked leaves into a pile. "I won't pressure her, but by the same token, I won't wade in any deeper and risk my daughter getting hurt. It's better to play it safe and step out of the picture. Lily and I are doing fine on our own. Do you know how long it's been since she had a stomachache?"

"You're a wonderful daddy, Aiden, and I know Lily loves you very much, but there's one thing you need to keep in mind. Years from now, your little daughter will be all grown up. You won't come first for her anymore. Don't you think you'll be lonely if there's no one to share your life with?"

"Mom, I'm not ruling out the possibility of that in a year or two or ten. Who knows what the future has in store? Somebody else may come along who catches my attention the way Rose did. Or maybe I'm fated to love only her. All I'm sure of is this—my priority is to safeguard my daughter. Everything else will take care of itself. Can't you see where I'm coming from?"

"I understand, but I wish you'd give this more thought. The expression I saw on your face when you talked about Mira was so full of sass and pizzazz that I had to bite the inside of my cheek to keep the tears from welling up. You say you want Mira to be happy. Well, I'm your mother, and you know what? I want happiness for you too. What's more, I know Rose would feel the same way."

"Thanks, Mom. But maybe the timing just isn't right." He crossed his arms and wished she'd let it go.

"Honestly, son. Sometimes you can be so…" She stopped short, and he turned curiously to face her. "Look at that." She pointed at the miniature rose plant on the floor.

Three small bright red blossoms met his gaze. He couldn't remember the last time the roses had bloomed. *Some sort of sign?* He wasn't sure he believed in such things, but if it was a sign, it had come along way too late.

Chapter Twenty-Seven

The day before Thanksgiving, final preparations for catering orders kept Mira preoccupied. Customers flooded in endlessly to pick up pies and baked goods for the big day. Tally rang up receipts while Mira prepared lattes and chai tea for frenzied customers before they scurried off to finish last minute holiday preparations.

Mira kept her eye on the clock. Tally had promised to let her leave early since she had put in so many extra hours in the past week. There were a boatload of things to do at home. She had talked Elise into letting her bake pies—one pumpkin and Tom's favorite, pecan—for Thanksgiving dinner. They needed to be spectacular, something to be proud of. Especially with Carolyn and Kat in town. Both were due to arrive later in the day. For all Mira knew, the girls and their significant others might already be at the house waiting to meet her.

When one o'clock arrived, Mira untied her apron. "You don't mind me leaving, do you?"

Tally looked up from the list she'd been using to check off pick-ups. "The bulk of the orders went out this morning, and traffic is starting to thin. I can handle it. Honestly, I don't know why you didn't bake your pies here. You'd have saved yourself a lot of time."

"Oh, no. There's something special about the scent of a pie in the oven. I'm sure you understand. It's part of what I want the Beckers to experience. Elise always orders holiday meals from a restaurant. She says it's easier that way."

"A lot of folks don't like to cook. It's what helps keep people like us in business." Tally grinned. "You have yourself a nice day, sweetie."

Mira paused at the door. "Are you sure you don't want to come over tomorrow for dinner? I hate to think about you being alone. I know Elise wouldn't mind. Plus, there's a couple of things I'd like to ask you about."

"To tell you the truth, Thanksgiving is a day of rest for me. The café is closed. I can take off my shoes, sit back, watch old movies, and relax. Sheer heaven. Things will be different soon enough when I'm in Colorado with my family."

The remark turned Mira's mindset from concern to contemplation. "I've heard it said that what you do now will change your future. I guess that's meant to motivate people, even if you're not sure how your choices will turn out."

"I suppose you're right." The phone rang, and Tally waved a cheerful goodbye before she picked up the call.

Mira dashed for the parking lot, her mind occupied by all the things she needed to do. Shower and clean clothes for sure. Then she envisioned spending time with Carolyn and Kat. Would they be welcoming or standoffish? Pleased to see her, or resentful? Were they the type to hang out in the kitchen while she put pies together, or would they prefer to sit in the hearth room while the gigantic big screen television blared? When it came right down to it, Mira hadn't the foggiest idea what to expect from them.

Then before she knew it, Aiden sneaked into her thoughts. She needed to call him and explain. Assuming, of course, he wanted to hear from her. How would he respond? She clutched the steering wheel and considered a wild array of possibilities—none of them good.

When she pulled into the driveway at home, there wasn't a single unfamiliar vehicle parked there. *Tom probably insisted they put their cars in the garage.* But when the garage door lifted and Mira pulled her van inside, she didn't see anything except Tom's BMW and Elise's Mercedes. The girls must not have arrived yet. Her fingers relaxed. At least she'd have time to get ready without heading straight into an agitated whirlwind of activity.

She stepped from the garage into the kitchen. Mrs. Caldwell was perched atop a tall bar stool tapping on her iPad.

"It's so quiet in here," Mira said as she grabbed a yellow apple from the woven basket on the counter. "I thought the house would be buzzing by now."

Mrs. Caldwell pushed aside her iPad. "There's been some unanticipated problems."

"Oh?" Mira lifted the apple to take a bite. "Is there something I can do?"

"Kat called this morning. Her agent arranged a last-minute booking. She has to travel tomorrow, so she won't make it for Thanksgiving."

Mira's arm dropped to her side. "I'm sorry to hear that. Elise and Tom will be disappointed."

"Carolyn won't be here either."

"What?" Mira looked at the apple in her hand, appetite suddenly vanishing.

"The veterinary clinic where Carolyn works is owned by the city. There's been some snafu with funding, and Carolyn will be working all weekend to straighten things out."

"I can't believe this. Elise was so excited about having them here."

"She had a beautiful dinner planned, too. Unfortunately, we've gotten used to last-minute cancellations. I thought this time it might go off as planned, but…" Mrs. Caldwell shrugged.

"How awful."

"Mrs. Becker wanted everything to be perfect when you met the girls, but so it goes. They're busy and wrapped up in their own lives. I suppose it's to be expected when children grow up and move away." She sighed. "Mistakes have been made in the past on both sides, but I wonder when it will end? Well, I've said too much. I'm glad you're here. It will help soften the blow."

"Where's Elise?"

"She has a headache. She's in her room lying down."

Mira swallowed her own disappointment. She knew it paled in comparison to how Elise must feel. Her hands twitched with the need to do something, so she grabbed a bag of apples from the pantry and placed them on the counter. "I'll clean up and then get started on the pies."

Mrs. Caldwell touched Mira's arm and nodded.

Thanksgiving morning dawned with heavy gray clouds and a distinct chill in the air. Mira felt restless and vaguely unsettled by the house's sad silence. She was used to helping Pauline in the kitchen on Thanksgiving Day, while friends popped in and out for a drink or to share an appetizer. The guest list in Key West was always a surprise. They never knew for sure who would show up, but everyone who came brought containers of food, creating an eclectic feast. The meal always included much more than turkey. She remembered sides of apple sage cornbread stuffing, pepper-roasted vegetables, cranberry compote, and lobster bisque, not to mention an abundance of seafood. Their unconventional guests usually arrived in flip flops. Some were quick-witted. Others bordered on zany. Pauline welcomed one and all to her table.

A pinprick of pain formed in Mira's chest. How different this holiday would be. Far from the only home she'd ever known. Friends left behind. Her mother gone. Mira's eyes filled, and she let the tears spill unchecked down her cheeks. Why did loss seem so much harder on a holiday? She considered the question for a while before it dawned on her. Holidays meant getting together with the people you love. How do you celebrate togetherness with everyone so far apart?

She plucked a tissue from the box by her bedside, dabbed under her eyes, and then blew her nose. There wasn't time for a pity party. In the blink of an eye, dinner had been snipped from seven people to three. The Beckers would be somber enough without dragging a down-in-the-dumps meal even lower. With a little thought, maybe she could come up with a way to lighten the mood for all of them. Mira turned on the shower and waited for the warm water to set her brain into motion.

While drying her hair, an idea materialized. Leaving her room to trot down the staircase, Mira headed straight for Elise's office. She knocked on the door and waited until a soft voice called out, "Enter."

She pushed the door open to see Elise behind her desk, her posture a bit less straight than usual.

"Good morning. Is your headache better?"

"Yes." Elise heaved a deep sigh. "I'm sorry about missing dinner last night. I should have come down, but I just didn't feel up to it. Mrs. Caldwell said she told you about Carolyn and Kathryn not being able to join us."

"I imagine you feel frustrated. I am, too, but we'll eventually meet. Just not today."

"Adult children need their own space, but sometimes it's hard to let them go of them."

"How about this? Let's call the girls later. I'd like to wish them a happy Thanksgiving."

"As a matter of fact, they suggested we do a virtual get-together before dinner."

"Why didn't I think of that? People do it all the time."

"A virtual visit isn't the same as one where you can hug each other."

"True. But it's still a way to connect. And if they weren't interested in connecting, they wouldn't have suggested it."

A ghost of a smile crossed Elise's face. "That's what Tom said."

"He's right. We'll have a lovely chat and then a wonderful meal. Mrs. Caldwell told me about the menu. It sounds delicious."

"I understand you made pies. I caught a whiff of them baking. It reminded me of when I was a little girl. My mother wasn't much of a cook, but she did love to bake. I'm sure your creations will be delectable."

"They better be. That's how I planned it."

"All this food for the three of us and Mrs. Caldwell. Tom doesn't eat leftovers. It feels terribly wasteful."

"I don't like wasting food either. What if we invite someone over for dinner?"

Elise lifted her chin. "I like the idea. Since the girls won't be here, do you want to call Neal?"

Mira kept her gaze locked on Elise's. "Neal is a nice man. Too nice for me to let him think anything will ever happen between us."

"Oh, I see." Elise shuffled through some papers on her desk. "I suppose the person you want to ask is Aiden."

Mira's mouth curved up. "Yes, if you don't mind. I'm not sure if he'll come, but I'd like to try."

Elise nodded. "Please do."

"I'll let you know what he says." Mira pivoted toward the door.

"Wait, darling." With a knowing nod, she added, "Don't forget to invite Lily."

"I won't." Mira beamed as she left the room. Pulling her phone from the back pocket of her jeans, she took a deep breath and called Aiden's number.

His cell rang and rang and rang. While Mira argued with herself over whether she ought to leave a voicemail, he picked up. She swallowed to steady her voice. "Hi, it's Mira."

"I know." He sounded cool and businesslike, as though talking to someone who had called the fire station for advice on smoke alarms. "What can I do for you?"

"I wondered how you are. Feeling better?"

"I'm okay. Looks like I'll be back at work soon."

"That's great. I know the guys are like family. You must miss them."

Aiden paused. "Yes, I do."

Mira waited for him to say something more, but he didn't speak. *So much for conversation.* Undeterred, she plowed on. "I know this is last minute, but would you and Lily like to come over for Thanksgiving dinner? We'd love to have you."

"We're going to my parents' house. Thanks for the offer, though."

"I understand." She chewed her lower lip. "What about the two of you joining us for dessert? I baked pies. Pecan and apple. For fun, I also made some chocolate croissants."

"Mira, why are you doing this? Is there something you want?"

His remark stung. "All I wanted to do was see you and Lily."

A brief silence and he spoke again, his voice quiet. "I saw you holding hands with your lawyer friend at the café. It's obvious you have eyes for him. That's your business, not mine, but I'm going to be honest. Lily and I have been stumbling along like two lost souls for more than a year. I didn't think I'd ever find anyone who made me feel the way Rose did—until you came along. You let me see hints of something better. The possibility of creating a new life. Since it's obvious you don't feel the same way, I'd rather not set myself or my daughter up for more misery." He exhaled heavily. "I'm sorry. That's probably more than you wanted to hear."

Her heart threatened to bounce right out of her chest. "But, Aiden, you misunderstood. What you saw at the café was me telling Neal we'd never go beyond friendship. I wish you hadn't left before I talked to you. We could have avoided all this confusion."

"Confusion? Exactly what are you trying to say?"

"Don't you get it? When I see you, my heart smiles. When we kiss, my skin prickles like some sort of chemical reaction occurred. There's never been anyone else who makes the ground under my feet seem more solid. I want to see where this leads us."

"You're sure?" His voice, thick with emotion, had her eyes pooling.

"I couldn't be more certain," she finally managed to say.

He paused so long, her fingers tightened on the phone.

"If that's true—if you really want to take a chance on me—on us—then I want to clear up something before we go one step farther. I've talked a lot about Rose to you. Who she was and what she meant to me. If it turns out what you and I have is as real as I hope it'll be, I don't want you to ever think I'd consider you second best."

"Oh, Aiden. I know you'll always love Rose, but your feelings for her have nothing to do with learning to love someone new."

"I wish we were having this conversation in person."

"Why?"

"I'll show you when I get there. What time do you want us for dinner?"

Her eyebrows slanted up. "You said you were going to your parents' house."

"I'll stop by and explain it to them. They'll understand."

"Dinner is at seven o'clock."

"Good," he replied, his voice warm. "We'll see you then."

The virtual meeting they had with Carolyn and Kat on the big screen television in the hearth room, went surprisingly well. At first, it felt more stiff than comfortable. But within ten minutes, the room's aura warmed. They discussed jobs, tossed out teasing comments, and even laughed aloud a few times. Carolyn's new husband, Rio, and Kat's steady boyfriend, Mac, were both funny but quiet, so the three girls dominated the conversation, with Elise and Tom looking on, as spellbound as Mira had ever seen them.

As fun as the conversation was, Mira couldn't help noting that the only topic carefully avoided was her relationship to the Becker family—as if the subject had been branded taboo. The elephant in the room no one wanted to discuss. Still, by the time the call ended, Mira felt pleased enough. She genuinely liked the girls, and unless they were exceptionally good actors, they also seemed to like her. Elise's expression showcased her feelings. She sat next to Tom and held his hand, her face radiant with joy.

When the front doorbell chimed on the dot of seven, Mira took time to adjust the tangerine scarf wrapped around her neck. She beat Mrs. Caldwell to the door. Aiden stood on the porch with Lily at his side. He had a bouquet of wildflowers in every shade of the rainbow tucked into a clear glass vase. It wasn't lost on her that the flowers echoed the color scheme on her VW.

She chuckled. "They're beautiful."

"I helped Daddy pick them out," Lily boasted.

"You did a great job." Mira hugged her. "No Siggy today?"

"I left him with Memaw and Papa so they won't be lonely."

Lily is growing up. Mira straightened with a smile. Aiden looked at her, with aqua eyes turned silver as a storm-tossed sea, and slipped his arm around her. Without a single word, he pulled her into such a thorough kiss that she fumbled with the vase, nearly dropping it.

Lily giggled with glee and clapped her hands. "Do it again, Daddy."

He smiled and obliged his daughter's request. When he finally let her go, Mira had to steady herself by taking Aiden's arm. She led him and Lily into the hearth room, where Elise and Tom waited. Louie barked and raced toward them, his tail blurred with excitement.

"This is Aiden," Mira announced.

Elise and Tom both rose, and Tom shook Aiden's hand heartily.

"We're pleased to finally meet you," Elise said.

Louie put his front paws on Lily's leg, begging to be picked up. The child lifted him and then tugged on Tom's sleeve. "Can we make popcorn again?"

Tom squatted down to Lily's level. "It's time for dinner now, but we'll do it soon, I promise."

The moment made Mira feel a touch woozy, like she had downed three margaritas, even though she'd been too keyed up all day to even take a sip of wine.

Aiden reached for her hand and gave it an encouraging squeeze. "Before we go to dinner, there's something I want to say, and I'd like everyone to hear it." He didn't let go of her fingers and kept his eyes locked on hers. "I know it's your dream to have your own business, and I've already told you I hope you'll stay in Kansas City. You said you need a loan to buy Tally's place. I'd like to help you. Will you let me co-sign?"

Mira's mouth rounded into an "O" of surprise.

"What's this?" Tom asked.

"Are you thinking about going somewhere?" Elise's voice scaled higher.

Three questions. And each one required an answer.

Only Lily said nothing, looking up at her father with a puzzled expression.

"Aiden, that's one of the most generous things anyone has ever done for me." She swallowed hard. "But the truth is, I'm a few steps ahead of you. I set an appointment with a small business specialist to talk about a loan. I was only looking for information, but when I told her the whole story, she pointed out things I'd overlooked. Things like the bank's Women in Business grant that offers seed money to help with down payments. She said the deadline was pending, so if I wanted to be considered, I had to apply right away. Then there's the apartment over the café. I could rent it to a tenant for extra income, or I could live in it whenever I leave here. By the time we finished talking, I decided to go for it."

"Leave?" Elise's voice held a pleading note. "We'd love for you to stay as long as you want."

Mira smiled at Elise. "I appreciate everything you've done, but I never planned to stay in your house forever. I should know something about the loan soon, and when I get the answer, I'll take it from there."

"Remember, if you have any problem," Aiden said, "I'll co-sign."

Elise turned to Tom. "We could help Mira buy the café, couldn't we, dear?"

Tom wrinkled his brow and then nodded.

"Thank you, but no," Mira said firmly. "I need to do this on my own."

Aiden's thumb gently stroked Mira's fingers. "No matter what happens, I'm here for you. I hope you stay, but if the loan doesn't work out for whatever reason, and you decide to go back to Key West..." he shrugged, "well, relationships can be tricky enough without trying to work out how we feel with a few thousand miles between us. Wherever you go, Lily and I will somehow find a way to see you."

His remark zinged straight to her core. She kissed his cheek and caught the familiar scent of cedar and citrus. "I woke up this morning missing Pauline and feeling sorry for myself. You all just reminded me how much I have to be grateful for."

Chapter Twenty-Eight

A few days after Thanksgiving, Mira readied herself for a new workday. She moved at a snail's pace, even though the hour wasn't as early as her normal start time. Aiden had taken her to a movie two days earlier. Last night, he'd treated her and Lily to an afternoon touring an organic commercial farm. Lily had been enthralled by the cows, horses, and chickens, while Mira inspected the fields and peppered the tour guide with questions about produce. She loved the way Aiden had taken a lively interest in her passion, even though she knew he sometimes felt out of his depth.

Louie barked and lifted his front paws from the floor, bobbing them up and down.

"You little beggar, you. I should never have let on I keep treats in the dresser drawer. Are all dogs so smart?"

She grabbed the bag of treats and tossed a morsel toward him. Louis caught it mid-air. Mira hadn't seen him miss one yet. With the prize in his mouth, he leaped on the bed, laid down, and chewed. Mira grinned and patted his fluffy head, thinking about what Aiden had suggested they do on his next day off. They were going to the shelter to pick out a puppy. Mira, with Elise's permission, had volunteered to keep the pup until Christmas. Lily would be positively euphoric.

Her phone burst into a musical trill, and she glanced at the caller ID. "Midwestern Bank." *Uh-oh.* She picked up her phone, throat dry as a sandy beach in summer.

"Miss Gordon? This is Vickie Harrison from Midwestern Bank."

"Speaking." It was scary to know how one's entire future could hinge on a single phone call.

"We have a few details to work out, but I'm delighted to say you've been awarded the grant funding and your loan has been approved."

"It…has?" Mira dropped to a seat on the edge of her bed.

"The business plan you submitted for the grant was quite thorough. Between the grant money and the funds your mother left, the scales tipped in your favor. As part of the grant, you'll be assigned a mentor who will help as you get your café off the ground. Our grant recipients find the mentor program to be extremely useful."

"This takes my breath away. Thank you. I'd never have known about the grant if you hadn't told me."

"Assisting a woman to start her own small business is my specialty. I'm glad I could help."

"I wasn't sure I'd qualify for anything, so I haven't made an offer to the café's owner yet."

"I'd recommend you move on it right away. In the meantime, I'll set an appointment to sign the necessary paperwork. And remember, if you have questions or need additional support, don't hesitate to call. Congratulations, Miss Gordon."

The phone went dark.

Mira waited for it to happen, but the prickle of an itch never came. Unsure of whether to laugh or cry, it stunned her to know that at last she was on the verge of her dream blooming into reality. Her mind hummed into awareness and quickly gathered momentum. There was so much to do. Update equipment. Get bids on expanding oven space. Her mind rambled on. Open the dining area. Add tables. Mira picked up a pen and searched for a pad of paper.

Hold everything.

An appalling thought intruded. *What if Tally had already accepted a deal from the developer? The one who wanted to turn the café into a pizza joint. Ugh.* She dropped the pen from her fingers, and sped back to her phone to place a call. After a few rings, Tally answered.

Mira didn't even bother to say hello. "Have you heard any more from the developer who wants to buy the café?"

"We haven't signed anything yet, but he made a decent verbal offer. He wants to bring by a check sometime this week. Why?"

"Tally, please don't sell it to him."

"Sweetie, you know I can't wait any longer. I already signed paperwork on my new condo. I can't back out now."

"I have big news. My plans changed. I didn't want to tell you until I was sure, but I applied for a loan and a business grant. I just found out I was approved for both. I want to buy the café. Please don't take a check from anyone else until we talk."

Tally stayed silent for at least one full minute—which felt more like an hour. "It's about time you came to your senses. I don't want my café turning out stacks of re-heated frozen pizza. Everything has turned out just like I hoped it would. Sounds like you studied the angles and made the right decision. Now get your fanny over here so we can discuss the details."

Mira slid a pan of croissants into the oven as Tally set up for the day. In easy camaraderie, the women chatted while they worked.

"I have a million things running through my mind on what I'd like to do with this place. Remodel. Redecorate. Change the menu. I'm so excited I can hardly stand it."

"If you want my advice, take one thing at a time." Tally pulled a folder from her bag and opened it. "Here's the contract my attorney drew up when I told him I wanted to sell." She pointed at the papers. "Everything goes with the café except my personal belongings. Equipment, tables, chairs, you name it. I suggest you go over this with your lawyer."

"I'd like to go ahead and give you a check for earnest money today."

"That can wait. I trust you completely."

"Nope. I want to do everything the proper way. Like any new business owner would."

"Okay," Tally laughed and glanced at the clock, "future business owner, it's time to begin the day."

Mira turned over the "Open" sign of the place that would soon be hers, and unlocked the door.

"Are you going to keep the same name or do you have something snazzier in mind?" Tally straightened a stack of menus on the counter.

Ever since Mira applied for the loan and grant, she'd been considering ideas. A silly pastime, but one that had thoroughly entertained her. "With the changes I have in mind, I think it needs a whole new rebranding, which includes a new name. Tell me what you think about this: Pauline's La Vie en Rose—Pauline's for short."

"La Vie en Rose. What does that mean?"

"Literally, it means life in pink. Looking at the world optimistically. The way Pauline always did. Don't you think the name has French flare?"

"I like it. Maybe you can put black and white tile on the floor. Add more bakery cases and wooden racks. Make it look like a real French bakery."

"All great ideas. Tonight I'm going to research and do a few sketches. But first," Mira picked up her phone, "I have calls to make before we get slammed. There are people who will be over the moon when they hear this. Is that okay?"

"You're soon to be the owner. Why are you asking me?"

Customers began to filter in, so she kept her calls short. Elise bubbled over with ideas and strategies when she heard Mira would be staying in KC. Tom surprised her by announcing that he would personally go over the sales contract. Aiden didn't answer his cell, and she remembered he had physical therapy. Leaving him a quick text message with the good news, she put away her phone in a soft glow of happiness. Her feet barely touched the ground the rest of the day.

On the way home from the shop, clouds billowed heavily in the sky. The air held a damp chill, but Mira glowed with warmth thanks to her new emotional state, a peculiar combination of exhilaration, impatience, and eagerness. Who would have dreamed so many wonderful things could happen so quickly? From Aiden to the loan and grant to buying her own business. It hardly seemed possible. *Speaking of Aiden…* She checked her phone again. No return call or message, which seemed odd, given how interested he had been in helping her buy the café. She thought he'd at least have texted a thumbs-up emoji even if he didn't have a moment to call.

Her own café. Mira's joy in the purchase had been tempered by only one thing. A sad silent obligation that lurked beneath the surface of her happiness. She finally broke down and did what she knew couldn't be avoided any longer. Pulling into a parking lot, she called Dinah, who listened silently as Mira blurted her news.

"Joe and I thought for sure you'd eventually come home. Then, as time went by, I started to wonder."

Mira's eyes prickled. Even as she tried to smooth over Dinah's feelings with a promise to bring Aiden and Lily to the Keys for a long visit, one truth startled her, though she didn't say it to Dinah.

In recent weeks, something within her had shifted. She had begun to think of Kansas City as home, not Key West. Had she forsaken the place Pauline loved? She blinked away the guilt and all but wrangled a promise from Dinah to bring Joe and the kids to the grand opening of the café she'd begun to think of as Pauline's.

Heart edged with heaviness, Mira drove herself home and pulled into the driveway. She pressed her remote. The garage door didn't budge. She pressed the remote again. Nothing. Even a third try didn't work. She either needed new batteries or else the opener had flatlined. Mira parked her van in the driveway, hoping Tom would understand. She got out of the VW and slammed the door. Right away, something cold and damp splotched against her cheek. *Now what?* She looked up.

Fat wet snowflakes were falling. With her face turned toward the sky, the flakes melted no sooner than they hit her skin. Icy cold but…as beautiful as she'd thought they would be. The snowflakes swirled down harder, and Mira admired the beautiful scene. It felt like she was in a snow globe. She let the powdery fluff collect on her coat until she started to shiver, and then reluctantly headed for the front door. Reaching for the knob, she tried to turn it.

Locked. *What in the universe?* Mira shook her head at the odd set of circumstances and rang the bell.

Mrs. Caldwell opened the door. "Goodness, you're all wet. You must be freezing."

"I've been enjoying this gorgeous winter wonderland." She stepped inside. "The garage door wouldn't go up, and I don't have a key to the front door."

"I'm sorry you had to stand out in the cold. The garage door isn't working properly."

"Are Tom and Elise here?"

"Yes. They're in the hearth room waiting for you." Mira removed her damp jacket, and Mrs. Caldwell took it from her. "I'll hang this up so it can dry."

"Did I miss dinner? I'm starving."

"No. Mrs. Becker asked me to hold dinner until you got home. They're thrilled about your news. Congratulations, young lady."

"Thank you. My head is still spinning."

Mira left Mrs. Caldwell and made her way down the hall. She reached the hearth room, and her eyes flew wide open.

Seated around the fireplace were Tom and Elise, Bob and Betty Stewart, and Aiden, with Lily at his side. The adults rose to their feet, raising a goblet in her direction. "Congratulations," the chorus of voices called, while Louie barked his silly little head off.

"Hush, Louie." Elise glided over to take Mira's hand. "We are delighted and so very proud of you."

"But…what…how…" Words failed Mira.

"A celebration appeared to be in order," Tom said. "Sorry about the deception. The garage is housing some extra cars. Or should I say hiding some extra cars?"

The Stewarts each took a turn hugging Mira. "I'm so happy for you," Betty said. "Owning a bakery sounds like such fun."

"I've tasted those croissants. You'll do a booming business," Bob added.

Lily threw her arms around Mira's legs. Mira bent and smoothed a wayward curl off the girl's forehead. "Miss Lily-Lou, I'm glad to see you again."

"Look," she said, spreading her mouth into a wide grin. She had a gap in the tiny neat row of lower teeth.

"How cool. You lost a tooth."

Someone approached her from behind, and Mira caught sight of Aiden. His appearance—self-assured and relaxed, with one eyebrow slightly raised—heated her insides until they all but liquefied.

"I imagine the tooth fairy will pay us a visit tonight," he said, grinning at Lily before he turned his attention to Mira. His aqua eyes caressed her. "Congratulations. You definitely deserve this."

He put his arms around her and pressed an appropriately G-rated kiss on her mouth. She felt his lips move into a smile and wondered if he wished they were alone as much as she did.

"It's still hard for me to believe this is really happening. The woman at the bank was so nice. Without her help…"

"You know I would have gladly co-signed for you."

"I know, and I appreciate the offer. But doing this on my own makes it all so much—" she paused to search for the right word, "sweeter."

"You're a stubborn woman. Here I am trying to prove how much I care, and you won't let me." Aiden touched her cheek. She felt the rough places on his hand from where the burns were healing, and a brand-new sense of pride in him filled her.

Tom cleared his throat loudly. She'd been so absorbed, she hadn't even noticed him standing next to them. "Pardon me, Mira, but will you come with me to the library? There's something we need to discuss."

"All right." Mira slanted a quick look at Aiden, who looked as surprised as she felt. Tom's casual request was curious under the circumstances, but his steps were purposeful as he walked beside her. They went inside the library, and he shut the door.

"I hate to pull you away from your party, but Elise and I decided we didn't want to wait to share this with you." He drew an envelope from the breast pocket of his jacket. "The results from the DNA test came today. They're addressed to you."

Tom handed her the envelope. It hadn't been opened. Mira inhaled a deep breath to steady her voice. "I'm a little afraid to see what's inside."

"There's no need to open it now if you'd rather wait." He had carefully shuttered his expression like a seasoned poker player. She hadn't even a vague notion of what might be running through his mind.

Her gaze dropped to her name and the Becker's address on the envelope. She stared at it until the letters blurred and ran together. Turning the envelope over, she slid her fingers across the seal.

How totally unexpected. On the day she'd figured out her future, a key to the secrets of her past lay in her palm, as objective and impersonal as the handshake of a stranger.

Chapter Twenty-Nine

In the silence, a faint murmur of conversation from the hearth room drifted into the library. A woman—*Betty?*—laughed out loud. Mira opened her mouth to say something and then clapped it shut, wishing she had a glass of water.

"Maybe this isn't the ideal time for us to talk with so many other things going on," Tom said. "If you'd rather, you can put the envelope away until later and read it when you're alone. Take as much time as you need."

A dozen reasons to open the envelope right this second fought for attention in Mira's head. She restrained herself from flicking an uneasy look at Tom. No more guesses. No more opinions. Only a medical report with factual evidence of the truth. It was what Tom had wanted—and, as her doubts grew, what Mira had wanted as well. Proof, one way or the other, of what Pauline had told her. An answer, and, if nothing else, an opportunity for closure.

Uncertain at first how to choose her words, she started slowly, carefully, to explain the strange mosaic of feelings.

"From the first time Elise heard my story, she treated me like her niece. You were more cautious, and I understand that. But in the weeks since I moved in, I had hoped you would come to see something in me other than a person who deserved your mistrust." She tapped the envelope against her hand and then gave it back to Tom. "I don't need any proof. I know what the truth is. You and Elise are my family."

If she'd surprised him, he didn't show it.

He regarded her steadily. "You don't want to see the report?"

"Nope. You wanted me to take the test, so the report is yours to use in whatever way you see fit."

"You do understand my position, don't you? I'm a skeptic about a lot of things, but I also need to protect Elise. She never got over what happened to her brother. A sudden accident with no chance to say goodbye. It changed her. Made her overcompensate, trying too hard to protect the people she loves. Always afraid she'd lose somebody else." He shook his head sadly. "I thought you were only here for whatever money you could get from us, and then her heart would be broken all over again."

"Money was never my reason for coming."

"I know that now. And just in case you're interested, Elise told me in no uncertain terms she has zero interest in looking at this either." He sighed. "In point of fact, I'm not sure I even want to." Tom lifted the envelope and tore it down the middle. Then he tore it again and tossed the pieces into a nearby trash basket. "I hope you can forgive me."

"Forgiveness. My mother told me it's the most healing decision a person can make. She was right." Mira inclined her head toward the basket. "Will you regret throwing away the report without reading it?"

"I don't think so. What about you?"

She wrinkled her brow. "Not for one second."

His mouth firmed. "Mira, there's one other thing I need to tell you. Let's get this on the table now because it's important, especially with you taking on a major responsibility. After Jim—your father—passed, we went through his things and found a life insurance policy. Elise didn't want to touch the money. She thought maybe someday we'd give it to the girls."

"Did you?"

"You know how it is. One of those things that simmer in the back of your mind, but you never get around to doing it. Elise and I discussed the money today, and we agreed you should have it. It's enough to give you some breathing room as you launch your business venture." He stumbled over his words. "Jim would want it that way. A gift from him to you, for all the years the two of you missed out on."

A sea of tears welled up in her eyes and rolled down her cheeks. If only she'd been fast enough to blink them away. "Sorry. I think I'm on surprise overload today."

"Elise will have my hide if she thinks I made you cry." Tom pulled a handkerchief from his jacket pocket and handed it to her.

Mira mopped her face and blew her nose. "I'm all right." She looked at the handkerchief. "I'll wash this before I return it."

Tom lifted his chin and laughed. "Elise keeps me well supplied. It's yours. I must say, I am a little disappointed with myself. I'm not usually wrong at judging the content of a person's character. I've learned to respect you. And to care about you, as well. As you said before, Elise has from the beginning." He offered his arm. "Shall we join the others?"

Mira linked her arm around his. "It was sweet of you and Elise to plan a celebration. I sure didn't expect it."

He chuckled. "Credit where credit is due. All we did was offer a location. The party was Aiden's idea."

Surprise set a pleasantly warm flow of blood racing throughout her body as Tom escorted her back to the hearth room. Lily sat on the sofa near Bob and Betty, chattering away. Aiden leaned against the fireplace's stone wall in conversation with Elise. Mrs. Caldwell moved quietly around the room, passing a tray of appetizers. Mira winked at Tom and headed straight for Aiden. She grabbed hold of his jacket lapels, turning him to face her. "I hear you planned this party."

She loved seeing him flush. Pulling him lower, she kissed him—not quite the way she wanted to, since they did, after all, still have an audience. Color deepened on his face to a delightful shade of lobster red.

"I had help from Mom and Elise," he finally said.

"Aiden had this brilliant idea, and we all pitched in to make it happen." Elise radiated goodwill.

Aiden and Elise on a first name basis. I like it.

Betty brought Mira a goblet of sparkling wine. "I am so excited for you. If you need help with the café, call me. I have way too much time on my hands, and I could use something to do. Otherwise, I'll have to buy a whole new wardrobe from sampling too many of the things I bake at home.

"I hadn't thought about it yet, but you just gave me an idea. There's no way I can run the place by myself. It would be fantastic if you'd consider working with me. Your cinnamon rolls certainly belong on the new menu. No pressure, though. You have plenty of time to decide."

A gleam entered Betty's eyes. "I don't need any time. Bob won't mind, and I'm getting excited just thinking about it." She lifted her empty goblet. "Another reason to celebrate. I better get a refill. Elise, this is the best champagne I ever tasted." She turned toward the bar.

"You mentioned the café comes with an apartment." Elise sipped from her glass. "With all the remodeling you want to do, how soon will it be before you can rent it to someone?"

Get it out there now. "Elise, I've loved staying here with you and Tom, but I've decided to move into the apartment myself. It'll be easier to oversee things."

A flicker of disappointment crossed Elise's—her aunt's—face, but, to her credit, it didn't last long. "You know we have more than enough room for you."

"I'll only be a few miles away, so we can still see each other as much as we want. The thing is, I've never been on my own before, and I want to find out what it's like. But

I'm not about to forget I have a family. An aunt, an uncle, and cousins."

Aiden lifted a curious eyebrow. "What did you say?"

"We're going to announce the details at dinner." Elise's voice softened. "It's strange how fear can bend a person's perspective. I understand you need your independence. I know that's what Carolyn and Kathryn wanted too. Children grow up. It's the natural order of things and I don't intend to waste any more time trying to orchestrate decisions that belong to somebody else."

Tom slipped an arm around his wife's waist. "We've been thinking, Mira. It would be simple for me to file paperwork and legally change your last name to Todd. Elise would love it if you had her brother's name. As far as that goes, if you want, I'd be proud to help you change your name to Becker."

Her eyes felt as gritty as if she stood on a windswept beach. Aiden watched her face and then reassuringly pressed her hand.

"Your offer means a lot to me, but I want to keep my name—Pauline's name—for now." Her voice cracked at the end. *If only she was here to share this with me.*

A strangely cool draft caressed the back of her neck. Odd, since Mira stood next to a blazing fireplace. Then a fleeting thought occurred to her, raising goosebumps on her arms. Perhaps a lost loved one is never really gone. Perhaps they appear in subtle nearly unnoticed ways to help celebrate happy occasions and provide comfort through sorrows. She could almost feel Pauline's presence this very minute, proud and loving as she had always been. And Rose. Perhaps even…James Todd. Her father.

Aiden brought Mira's hand to his lips. The gesture grabbed her attention with a delicious shiver, despite the warmth from the fire. With his gaze leveled on hers, he whispered, "I hope you don't rule out the possibility someone else might be interested in changing your name someday." His eyes teased hers with meaning.

Lily put an arm around her father's leg. He picked up his daughter and settled her on his hip. His other arm opened to Mira, who stepped into the circle. She brushed away a curl drooping on the child's forehead, remembering how not so long ago she'd come from Key West to Kansas City anxious and alone.

Life certainly wasn't static or predictable, nor would it ever be. As with the changing roll of the sea, anything could happen. Yet she had never felt stronger or more certain of herself.

Mira looked up at Aiden through lowered lashes and peace expanded her heart. His mouth curved into a sweet, crooked smile as he leaned closer to kiss her cheek.

Epilogue

Christmas Day, One Year Later

Torn wrapping paper lay scattered across the floor, along with colorful tangles of ribbon, beneath a magnificent Christmas tree. This year's display towered more than fifteen feet tall, its branches sparkling with soft white lights that reflected on ornaments of red, green, blue, and silver. Decorating the evergreen had taken the combined efforts of the Stewarts, the Beckers, and Mrs. Caldwell—plus a tall stepladder.

Up until last year, Mira's first Christmas in Kansas City, Elise had hired someone else to do the work, but after Mira had pointed out how much fun a decorating party would be for Lily, Elise had jumped on board immediately. There were few things she or Tom wouldn't do for the little girl. As it turned out, they'd all enjoyed the event so much the last holiday season, that Elise decided to make the party an annual event. This year's guest list included Aiden's parents, and the group had worn themselves out with laughter.

Now, the hum of many voices in the hearth room made it tough to think, but Mira didn't mind. It was a gleeful sound, a happy sound that reverberated around her and echoed in her heart. Last year, Christmas had been lovely, but quiet, with only Aiden and Lily to celebrate the season with Mira, Elise, and Tom. This year, Elise had invited the Stewarts. On top of that, Carolyn and Kat—her cousins—were both in town to celebrate the holiday, even if only for a few days.

Mira's cousins had each visited a couple of times during the past year, but separately from each other. Now they were all finally together in the same place at the same time. Carolyn and her husband, Rio. Kat and her fiancé, Mac. The result could only be described as comfortable chaos. It reminded Mira of her past in Key West.

"You seem distracted," Carolyn said as she sat beside her on the sofa. "What are you thinking about?"

From her peripheral vision, Mira noticed the sweet way Carolyn's husband, Rio, stood with his arms crossed, listening to Aiden and Betty, while keeping a protective eye on his wife. Carolyn had experienced a miscarriage earlier in the year but was now in the fourth month of a new pregnancy. Thankfully, this time, all the signs looked good. Even the stress of running her vet clinic had subsided, thanks to the combined efforts of the staff Carolyn had assembled.

"I've been thinking how glad I am everyone could be here. It's fun to spend more than a few hours with you and Kat."

"Did somebody mention my name?" Kat joined them on the sofa. She carried her tiger-striped feline companion, Charlie, who purred like a motorboat.

"I've never seen an animal as relaxed as he is." Mira pointed to the cat.

"He's like his mom. We're both chill," Kat replied. "He only gets annoyed when Stella or little prince Louie pesters him."

Stella, a rescue dog adopted by Carolyn and Rio, had quickly charmed Mira with her perpetual Staffordshire Terrier smile. "I don't know. Stella looks more innocent than Louie. I think Louie is making the most of getting reacquainted with Charlie."

"Or picking on him," Kat stroked the tabby's head. "Hey, have either of you seen my man?"

"Mac and Bob and Daddy headed toward the kitchen. I think they're after some early morning Christmas cheer." Carolyn grabbed her sister's hand. "Show me that rock again."

Kat raised her hand and wiggled her fingers, so the radiant-cut diamond flashed with fire. "This beauty sure catches the spotlight whenever I sing. Mac has good taste, doesn't he?"

"I'll say," Mira chuckled. "Have you settled on a wedding date?"

"Uh-uh. Mac's dad and his brother want us to elope like…yesterday, but I have more gigs coming up. Good news is the end of school is in sight, to which I shall sing Hallelujah. Can you believe this?" Kat widened her eyes at

Carolyn. "Mother and Daddy told me they're fine with however we want to handle the wedding."

Carolyn elevated both eyebrows. "My, how things have changed."

"Ain't that the truth." Kat turned to Mira. "Now give us the scoop on you and Aiden. Are the two of you marching in the direction of wedding bells?"

"Could be, but we're in no hurry. He's busy with his job, and I'm only just getting the café where I want it to be. Thank goodness for Betty. She's made running the place a thousand times easier. Now that Lily's in third grade, Aiden let her sign up for dance lessons, soccer, and gymnastics. Things she didn't get to do before. She practically needs her own chauffeur to get her to all her practices and games." Mira glanced fondly at the child, who batted around a new soccer ball, accompanied by her shaggy pup, Clover.

"You want to know what I think?" Carolyn placed a careful hand on her belly. "Getting to know the Stewarts has been good for Mother and Daddy. Mother talks about Lily all the time. I suspect she'd love for you to officially make her a step-grandparent—or, should I say great-aunt?—and the sooner, the better."

The hint of past sorrow in Carolyn's voice prompted Mira to shoot a plea heavenward. *Pauline, I know by now you've got some influence up there. Make sure all goes well for this new little one.*

Aiden's voice came from behind Mira. "How are you doing?" He leaned over to rub the place on the back of her neck that knotted up whenever she worked a long day.

His touch sent the usual jolt through her. "Couldn't be better. Look at your daughter and that wild-eyed puppy of hers. Between the two of them, what a whirlwind. I think it's safe to say, Lily's having fun."

"What do you expect? It's Christmas Day, and, as you know, wild-eyed is Clover's norm. She's still all puppy. I guess as long as Tom and Elise don't mind them galloping around the room, I'm fine with it," he said.

"Mind?" Kat chuckled. "Don't kid yourself. They love it."

Tom and Elise made their way to the center of the room, catching Mira's eye. Tom cleared his throat and in his courtroom voice said, "Excuse me, everyone. I have an announcement to make."

Mira shot a questioning glance at her cousins, who appeared just as bewildered.

"Elise and I are privileged to spend the holiday with all of you who are so dear to us. There's something I'd like to say. Over the past few months, I've been thinking about a lot of things. There were many special occasions and events where I could have spent time with my family. Instead, I took on a bigger workload and left my wife in charge, when she could have used my support." He flashed a repentant grin at Elise. "It's easy to be the good guy who flits in and out of the picture. Somebody who tells himself he supplied his family with a great lifestyle and no need to bother about anything else. I've decided I don't want to be that person anymore. After the first of the year, I'm cutting back on my work hours. Elise and I have booked a cruise to relax and get…reacquainted."

Pink bloomed on Elise's cheeks. "It's something we've talked about for a long while, but we never found the time. I've given up some of my charity duties so we can enjoy the trip, but don't worry. We won't miss a single important event. Whether it's a dance recital, an engagement, a wedding, or a new baby, we'll be here."

The declaration was met at first by stunned silence from the family, until Aiden started to clap. Within a moment, the rest of the group stood to join him in giving Tom and Elise an enthusiastic salute.

Mira raised a glass toward her uncle and aunt. She couldn't believe it. Tom and Elise were finally going to dial back and simply…be. "Congratulations," she called out. "When your cruise ship is sitting in the middle of the ocean, remember to look up at the stars."

"Yes, sir," Kat said. "I believe y'all are gonna let the good times roll, and the sooner you get started, the better."

"Here, here," Carolyn added.

Mrs. Caldwell stepped into the room, interrupting the celebration with a smile. "Breakfast is served. I hope everyone is hungry."

Aiden reached for Mira's hand. "Sounds like there's gonna be some interesting table talk ahead. Are you psyched up to hear it?"

Mira squeezed his fingers. "Without any doubt."

Acknowledgments

When I envisioned *Pathway to Home*, the third and final book of the Becker Family series, I never dreamed I'd be writing it during a global pandemic. Staying focused with so many scary things happening became a major obstacle. Instead of writing, my attention went in a hundred different directions, like searching for items on empty store shelves (toilet paper, really?), buying an array of face masks, and worry over family and friends. I mourned the closure of businesses and lamented the inability to hug and kiss loved ones. Writing went to the back burner. I figured I'd start again when things calmed down—except they didn't.

Finally, as people have done during frightening times throughout history, I realized the only thing to do was settle into this strange "new normal" and get back to work. As the words slowly emerged, I found that my own feelings of stress, powerlessness, and anxiety began to fade. Like Mira, Aiden, and others in *Pathway to Home*, I hacked through my own tangle of fear and loss, until the possibility of hope glimmered.

It is my sincere wish that this story did the same for you. Now, onward to the people who helped make *Pathway to Home* possible.

Writer friends. What would I do without them? My deep gratitude to everyone who provided feedback and encouragement for this story, especially Coffee and Critique, a group made up of the most wonderfully eclectic, clever, and adaptable people on earth. Not even a global pandemic kept us from gathering—once we all learned how to navigate Zoom meetings. Special thanks to Alice Muschany, a beta-reader and editor who is not only a talented writer, but brilliant at noticing problems and offering insights.

I'm fortunate to be part of another fabulous local writing group. Saturday Writers, you are a dedicated and hard-working bunch. It's a pleasure to learn more about our craft with each one of you at monthly meetings and workshops throughout the year.

To the staff at Joy Editing, thanks for helping to keep me on track while we mold a manuscript into a story.

Jenny Quinlan at Historical Editorial, I love your cover designs. You have a talent for taking my ideas and bringing them to life. Thank you.

Formatting a book is a skill and an art. Many thanks to Jeanne Felfe. I could never publish a book without your help.

My dear family, what a year it has been. Your support means everything to me. Here's to all the hugs and kisses we'll share when the time is right in 2021.

And, as always, thank you to my readers. It's truly an honor to know that among millions of possibilities, you chose my book. I'm humbled and grateful for your support, as well as for the lovely messages of encouragement you've been kind enough to send me.

A Note to Readers,

Thank you for reading *Pathway to Home*. I hope you have enjoyed the Becker Family series as much as I enjoyed writing it. I'll miss the characters I've grown to love, but I'm excited to announce my return to historical fiction. The story will feature another notable woman from history who called Missouri home.

For more, please connect with me on the following social media platforms. I am most active on Facebook.

Website: PatWahler.com

Facebook: Pat Wahler, Author

Twitter: @PatWahlerAuthor

Instagram: patwahler

I am also on BookBub, Goodreads, and Pinterest

Many people discover stories via a friend's recommendation, or after reading a review. Reviews and recommendations are vital, as they help other readers choose their next book.

I would be most grateful if you would take a moment to leave a short review of this book at your favorite retail site. Your opinion is important to me and helps provide the encouragement to create the next book just for you! Here's a link for your convenience. Thank you. https://books2read.com/u/4jLLAv

With warmest regards,

Pat

ABOUT THE AUTHOR

Pat Wahler is a Missouri native and avid reader with a love for a story well told.

She is also an award-winning author who writes in multiple genres including historical fiction, essays, short stories, poetry, children's fiction, and romance.

Pat's work has appeared in nineteen *Chicken Soup for the Soul* books as well as *Sasee Magazine, Storyteller Magazine, Reader's Digest,* and many other publications.

Her literary memberships include the Missouri Writers Guild, Saturday Writers, the St. Louis Writers Guild, Romance Writers of America, and Coffee and Critique. She has learned to schedule her life around the demands of one pampered rescue pup and a rescued tabby who rules the homestead with plenty of attitude.

Pat is currently at work on her next novel.